PRAISE FOR *THE BIG GET-EVEN*

T0025606

The
BIG
GET-EVEN

The
BIG
GET-EVEN

PAUL DI FILIPPO

**BLACK
STONE**
PUBLISHING

Published in 2019 by Blackstone Publishing
Cover and book design by Kathryn Galloway English

Printed in the United States of America

First paperback edition: 2019
ISBN 978-1-9825-4645-8
Fiction / Thrillers / Suspense

1 3 5 7 9 10 8 6 4 2

CIP data for this book is available
from the Library of Congress

Blackstone Publishing
31 Mistletoe Rd.
Ashland, OR 97520

www.BlackstonePublishing.com

To Deborah, who makes everything possible.
To Brownie, who showed the path.
And to Richard Curtis, who believed.

PROLOGUE

These days, I obey all the laws. Even the stupid ones. With three years of parole still hanging around my neck, I can't afford to put a foot wrong. Too many vindictive people—mostly those I had stolen large sums of money from and who were never recompensed and were never going to *get* recompensed—would be delighted to see my ass back in jail.

This newly civic-minded attitude of mine explained why I was sitting at a traffic light, idling behind another car at 3:20 a.m. on a frigid December night, while the exhaust-belching beater ahead of me had not moved for three full cycles of green-yellow-red.

Even though no other car had passed through the intersection in any direction for several minutes, I didn't want to zoom around this blockhead, just in case a police cruiser should happen to swing by at that very moment. I had just enjoyed three generous mojitos, over as many hours, at Danny's Cavern (and left without getting so much as a phone number). So while, by my reckoning, I was sober as an owl, I did not want to chance blowing even a hair over the legal limit.

But my patience was wearing thin. Not that I had anyone

waiting for me at home, or any job to get up for in the morning. Nonetheless. So I focused my growing annoyance on the back of the driver's shaggy head, spotlighted in the muted blue radiance of the corner streetlight, and tried to send a telepathic message to move. No luck. Was he looking at his cell phone? I applauded his considerate wisdom in not texting while his car was in motion, but my inconvenience had to count for something.

Finally, I did what I had been avoiding for fear of waking up the whole very proper suburban neighborhood where we sat frozen in place. (That damn cringing, overcautious whipped-dog attitude again. Two years of prison, even in the relatively country-club atmosphere where I did my stint, had really taken the starch out of me.) I lay on my horn for an earsplitting second or two.

I might as well have whispered at him for all the response I got.

With a long, self-pitying sigh that felt all too familiarly satisfying, I put my car in park and, leaving the motor running, stepped out. The cold air hit me like falling into a mountain stream. With the clean scent of approaching winter stinging my nostrils, I crunched over the gritty ice on the roadway to the guy's door.

My first quick impression was of your standard mook. Ugly-handsome, wearing a leather jacket unzipped over a garish sweater cut low enough to reveal a thatch of chest hair adorned with a gold chain. I had seen his type often enough coming through the law offices, usually seeking our help against one minor felony charge or another.

My second quick impression told me the guy was dead.

His face was pale and clammy like a frog's belly. His lips were bluish, and not just from the streetlight. His eyes stared without seeing, his pupils the size of poppy seeds. His stiff right leg, foot jammed on the brake, was the only thing keeping his car from moving.

I jerked open the door and brought my head close to his. Booze and body spray.

Faint but stertorous breathing told me he hadn't quite croaked. And I knew what had hit him—I'd seen it often enough before.

I sprinted back to my car and grabbed the Narcan kit from under the front seat. I fumbled out the nasal injector and sprinted back to the mook's car. I had to wrangle him to tilt his head back and maximize the dose. The car started to roll forward, and I abandoned him for the shifter. After slamming it into park, I pushed the injector deep into one nostril and blasted the naloxone up into his skull, then laid him back down on the seat.

Almost immediately, his condition improved. His breathing got easier, his skin changed color, and he began to twitch.

If only this miracle stuff had been around when I was using. But it wasn't, and I had seen several of my dope friends and fix acquaintances buy the farm for lack of it.

I called the cops on my cell. They roared up in no time, as if they were actors waiting just offstage for their cue. Their strobe lights painted the scene as if for an early Christmas.

One cop went to attend the mook, while the other came to me. The blond, smooth-faced kid questioning me looked so young and earnest, I felt like my own father. But he still regarded me with that innate suspicion all cops quickly develop, as if I must be guilty of something.

"Your name?"

"Glen McClinton." I already had my license out.

"You called this in?"

"Yes." I explained the circumstances.

"Please wait right here."

He went back to the car and ran my information. When he

returned, he was trying his best not to look especially crafty, and I resigned myself to some hassle.

"Mr. McClinton, the terms of your parole do not include a prohibition on alcohol, so I won't ask you to take a Breathalyzer test. You seem quite sober. I hope you'll appreciate this special consideration."

"Thanks." I suspected what was next.

"Okay, then. So maybe you'll be up front with me. I need to know if you were meeting this person to make a heroin buy."

"I was not. I have been clean for over two years."

"Yet you carry a Narcan kit with you."

"I just don't like seeing people die if I can help it."

"Isn't it quite a coincidence that an ex-addict like yourself should happen to be tailing a current addict?"

"I wasn't tailing him; I was driving home. It's not much of a coincidence anyhow, two dopers in a line of cars, given the growing number of junkies around town these days."

"What made you intervene, then, if you didn't know him?"

I experienced a sudden weariness at that moment. I felt stupid and ridiculous, my whole life a pointless exercise. So I indulged in a little snark.

"I told you, I have an objection to useless deaths. Hard as it is to believe, even an 'ex-addict like myself' can be a Good Samaritan. God works in mysterious ways, right? He even saw fit to make you a policeman."

The young cop looked as if he was about to object to my mild sass. But then the ambulance pulled up in a confusion of noise and lights, and the guy's partner left the EMTs to their job and came over to us. He was older and, I hoped, smarter.

"Jack, we can stop questioning Mr. McClinton now. You can be sure there's no connection here. The vic just got out of jail this morning, upstate. He rode a bus most of the day, arrived here in town, bought this car around 6:00 p.m. He barely had time to get his own fix, never mind setting up a deal."

Jack seemed reluctant to let it go. But a stern look from his partner convinced him.

"You're free to leave, Mr. McClinton. I'd be sure to report this incident to my parole officer if I were you."

"If you were me, then I could be someone else, and I might be a lot happier, although you'd be miserable. But that's not gonna happen."

The young cop scowled, and the older one laughed. Then I was back in my car and on my delayed ride home.

I figured that would be the last I ever heard of this poor overdosed jerk.

Ha.

PART ONE

1

Back in the good old, bad old days, I used to drive a Porsche Cayman, Black Edition. Once the dealer got it tricked out to my specs, it had cost me seventy thousand. I loved that car like the daughter I never had (and now probably never would have). The interior was like sitting cozy in God's palm. Once, I took it to a track and got it up to 160. There was a stretch of highway on the coast where I'd regularly break 120. Ghent, Goolsbee & Saikiri, my employers, even paid my speeding tickets.

But that car was long gone, auctioned off by court order, along with all my other possessions of any value, to repay at least some bare pittance to the clients I had bilked. All my savings accounts, IRAs, stocks, and other financial instruments and investments had been liquidated as well. I had gone into prison with a net worth approximating zero. And even then, my victims felt I hadn't been punished enough. Bernie Madoff, *c'est moi*—a pint-size version, anyway. I lost track of exactly how much I stole—the heroin was partly responsible for my slovenly illicit bookkeeping—but it was in the vicinity of only five or six million—nothing like Bernie's tab of eighteen billion or so.

In any case, when I got out of prison (curing my drug habit almost made that hellish stay worth it), I entered a halfway house as a penniless penitent. The counselors tried to fix me up with one dead-ass job after another, but I bailed on or got fired from all of them. It wasn't that I thought such work beneath me. Most of the companies the counselors placed me with provided valuable or at least not-harmful things and services, and their employees labored harder and more honestly than I ever had at GG&S. No, I just couldn't stand the contrast between my old life and this new one. Nor did I enjoy, as the break-room talk turned personal, sharing my fall from fortune with all these regular joes and janes.

They never got mad or judgmental with me over what I had done.

It was always pity I saw in their eyes. For I had thrown my life away, along with all its opportunities and rewards and privileges that they would never know.

They were right, of course, and I just couldn't take knowing they were right.

When it came time for my transition out of the halfway house, I had to meet for the umpteenth time with Anton Paget, my first and current parole officer.

Paget was no bleeding heart. About ten years older than me, he reminded me of a dwarf out of some fantasy movie, right down to the beard dense as a Texas mesquite thicket. He favored work boots, cargo shorts, and madras patch shirts that could make your eyes bleed. During ten years at this job, he had handled enough poor slobs like me not to be overoptimistic about the success rate of his clients.

"McClinton, you are a grade-A fuckup."

"Yes, sir."

"How, exactly, do you plan to reintegrate yourself back into society as a useful citizen if you can't even slap a hamburger together?"

"I do not wish to reintegrate, sir. I just want to live in isolation like a gut-shot animal and lick my wounds until I finally expire and am no longer a burden on society."

Paget restrained a grin. "Highly inspirational. Maybe we can get you a speaking gig at the local high schools. 'Scared Shiftless.'" His eyes narrowed. "Seriously, how do you intend to support yourself?"

"I have a relative who will take me in, at least until I can piece together what I want to do. My uncle, Ralph Sickert."

Paget needlessly consulted some forms—only to avoid holding my gaze, I suspected. "Your parents are both gone, correct?"

"Yes, sir."

My father, Aaron, had died of an aneurysm while I was still a young, high-flying legal eagle. But my mother, Christina, had died while I was in prison, her chronic illnesses no doubt aggravated by my fall from grace. I couldn't even get a day pass to attend her funeral.

"This Uncle Ralph—he's got a stable lifestyle? Good home? Willing to let you coast on his nickel?"

"He's retired, and he owns his own place. He says he could use my company."

"Well, we'll have to make a site inspection, but tentatively it sounds okay."

* * *

Leaving the parole office, I took a crosstown bus to Uncle Ralph's house and got busy.

What I hadn't told Paget was that Ralph Sickert was a stooper. That's the guy who picks up intact discarded tickets, looking for inadvertently abandoned winners. It's about as low as you can descend in the racetrack pecking order. So Uncle Ralph was gone from his modest house from sunup till late at night, coming back just to eat a little junk food and sleep before starting the next day all over again.

Ralph had married my mother's sister, Gillian. He had always been a devil-may-care playboy type who drove my sober and sedate aunt to distraction with his wild ways. But he had provided a good living for himself and his wife, thanks to his skills as an old-school chef, working at various high-end steak houses around the state, the kind of place that focused more on portion size than quality of the beef. When Aunt Gillian died, Ralph—left improvidently with no savings but with a free and clear deed to his house—retired on a decent Social Security check. That was when he developed a problem with the horses. He blew most of his check on the ponies within a few days after it hit his account. And for the rest of the month, he became a stooper—an ignoble profession at best.

But Uncle Ralph didn't seem to mind. Anything to stay active at the place where he felt most at home.

Consequently, Ralph's actual home looked as if the tenant had died a year ago and the corpse still hadn't been discovered. There were cobwebs older than my sentencing date, and the dust bunnies had mutated into jackalopes. The kitchen was piled high with moldy take-out containers, so that the place looked like the tomb of a pharaoh with an addiction to KFC and Subway.

That day, I spent a solid eight hours cleaning, until about 10:00 p.m., when I heard Uncle Ralph's tired old Impala pull into the driveway.

Hollowed out by his current schedule, lifestyle, and obsessions, the big man I recalled from my youth was now a beaten seventy-two-year-old washout. He didn't look particularly surprised to see me after so long. Neither welcoming nor rejecting, but neutrally curious, he listened to me explain what I needed from him.

"So you'll promise to be here all day this first time when the social worker is going to come by? And you'll make out like you're a quiet old shut-in who just can't wait for his nephew to move in?"

"Sure. So long as you can come up with a hundred dollars. That's what I make on a good day at the track." Ralph suddenly had a suspicious look. "Where you gonna get a hundred bucks from if you don't have a job?"

"Don't you worry about that," I said. "Listen, I gotta run now, to beat the curfew at the residence."

As I trotted down the sidewalk, Ralph called out, "Glen! Your mother always said right up to the end that you were a good boy!"

That was the first time I cried since my life went pear-shaped.

* * *

So, to put everything in a very small nutshell, the inspection went fine, the Department of Corrections approved, and for the past year now I had lived with Uncle Ralph. It was a mutually beneficial arrangement. I kept the place reasonably clean and saw that he ate better. He gave me a roof over my head, and a stable address where Anton Paget could regularly come and see I was not violating any terms of my parole, despite my slackerly lack of ambition.

And I even got the use of a car. Not a Porsche, but it was wheels.

Uncle Ralph's Impala hailed from the mythic year of 2002— precisely the model year that logged the most owner complaints. Something was always going wrong with it, and it fell to me to get the beast repaired.

It was only fair. I had access to the car pretty much all day. In the mornings, I would drop Uncle Ralph off at the track. I used to have to collect him, too. But over the past few months, he had been getting a ride from a lady friend his own age. Her name was Suzy Lam, and she resembled every plump Chinese auntie I had ever seen buying lottery tickets at the Asian markets. She could swear like a Marine drill instructor and smoked off-brand cigarettes by the carton. Suzy was just as hooked on the horses as Ralph, and apparently they had hit it off right from their first encounter. That meet-up occurred when Ralph, unbending after snatching a ticket from the filthy pavement, knocked the plastic cup of beer right out of Suzy's hand. It splashed a bystander, whom she dissuaded from punching Ralph by reeling off a gale of profanity in her tobacco-cured rasp. By the time she consumed the last dregs of the replacement beer my uncle had bought her, they were a couple.

I had a vague hunch that Suzy might be thinking about moving in with Ralph, in which case I would be a definite third wheel, forced to find alternative housing. But with my usual lack of interest in my own life, I couldn't get too worked up about the prospect until it happened.

On the morning of the August day that was to change my life, the Impala refused to start. Ralph hailed Suzy for a ride to the track, and a call to my regular garage got the balky machine hauled off. Later, I got the diagnosis: ignition shot. Two hundred and fifty for the repairs.

I went down to the basement. Built in the 1940s, Ralph's house featured a working cellar fireplace. He stubbornly continued to burn paper trash there now and again—mostly nonwinning tickets he carted home to sort—just as if he were living in some bygone decade before pollution laws.

Scraping aside the ashes, I uncovered the loose bricks. I worked them out of place, getting my fingers all sooty, and reached into the cavity for the little fireproof SentrySafe, about the size of a flat-wrench box. I unlocked it by spinning the three mechanical reels to the proper combination.

Inside were some two hundred gold Panda coins, thirty grams each, issued by the Chinese government. At current market value, each coin was worth about thirteen hundred dollars, although the guy I regularly sold them to, a shady coin dealer named Bert Deluca, would give me only a thousand apiece. The discount was consideration for his keeping the transactions unrecorded. So the total contents of the chest were worth somewhere between two hundred thousand and a quarter of a million dollars.

Not too many lawyers had an *actual* golden parachute—especially a lawyer deemed bankrupt by every court in the land.

2

Returning home in the repaired Impala, I had occasion to think about my future. Converting the latest gold Panda had turned my thoughts in that direction. Minus the garage guy's share, the remaining cash from the thousand that Deluca had given me weighed heavily in my pocket. Once, that sum would have represented a not particularly extravagant night on the town, a few bottles of good champagne, and some C-notes tucked into the waistband of a stripper's thong. Now it felt like one more bloody slice out of a dwindling legacy. I would piss the money away on boring necessities, maybe springing for something as wild as a movie ticket and a few happy-hour drinks at Danny's Cavern. This was a train of thought that always left me feeling numb, angry, confused, and helpless.

After being permanently disbarred, I could do nothing with all my expensive legal education and years of experience at GG&S. To all my old contacts, the back-slapping guys I had schmoozed and boozed with, I was radioactive waste. I had given up junk, and confronting myself in the mirror each morning, I felt anew, with genuine surprise, that the craving had truly and completely left my bones. So I couldn't even dream my time away in an opiate haze. No other pursuit really appealed to me. Since my teenage years, I had never had a predilection for anything but making as much easy money as fast as I could, and had chosen law school as the quickest route to that goal. And then I had chosen larceny as an even faster path. I supposed I could force myself to adapt to some new and decent-paying career. Pick up some fresh skills. Job training, sure. A new degree in bleeding-heart social work, maybe. Tractor-trailer driving school. Although, with my criminal record, the prospect of someone hiring me was no sure thing. Maybe I could buy into a glamorous and lucrative Dairy Queen franchise. But no likely alternative career was going to get me back into the stratosphere of one-percenter wealth and luxury that I had formerly inhabited.

A quarter-million dollars in gold. It sure sounded like a lot, even for someone who had boosted five million—until you realized that the stash was all there was or would ever be. That sum worked out to twenty-five K a year for ten years—a decade at chump wages.

My trapped mind ran down familiar channels, like a rat trying to earn some science cheese. Maybe I should think about relocating to a different country after my parole ended. Some stable, peaceful tropical place where life was easy and expenses were a fraction of what they were here. Beautiful half-naked native girls serving exotic drinks while I lolled in a hammock, shaded by palm trees. But did any such place actually exist anymore in this crazy, dangerous world? And what would such a backwater offer in the way of sophisticated pleasures that wouldn't get stale after the hundredth go-round?

I put the Impala in park and shut off the engine. Walking to the front door of Ralph's house—I refused to think of it as mine; that would be just too depressing—down the cracked pavement whose summer-strengthened weeds I kept meaning to grub up,

I continued uselessly going over my limited options. It was like riding a carousel past the same unreachable brass ring that gleamed just beyond my too-short child's arms.

Still distracted, I had my key in the lock when a big, heavy hand dropped onto my shoulder from behind, even though I had heard no one approaching.

My first thought was Anton Paget. He'd been spying on me in his sneaky parole-officer way and saw me cash in that Panda, and now I was royally fucked.

My second thought was that a pizza-delivery guy got shot a block away from here only a week ago.

My third thought was that I should slowly turn around in a nonthreatening manner and find out who this was.

Who it was, was the mook. The guy whose life I had saved back in December, over half a year ago.

But today he didn't look so mookish, and I began to form a new, more respectful opinion of him that would deepen with time.

No longer slumped dead in the driver's seat, and standing much too close inside my personal space, he proved to be a few inches taller than I. He had a lot of muscle on him, and some comfortable fat around the gut. Wherever he had been for the eight months since his overdose, it probably hadn't included the Fashion Institute of Technology. The electric-blue silk shirt, featuring various images of cavorting African wildlife, showed off even more chest foliage than his winter sweater had. He had dialed back the jewelry to a single silver Italian horn on a silver chain around his neck, but the decorative cornicello was as big as my middle finger. His sleek brown pants were of some form-hugging synthetic that displayed his topography in more lurid detail than if he had worn one of those Speedo marble bags. Brown tasseled loafers, sans socks, completed the ensemble.

Only after I had taken all this in, with the stranger's hairy paw still draped familiarly on my shoulder, did I notice that he was smiling, putting me vaguely in mind of a snarling grizzly. Okay, that was supposed to make me feel a tad more reassured about his innocent intentions.

"I'm Stan Hasso," he said, pushing a shaggy brown lock off his forehead as if to reveal a confirmatory trademark. "You're Glen McClinton, and you saved my fucking life."

"Um, yes, that would appear to be correct. No big deal."

The ursine face darkened. "Whatta you mean, 'no big deal'? It was a *huge* fucking deal! For me, anyhow, it sure was!"

I tried to back straight through the closed door. "Yes, of course," I stammered. "Saving someone's life is a very big deal! I just meant, it was, uh, no particular burden on me. No obligations. Happy to do it. Any old time."

Stan Hasso grew friendly again. "Okay, so we agree. You saved my life, and I owe you big-time. So listen, I'm gonna do something good for you. To repay you, like."

In a fleeting moment of baseless absurdity, I pictured Stan Hasso introducing me to some woman, a friend of his own hypothetical girlfriend, and the four of us going on a double date.

In the months to come, I would recall that visionary flash and marvel at its off-kilter accuracy.

Stan Hasso leaned in close to me, his thick, spicy cologne swamping my senses and even causing my eyes to blur. "How'd you like to get rich, Glen? Five million dollars rich. Sound good to you?"

At first, I couldn't think. This whole freaky scene was playing out as if he had been reading my mind for the past few hours.

But when my brain got revolving again, I said, "Stan, my friend, let's go inside, where you can tell me more."

3

Inside the stuffy house, I opened some windows and got two beers out of the fridge. The cheap stuff I could afford. I didn't bother with glasses. Such delicate hostess touches had vanished with my old life. I didn't think Stan Hasso would mind a cold, sweaty bottle on a hot August day, and he didn't.

Uncle Ralph's house had no air-conditioning, so I set a grimy plastic box fan wobbling in one window to push the heat around.

Hasso had gravitated inevitably to the most comfortable chair in the room, one suitable for his bulk. The parlor featured Aunt Gillian's best furniture, ground down by the unforgiving years into a suite of flophouse castoffs. Uncle Ralph's slovenly lifestyle had not been kind to Aunt Gillian's pride and joy. Unfortunately, she had favored for her set white fabric dotted with small blue flowers, and it showed every stain of the subsequent decade. Sprawled with his legs stretching almost to the center of the small space, Hasso resembled some Long Island disco-era prince unwinding after a funky time on the dance floor.

I took the seat farthest from him and closest to the front door. He seemed harmless, even a potential new best friend, especially if he was somehow going to put five million dollars in my hands. But as with all dealings involving money, tempers could flare, and Hasso's earlier lapse into anger had shown me he might easily find a reason to do me harm. It did not escape me that I sat here, incommunicado with anyone else who might care about my welfare, sharing a beer with an unknown ex-con and holding seven hundred and fifty dollars in my pocket. In these situations, having saved a guy's life bought only so much goodwill.

And yet, I could not regard Hasso as a menace or a scammer. Sure, such a guy would always be looking out for himself. But some oddly ingenuous, even faintly naive vibe underneath the bluster convinced me he might also do me some good along his selfish path.

I didn't open the conversation. After draining a third of his drink in the first pull, he said, "Let me tell you a few things about Stan Hasso, so you can get an idea of where I'm coming from."

"Okay," I said. "But you have to promise me one thing."

"What's that?"

"You will never refer to yourself in the third person again."

Hasso's face flashed confusion, irritation, and amusement in quick succession. "You got it." He squirmed his butt around as if to reconfigure the ridge formed over the years by Uncle Ralph's bony ass groove, and began.

"That night in December when I almost cashed my ticket, I had just got out of the can. Released that morning. Served three years for felony arson. When I went in, I had a habit. And the first thing I did when I got out was score. I'd been dreaming of a fix for three years, you know, even though I was clean after the first few months in the stir. Kept telling myself I needed and deserved it. It had gotten to the point where the dream had a life of its own. Looking back, I can see I didn't even really have any desire to shoot up. At least, not like when I was truly hooked. It was just like the dream was some old debt that had to be paid, or sort of a fuck-you to them for putting me away. Like my mind was an old video replaying itself. I was gonna get even with everyone, even if I had to cut off my own dick to do it. Any of this making any sense to you?"

I tried to figure out if Hasso's question implied anything about my own junkie past. How much did he know about me? He had tracked me down here, after all. Well, maybe the depth of his knowledge about me would come out later.

I thought about my own detox, how I had harbored similar fantasies and compulsions and anger that, luckily for me, had died out before I got released. Somehow, I had seen through the deceptions of my own addiction before I got into a place where I could resurrect old bad habits.

"Yeah," I said, "I hear you."

Hasso killed another third of his beer. "But Jesus, I hadn't realized how much the frigging scene had changed since I went in! Dealers these days, they don't think twice about cutting their stuff with enough fentanyl to croak a bull. People are offing themselves left and right, when all they want is a nice high!"

Hasso sounded genuinely indignant at the injustice of it all, revealing again that hidden and faintly ridiculous nobility of soul and sense of injured justice.

"So to cut to the chase, I got a hot shot like nothing I ever had before. And maybe, too, being clean, my body couldn't take what it used to. Whatever. You saw what happened. I OD'd right there at the stoplight where I put the spike in. If it wasn't for you, I'd be rotting today in one of those number-only plots with the other nameless street trash."

"Like I said, I was happy to be of help. So, no family, then?"

"Not one lousy second cousin or ex-sister-in-law to claim my unholy carcass. It's just me against the world. I don't even have a kindly old uncle, like some folks I could name."

He smiled big at the undeniable and purposeful hit. It seemed Mr. Hasso had done some homework.

"When I got out of the hospital, I expected to end up back in the can. But I lucked out. The judge was a goody-goody. She stuck me in this new kind of diversion program. That's where I been for the past seven months. Learning all about how to be a decent member of society by avoiding all my codependent triggering shit and how to reprogram all my failure modes, like. Then, when I finally got some free time, it still took me a couple of weeks to track you down and scope you out. The cops weren't too liberal with information. I had to pull in a few favors."

"This is your town, then?"

"Yeah, that's why I came straight back to the city after they turned me loose from the calaboose. Figured I knew the territory."

"You planned on, uh, resuming your old line of work?"

"Torching stuff? Nah, that's out. Not that I couldn't pick right up again. I didn't lose my touch. Best firebug this side of the Mississippi. No, they only caught me because of a tip. A bastard of a snitch turned me in—the very guy who hired me for that last job, in fact."

As swiftly as a tropical storm, a cloud of pure hatred passed over the face of Stan Hasso. I felt relieved to be sitting at some distance from him, and also not to have a place on his shit list.

"So that part of my career relates directly to how you and me and a couple of essential helpers I got in mind are gonna get rich. You'll hear all about it at the proper time. But the only way you're gonna understand how this'll pay off for us is to take a little tour."

My voice cracked a bit. "Um ... tour?"

"C'mon now, Glen, don't go all taffy-ass on me. I don't mean anything more than what I'm saying. We just need to drive around town for an hour to scope out a few sites. That sound like a small enough investment for a five-million payback?"

"Well, when you put it that way …" I had a sobering thought. "Should we be seen together, though? Two ex-cons associating?"

"Don't sweat it; no one's gonna recognize us. It's not like we're *Dog Day Afternoon* here. Just put on your shades and slump down in your seat if you're worried. And guess what? Your Big Brother Anton Paget is out of town this week. How do I know? He's my minder, too."

Hasso glugged the last of his beer and shot to his feet. He moved fast for a big man sunk down in an old sprung chair.

"Okay, then, Glen boy! Toss me the keys. I'll drive so you can focus on the sights. I don't have any wheels myself right now—had to take a taxi out to this dump."

Reluctantly, I handed over the keys to the Impala. At this point, there seemed no reasonable way I could refuse. I wasn't buying into anything yet, after all. I was just going for a drive. And I would actually feel safer out in public than in the house.

Still, I had to raise some mild objection to Hasso's dominance. "It's my uncle's car, you know."

"Don't get your panties in a twist. I'll treat it like the vintage classic it is. Now, let's roll."

4

The recently rebranded Seven Oaks neighborhood was an up-and-coming residential district on the west side of town. Back in my GG&S days, looking to get in on the ground floor of a solid investment, I had almost bought a place here before getting a better deal on a loft closer to work. Once home to various light industries associated with the garment trade, it used to be called Button Town. I remember my dad taking me there one Saturday morning when I was about nine years old. We trooped past stooped, bandanna-coiffed laboring women and across a noisy factory floor where hot cotton, rubber, and machine oil gave off a fascinating tang. At the other end was a seedy but neat office. There, my dad talked business with a guy sporting a mustache like Lech Walesa's—an exotic figure much on the nightly news at the time. While they dickered over the installation of a new sprinkler system in the shop, I was left unattended, to leaf with increasingly horrified fascination through an undergarment catalogue. Right around that long-ago year, the first Victoria's Secret store had opened in our local mall. I had been riveted by the sexy images and was hoping for something along those lines from this sales brochure. Instead, I found black-and-white photos of women who resembled my grandmother, wearing support garments fashioned after medieval torture devices. I still don't know how my sexuality ever recovered.

As Stan Hasso tooled the Impala down Callista Avenue, the memory made me smile.

I could have sworn Hasso had eyes only for the sparse traffic. His driving was competent and circumspect and surely striving to be unworthy of any police attention. But he must have caught my grin. Imperceptive, he was not. A good thing to remember.

"What's so funny?"

I told him.

"Now, that's a coincidence. I knew that building pretty good. Hadn't been a girdle factory for some time, but there were still a bunch of retail shops inside. That's one of the places I wanted to show you. We're coming up on it right now, in fact."

Hasso pulled into a curbside slot. I looked out and saw, not the factory from my youth or the arcade that replaced it, but a gleaming new condo building. A modest three stories tall, but it took up the entire square block. Elegant signage proclaimed this to be *The Phoenix Arms*. Brick and brushed aluminum, blue-greenish thermopane windows and passive solar features. Very tasteful.

"This is where that underwear factory used to be?"

"Yeah. It burned down somehow."

I pondered that acid-etched observation.

Hasso grinned. "I think the concierge here makes more a week in tips than any of those women got paid in six months. Your basic unit goes for one-point-five million. Get out of the car."

"Huh?"

"Get out of the car, go up to the front door, and read the plaque they got pasted there. Don't try no soliciting, though. They got a warning posted, and it's backed up by security guards."

Being bossed around by Hasso was annoying, but I wasn't about to get into any pissing contests with this behemoth. Besides, in this case it was nothing worth arguing about. I could show that I was bigger than his childish need to strut his authority. So I did as ordered.

The discreet bronze shield featured the bas-relief of an old-fashioned player piano, and this legend:

NANCARROW LOGISTICS TRUST MANAGEMENT, LTD.
"QUALITY RESIDENCES FOR QUALITY CLIENTS"

I returned to the car, saying nothing. Hasso didn't quiz me or shed any light on what I had read.

We drove out of Seven Oaks and soon found ourselves on the edge of town, not far from Giuffre Memorial Park, that popular riverside reservation managed by the state.

"You like baseball?" Hasso inquired.

"Yeah, well enough, I guess. I actually like basketball better."

"Me, too. But let's have us a look at a baseball stadium anyhow."

Hasso took us off the main road at the entrance to the new stadium for the Bandits, the Class A minor-league team that made its home here. The place had gone up while I was jailed, replacing the rickety old structure some miles away. I had not seen the new field since I got out. My first impression was of a well-wrought, functional, appealingly modest venue—fitting for the humble stature of the Bandits. It seemed as if the developer had not skimped on materials or design. I was willing to bet that a family could have a good, comfortable, inexpensive night out here.

Hasso pulled the car up next to one of the wide concrete pillars that supported the upper stories, and I saw a bronze shield featuring that same player piano.

NANCARROW LOGISTICS TRUST MANAGEMENT, LTD.

"RECREATIONAL FACILITIES THAT FOSTER COMMUNITY SPIRIT"

Hasso said, "You know what used to be here? A dairy farm. It lasted a hundred and fifty years in the same family. But Mrs. O'Leary's cow must've kicked over a lantern or something, because one night it caught fire, sudden-like."

We left the stadium behind and drove to several more spots, all of which featured Nancarrow properties that had arisen, according to Hasso's narration, from the ashes of vest-pocket infernos.

Our final stop was at the new Department of Public Works facility. Inside a chain-link fenced lot, big snow plows lay quietly in summer estivation, and I was reminded of the December evening when I saved Hasso's life.

Here, the Nancarrow plaque was more subdued, and subordinate to the city's own official seal.

NANCARROW LOGISTICS TRUST MANAGEMENT, LTD.

"CIVIC DUTY AND ENGAGEMENT THROUGH

ECONOMICAL DESIGN"

I said, "There used to be some kind of rectory or monastery here, wasn't there?"

Hasso put his large hands together palm to palm like a giant altar boy and looked skyward. "The Benedictine Sisters of Perpetual Adoration. Just two wrinkled, half-deaf old nuns squatting on twenty thousand square feet of falling-apart castle, on land worth a few million. Luckily, they both came down with food poisoning and were in the hospital when the place went up."

"Jesus."

"Yeah, that's who they were counting on. But neither the nuns nor Jesus nor any of these other owners could hold a candle, so to speak"—here he mimed a little bow from the driver's seat—"to the team of Nancarrow and Hasso."

I looked at him with what surely registered as stunned disbelief. He beamed with evident pride.

"Oh, sure, you won't find my name on any incorporation papers or nothing. I was kind of a silent partner, you see."

His face went dark. "Until there came a parting of the ways. On which the books ain't quite closed yet."

5

Reasons why I like Danny's Cavern: It's just a couple of miles from Uncle Ralph's house. The drinks are cheap. The seasoned, stolid, disdainful help, who have seen and survived every tragedy imaginable, leave you alone, neither disbursing nor soliciting sympathy. None of my old friends would be caught dead in this down-market dive, thus forestalling any embarrassment for me or them. And there are no televisions, flat-screen or otherwise, blaring at the patrons.

I estimated that Danny's was last redecorated sometime during the first Clinton administration. The booths featured lime-green vinyl, patched here and there with duct tape of roughly the same shade and trimmed with fat-topped brass nails. The bar stools, with their padded seats of an unlikely floral fabric akin to slippery chintz, would have pleased Aunt Gillian. I suspected a bargain job-lot purchase. Luckily, the gritty, Carhartt-clad backsides of thousands of working-stiff patrons had imparted some roughness to the seats, although patrons deep in their cups still tended to slide gradually floorward, aided by the slick fabric. From the spray-textured ceiling, sixty-watt bulbs shone through globes of pebbled ruby-colored glass. Below, the occasional missing linoleum tile revealed floorboards the color of buttery mashed potatoes mixed with cigarette ashes.

Stan Hasso and I had a booth in the rear section, next to the swinging kitchen doors, whose padded surface showed a million greasy handprints. Danny's Cavern featured a limited menu along the lines of cold-cut sandwiches, ready-made shrimp cocktail, stuffed cabbage rolls, and Jell-O of the same hue as the vinyl booths.

Hasso was working on an enormous grinder, washed down with a pitcher of Old Milwaukee. His latest bite bisected a pickled pepper, arcing a squirt of clear juice across the table in my direction. I had little appetite and was nursing a mojito, having long since become inured to taunts from some of the regulars about having a "girly drink." The tropical cocktail allowed me to fantasize about the Brazilian vacation I had taken at the height of my crimes, to experience Carnival. That existence felt increasingly like someone else's, which I had viewed in a movie.

Hasso finished his sandwich and all but half a glass of the beer. He belched contentedly and sat back.

"Okay, now that you had the tour around town, you're ready to hear the whole story about me and Nancarrow, including how he done me wrong. Then we'll talk about the plan I got to soak him for somewheres around twenty million. First off, you've heard of Barnaby Nancarrow before today, I bet."

"Yes, of course. He's one of the city's leading businessmen and philanthropists. Made a fortune in real estate, always giving away a couple of thousand here and there to various charities. Spreads small sums around rather than focusing on any one cause. Likes the ladies very much but has no special partner. Is eager to have his picture taken with politicians and other powerful people. I was actually at a party once where he showed up, but we never talked."

"Yeah, you traveled in special circles once upon a time, didn't you? Musta felt nice. Me, I never woulda been allowed in the same room as him when we were operating together, and certainly not now. Despite all I did for him. Anyhow, that's a pretty good short description, but it leaves out a lot. First thing is—which hardly anyone knows—he wasn't born Barnaby Nancarrow. He dug up the first name from some old TV show. Thought it sounded classy but kinda old-school like. Not threatening, folksy, and all that crap. 'Nancarrow' he took from some famous guy that played the piano a shitload of years ago. Pretends now that he's descended from this other Nancarrow, and that's why he uses the piano on his signs and letters and stuff."

"How do you know all this?"

"Because Barnaby Nancarrow—or, as he was then known, Algy Teague—grew up side by side with me. Algernon and Stanley, bosom buddies. Both our families were dirt poor. Food stamps, church pantries, charity coats in the winter. You remember that neighborhood they called the Gulch?"

"Sure," I said. "Now it's a mall and the water park and a lot of pricey restaurants."

"Well, back then it was piss-smelling alleys and roach-filled tenements and weedy lots where dead bodies tended to accumulate. Rival gangs of about six different ethnic types who all hated each other, all struggling for turf. That's where me and Nancarrow spent the precious days of our youth, hustling and angling for the main chance. But after a certain point, we went our separate ways. I dropped out of school and started scrabbling for whatever work I could find, on the shady or the sunny side of the street. But Algy—Nancarrow—he got lucky. Or maybe he was just naturally brighter than me. Some charitable guy thought he had potential, and took him under his wing and got him into some fancy college on the far side of the country, all for free. That's where he changed his name, all legal-like, and emerged four years later all polished up, shiny as a new penny straight from the mint. Why he came back to this stinking burg, I'll never figure. I guess maybe once the Gulch is in your blood, you can't escape it entirely. But his family was all gone, along with pretty much everyone else from the old hood, once they bulldozed the place. He musta felt safe returning to a place where he knew the ropes and no one knew him."

"All right," I said. "So Nancarrow comes back here and looks you up right away? Not too likely in my book."

"No, course not. He had zero idea if I was still alive or had screwed the pooch and got dead, like about 70 percent of the kids from the Gulch. And he wasn't holding on to any nostalgia for old pals. But when word went out that some anonymous big player needed a torch, my reputation preceded me, and the next thing I know, it's reunion time for Stan and Algy. He was a little nervous at first, coming face-to-face with someone who knew all about his real history and who could spill the beans if they chose to. Not that Algy even had much of a juvenile record to be ashamed of—just the usual misdemeanors. But the shabby start to his life woulda mortified him in front of his new high-class pals. I think maybe that's one reason he hired me: to keep me in his pocket and indebted to him so I wouldn't want to spoil his setup. Of course, my skills at making inconvenient buildings go up in smoke were the main reason."

"So you're telling me that Nancarrow's whole fortune is built on arson?"

"Well, maybe not his *whole* fortune, but a big chunk of it. You see, he only had a small stake when he came back, and he wanted to parlay it into a big one, and fast. That's the kind of lessons and ambitions the Gulch drilled into us. Make a killing any way you can, and make it quick. You never forget those rules, no matter how many fancy schools you go to. So he focused on undervalued properties. Places like the girdle factory. He'd snap them up for a song, then have me burn them down. To throw off suspicion, he used a lot of fake names and fake companies with no obvious connections to him. Worked like a charm. Nobody ever sussed out all these fires were connected to one guy. They paid off like a rigged roulette wheel. The insurance money would go toward the redevelopment. No trouble finding legit partners eager for easy money. And the property was always worth more without some shitty old factory on it than with. Big profits piling up faster and faster."

"Sounds like a marriage made in heaven. What broke it up?"

"Nancarrow felt he'd finally made it. He was gonna go totally straight. No more torching. That left me out of a job, and I made the mistake of sounding unhappy about it. If I hadn't been hopped up half the time back then, I woulda been smarter about shooting my mouth off. But the dope made me a little sloppy. So he ratted me out on another assignment—a job I did for someone else—and off to jail I went, to teach me a lesson. Luckily, the charge was for a smaller gig than any of the others, so I got out fairly quick."

"He wasn't afraid you'd take him down with you, before or after prison?"

Hasso looked genuinely affronted. "Number one, I am not a snitch—even against a bastard like Nancarrow. We were both Gulch rats, right? Number two, he put fifty thousand into my bank account the day I went in. Peanuts to him, but a lot to me. Number three, where was the evidence? It wasn't like I had signed contracts for all the work I did for him. It woulda been just my word against his—the street trash against the society suit. Maybe, just maybe, I coulda interested some cop in my story. And maybe, just maybe, that imaginary cop coulda come up with something against Nancarrow. But what were the odds? No, keeping my mouth shut was the only sensible thing to do. I figured I'd get back at Nancarrow my own way, once I was free again."

"And you want me to help somehow," I said. "I have to tell you, violence makes me puke."

Hasso snorted. "If I wanted to hurt Nancarrow some physical way, I could do it by myself. And if I couldn't do it by myself, well, no offense, but you're not exactly the extra muscle I'd pick. No, I'm gonna hit him where it'll hurt him the most. I'm gonna take twenty million dollars from him and make him look like an idiot. And that's where you come in. I need your smarts, and also something else."

"What else?"

"That quarter of a million in gold you're sitting on."

6

The dim light from the dirty red globes in the Cavern seemed to thicken and slow to a molasses crawl, as if the nature of time itself had changed. The cash in my pocket assumed a supernatural weight, as if the whole trove of gold hidden back in the fireplace had jumped into my pants to join the recently converted Panda coin. Breathing seemed like a new skill I had not yet properly mastered, and my limbs tingled with a strange exhilarated paralysis.

I must have looked like a steer on its way to the slaughterhouse, because Stan Hasso adopted an expression of genuine concern and distress.

"Hey, bro, unclench! No one's gonna hurt you. Your secret's safe with me. This is all about the two of us acting together for our mutual benefit. I'm gonna kick in my fifty thou, if you agree. That shows good faith, right? Anyhow, we're just talking at this point, okay? C'mon, now, relax. Here, drink this."

He handed me the pint tumbler with his last few ounces of warmish beer in it, and I automatically took it with one lead-weighted hand and slugged it back, although I am not normally in the habit of drinking backwash from a less-than-pristine glass. The very mundaneness of the Old Milwaukee's skunky taste acted like some kind of noxious antidote to my initial fright and confusion, and I began to feel slightly more like a sentient human being instead of a helpless chipmunk in the claws of an owl. Even the sixty-watt bulbs in the Cavern resumed their usual low-intensity ruby glow.

Now that my immediate crisis was past and I did not seem on the point of physical or emotional breakdown, Hasso looked pleased with himself. "I hit on the real figure pretty close, huh? Not bad for educated guesswork. Just call me No-Shit Sherlock, right?"

"But how … how did you even know about the gold?"

"I told you, I scoped you out for a while before I showed up today at your door. I had to know whether or not you'd make a good partner. If I'da had any doubts about that, I wouldn'a showed up at all, or maybe I mighta just stopped by to say thanks for saving my ass back in December. But I liked what I learned about you, Glen, and so that's why I was up front about your gold. Nothing hidden between us, right? Share and share alike. So how did I know about the gold? Simple. I followed you one day last month to Deluca's, and I braced the coin guy for info about what you and he were doing. He gave it up quicker than microwave popcorn by the way, which makes him a weak link for you if anyone else ever comes snooping."

"But guessing the amount?"

"Piece of cake. I just did some studying, then ran the numbers. First off, I knew how much you stole total, and how much you claimed you blew through, and how much the court clawed back out of your accounts. Them numbers were right there in all the media coverage. All the parts of the equation were supposed to balance out to zero left for you. The judge bought your story, but not me. I knew the numbers lied. If you were cashing in gold, then you had squirreled something away. But it wasn't life-changing amounts, or you wouldn't look so pitiful and hangdog whenever you had to sell a coin. That's where me being a student of human nature comes in. I can read people. Tricks I learned in the Gulch, just to stay alive. I hate to say it, but in spite of all your crimes, Glen boy—and I'm counting the stuff lawyers do that is supposedly legal—you're kinda innocent still. Man, I hope you never play poker, your tells are about as subtle as a billboard."

I got a little miffed then. "Okay, so I'm a babe in the woods next to you. What's the rest of your detective work?"

"Well, I started to think, how long would I want my raggedy little stash to last if I were in the same fix as ol' Glen? Maybe five years or so. You were cashing out a thousand about every five or six weeks. The rest of the business was just some multiplying I could do on my fingers."

What Hasso said made total sense. I wondered how I had ever hoped to fool anyone who tumbled to my dealings. I had been a better bluffer on dope, which gave me a kind of brazenness and audacity for the big lie.

"Okay, so I have a quarter million in gold. Big whoop. It's pathetic, isn't it? And it's actually a little less, at the rate Deluca buys the coins. But however little it is, I assume you want some."

"Some? I want all of it! For our scam! I'm putting in my fifty K, and I would add more if I could. You're gonna invest your quarter mil and get five mil back! Now, that's life-changing dough! Who else is gonna make you an offer like that?"

I was a little taken aback at Hasso's genuine sincerity. He truly did not want to appear as if he were strong-arming or black-mailing me or ripping me off. Taken with his earlier statement about never snitching, he appeared to be a crook with a certain code of ethics. Maybe I could trust him. Maybe he had a scheme that would work. Maybe we could actually pull something off that netted us a big paycheck. A lot of maybes. But I was starting to think that any number of maybes were preferable to the dull, diminishing certainties that were my only other future.

I said, "You keep talking about this scam to get millions out of Nancarrow. How's that gonna happen, exactly? Shouldn't I hear some details before I decide to invest?"

"Absolutely! You don't buy a pig in a poke, I know that. But this plan of mine is genius. And all it needs is your dough and your demonstrated talents for screwing people over. Like you did to the Evangelides broad."

I actually felt my face get warm. The elderly Harriet Evangelides, newly widowed and with a sizable legacy, had made the mistake of taking investment advice from yours truly. I had spun a financial web so convincing in its false complexities that even her husband's expert accountants had been fooled for a long time. As a result, Harriet no longer lived in the fine big house her husband had provided for her, but with a daughter and son-in-law, far from her familiar scene and friends, on a strict budget. The only palliation of my crime that I could summon up was that very feeling I had mentioned earlier, that the dope-suffused, sociopathic Glen McClinton had been another person entirely.

"Okay, so I can scam people. But Nancarrow is a scammer himself. What makes you think we can get anything out of him?"

"I know we can. We're gonna tap straight into his ego and his greed, just like with any mark. In the end, he's going to write us a check for twenty million or so, and be glad to do it."

"Twenty million? How's that work out to five apiece for us?"

"We've got to bring two other people onboard. And they both got something neither of us got. One's an expert with computers and shit. And the other one is a babe who hates Nancarrow's guts."

7

The musty retro-sleaze interior of Danny's Cavern had seemed much the same at 3:00 p.m., when Hasso was demolishing his sandwich and pitcher of beer, as now, at 11:00, when he chomped his way through a plate of buffalo wings and slugged down an accompanying quart of ghastly-sweet sangria. Perhaps the only difference was that now the ever-rotating but essentially interchangeable clientele seemed more desperate for some kind of connection, whether with the demigods of alcohol, the person on the adjacent chintz-slippery bar stool, or some numinous being that only they could see.

I wasn't feeling in top form. It had been an utterly exhausting day, its events too odd and numerous to fit into the same twenty-four hours. First the shock of getting waylaid by this hulking stranger on my doorstep, then hearing his life story, riding about town while being pitched a nebulous scheme to get even with his ex-employer, and realizing that my secret stash of gold Pandas was on the line—all this had left my head awhirl and my gut churning. And my couple of wings and small glass of sangria hadn't helped.

Hasso licked his fingers clean and washed down the final

remnants of hot sauce with a large belt of fruity wine. "Ah, man, now I can focus on talking. Mind's no good when the stomach's empty, am I right? You sure you don't need nothing else? Jesus, you didn't eat enough today for an anorexic cheerleader."

"No, no, I'm good."

"Okay. Get out your phone."

Without asking why, I dug out my primitive flip phone.

"Holy Christ, what is that? Nineteen ninety calling, bro! They want their technology back!"

Hasso's gibes pissed me off, and I found myself answering in kind. "Listen, smart-ass, when I was a lawyer, I always had the latest iPhone. Totally connected, always in my hand. I know what they're all about. But now I've got no use for one. I've got no one to call, no one to text, no Facebook friends. And I'm just not interested in most online shit. Plus, they're expensive. And you know what I found out in jail? Those things are a leash. I'm happier without one. The only reason I've got this simple model is that Paget said he and any potential employers had to have some way to reach me."

Stan Hasso regarded me with a sort of weird vicarious admiration and satisfaction, as if my mild backsass confirmed to him that he had not erred, that I was not a total wuss—competent and also mean enough to be his partner. "Okay," he said, "I hear ya. You're probably right—in some useless egghead way. But ya gotta have a smartphone if you wanna be a player. And just remember, a leash can be yanked from either end. Now, scoot over here and we'll use mine."

Reluctantly I came around to his side of the booth and sat down beside him. His large body radiated heat and a kind of animal vitality, along with the dwindling scent of body spray.

Hasso had his phone out—a glass slab the size of a trade paperback.

"I gotta hand it to you, Glen boy. You've been real patient with my meager details. Here I waltz into your life, talking about making millions in some kind of crazy revenge scheme against a well-connected guy, and you don't even press me for particulars. Well, now your patience is finally gonna be rewarded. And you're gonna say this is pure genius."

Hasso brought up on his screen the front page of the *Citizen Ledger Tribune*, the local paper of record (a desperate merger of what had once been three flourishing rivals). He scrolled down, found what he was looking for, and jabbed the headline with one big finger.

LOCATION OF NEW CASINO STILL A SECRET

"Can you believe this? That Vegas mogul Steve Prynne has everybody shitting their pants out of sheer frustrated greed. He's as wicked smart as that douchebag Trump imagines his own self to be. Prynne's swore up and down that he's definitely gonna build somewhere in the state. It's a market he wants. Totally underserved. Guaranteed millions in profits. But he won't say where. And why should he? The instant he names the property he wants, the price for it will shoot sky high. And values for the whole area will rocket up, too. Local owners'll make a killing. But maybe not the first guy to sell—especially if Prynne uses a front to buy the land for a song.

Whatever Stan's scheme was, the presence of Prynne in it confirmed to me that, potentially at least, big money was in play.

"Now, don't think Nancarrow isn't getting a boner over all this happening right in his own backyard. He sees himself pissin' in the same tall weeds as Prynne, maybe just a few rungs below him."

"What kind of weeds have rungs?" I said. "Jacob's ladder? Ladder fern?"

"Ha ha, that's a riot. I had a teacher back in the Gulch who always used to pick on the colorful way I talked. She never came back to the classroom after that time her brakes let go. Now, where was I? Oh, yeah. So, Nancarrow would give his left nut to somehow get in on this casino deal and make a killing, establish a connection with Prynne. Convince him they could be partners or something. Believe me, I know him. He can see his name in the headlines already. And that ambition and greed is how we're gonna hook him. We're gonna convince Nancarrow that we know Prynne's pick—that we have the rights to the secret chosen casino land and we'll sell it to him for the bargain price of twenty million. Now, when I say 'we,' I mean you as the legal owner. Ol' Algy can't suspect I'm anywhere in the picture, or he'll smell a scam for sure."

We had to interrupt our discussion as Harriet, a barmaid older than television, came by to ask if we wanted more booze. I flashed on how odd it must look for both Stan and me to be occupying the same side of the booth. But Harriet seemed to take it all in stride and left with our orders. Just another late shift at Danny's Cavern.

"How are we going to convince Nancarrow our property is the one Prynne wants?"

"Two ways. First, the old-fashioned way: bribing a state senator. Second, the newfangled way: by futzing around on the internet."

"Let's assume you can do it," I said. "Where is this land, exactly?"

"Upstate, in the region that everyone already figures Prynne is most interested in."

"It's got to be a pretty big chunk of land for the kind of operation Prynne has in mind."

"Five hundred acres."

"Five hundred acres? How can we afford that with my lousy savings and your pittance?"

Hasso started swiping through several screens. "But we can, no problem! The land's in a real dead zone—nowheresville with a handful of hicks living on it. Best of all, it's unincorporated land. No authorities looking over our shoulders."

Hasso angled his phone so I could better read the screen.

FOR SALE

BIGELOW JUNCTION

500+ ACRES

SEVERAL BUILDINGS INCLUDED

LARGE DEVELOPMENT POTENTIAL

CLOSE TO INTERSTATE HIGHWAY

Hasso snorted. "'Close to the highway' is true. The freeway runs right through the middle of the land. But they don't mention that the nearest exit ramp is twenty miles away from the center of the property, down a local road you can't drive more'n thirty-five on. Of course, if this *was* gonna be the casino land, they'd put in some new ramps right where Prynne demanded, faster'n a goose can crap. Anyhow, the price is right. Two hundred twenty-five large. Out of your quarter million and my so-called pittance, that still leaves us seventy-five thou for the bribe and other operating expenses, of which we're gonna have some. But not much, because this whole thing has to go down fast, before Prynne makes his real selection public."

I thought about the whole scheme. It seemed crazy—maybe just crazy enough to carry its own success in the terms of its outrageousness.

Hasso sensed I was verging on agreement. "Look, we're not even really gonna be doing anything illegal. We're gonna own some land all kosher-like, and Nancarrow wants to buy it. A simple, honest transaction."

"It's the misrepresentation that's illegal," I said. "I could cite you a dozen fraud statutes that we could be prosecuted under. Never mind bribing an official."

Hasso banged his big phone down with a loud *BLAM!* on the table and hollered, rousing the abstracted customers out of their alcohol-hazed introspection.

"Jesus Christ, Glen! Are you *afraid* to get rich? Or maybe you're just happy living like a broke-backed dog, lying in the gutter in your own puke!"

Echoing my own thoughts and even Paget's accusation of cowardly fecklessness, Hasso's words pushed me to a place I had never imagined going when this long-ago morning dawned.

"All right, all right, calm down. I'm in."

Hasso offered a fist bump. "Dude!"

"But I need encouragement, so next time could you tone down the unflattering imagery just a tad?"

8

Today would be devoted to finances.

Driving across town that sunny morning, my lockbox full of gold lying on the archaic worn-velour cushion that had been factory installed flush between the front seats of the old Impala, I wondered for the hundredth time since last night whether I was doing the smart thing. Or, if not exactly the *smart* thing, at least a potentially rewarding thing—a proactive course of action that would lift up my self-esteem without getting me jailed, killed, or otherwise badly damaged and that also might reboot the failed course of my life.

I just couldn't decide. Had I been bullied and seduced into an unwise and self-destructive scheme? Or just alerted to my own sloth and self-pity and jolted into taking the evanescent main chance for a life-changing payoff that was being presented to me?

I grabbed the can of warming ginger ale from the busted cup holder and tried to soothe my churning stomach.

Last night as Hasso and I left Danny's Cavern, I had a brief flash that he was going to ask to stay at Uncle Ralph's house, having finished up his residential treatment and been left with no place else to go. I was already mentally framing some kind of story to sell Uncle Ralph when Hasso said, "You mind driving me to my girl's place? Kinda late to get a cab—especially a driver that'll go to my hood. And that way, you'll know where to pick me up tomorrow."

"Sure, no problem."

Chalmers Street lay deep inside the district that the *Citizen Ledger Tribune* often colorfully referred to as "Slaughterville." I dropped Hasso off at number forty-six, with the only illumination coming from the last functioning streetlight, half a block away.

* * *

This morning, Chalmers Street had considerably more activity than last night, none of it especially scary. Truth be told, in my junkie days I had ventured into scenes that were a lot sketchier.

By daylight, number forty-six revealed itself to be a once-classy brownstone fallen on squalid times. The granite steps up to its front door, featuring colorful graffiti tags and flanked by overflowing trash cans, were chipped as if a bored kid with a ball-peen hammer had used them for a long game of Whac-a-Mole. Rain-stained cardboard substituted for a missing glass pane in the front door.

I was debating whether to get out and try to discover which apartment held Stan Hasso, when he emerged from the building with a woman in tow.

A fit match for Hasso's burliness, the big, tall woman probably outweighed me. But no one would think to call her fat after taking in her mind-blowing topography of bountiful and alluring curves. She wore flare-bottomed camouflage leggings that looked painted on by someone running out of paint, a gingham shirt with the tails tied to reveal a bare midriff; and rainbow high-heeled espadrilles.

Gold hoops that could have collared a standard poodle dangled from her ears, and a red bandanna secured her wavy black hair.

Hasso and the woman came around to the passenger side. Hasso grunted a weary introduction, as if he had not gotten much sleep. Or maybe the sangria had left him hungover.

"Glen boy, Sandralene."

Hasso opened the door, and Sandralene deposited her generous left haunch onto the seat, then slid it and the rest of her over in one fluid, sensuous motion, butting up against me as if she were trying to mold an impression of my shape with her own sumptuous flesh. She had on some kind of tropical musk that conjured up the rich wet soil of a primeval forest.

Sandralene's voice mixed the smokiness of Lauren Bacall with the brassiness of Fran Drescher.

"Hi, Glen, real pleased to meet you," she said, sticking out a beringed hand.

Somehow, without even knowing I was doing it, I had lifted up the box of coins as the woman slid in, and held it now on my lap, in a stupefied embrace. I managed to unclench enough to shake hands. Her grip was strong as a python's.

Hasso climbed in, and his bulk shoved Sandralene even closer to me. He slammed the door and said, "Okay, let's go."

I had forgotten how to activate the car. Being without a woman for so long had left me an empty vessel now overflowing with Sandralene's carnality.

"Wake up, stupe! What, are you at a middle-school dance looking at the girls or something? Here, gimme that box and drive."

Hasso took the lockbox from me, and I managed to get the car going and pull out into traffic.

"Where … where are we going?"

"First, to your guy Deluca."

I headed to Bert Deluca's coin store, saying nothing. Hasso was quietly stewing in the aftermath of last night's excesses, and Sandralene proved not to be a chatty gal. She stayed pressed against me in a nonflirty way that bespoke a simple comfortableness with her own Amazonian body.

At Deluca's Coin and Stamp Emporium, we all got out. Hasso said, "Let me handle this," and led the way into the store.

* * *

Bert Deluca resembled a character actor chosen by Central Casting to play "Morose Cop on Verge of Retirement." Balding and potbellied and with no fashion sense whatsoever, he always looked as if he was bored with the whole thing and just waiting for something less strenuous to come along. But when he saw Hasso, his expression became more animated by a high level of trepidation.

"Deluca, you remember me, right? We had a nice little private talk about your best customer, Mr. Glen McClinton here, who, as you can now see, is a good friend of mine. Me and Glen are here to cash out the rest of his gold. And we plan on getting somewhat more favorable terms than you have offered in the past."

Deluca looked nervously around the cluttered store, which was otherwise empty of customers, as if for help or reassurance. He certainly got none from Sandralene, who was admiring a sheet of Princess Diana commemorative stamps. She uttered small coos of pleasure at Di's classiness. And all I had to offer was a nervous grin.

Deluca ran his wrist across his brow. "Well, uh, yeah, sure, always happy to help out a good customer. But I'm afraid I really can't offer more than I've offered in the past."

Hasso whipped his phone out of his pocket, making Deluca

flinch. With swift fingers, Hasso brought up the spot price of gold, then thrust the screen in Deluca's face.

"Fourteen twenty-five an ounce. You're gonna buy these coins at fourteen hundred each. The shitty profit you receive today makes up for how bad you rooked my pal in the past."

"But, but—"

"But shit! These coins aren't hot. You'll be able to sell them aboveboard for more than you're gonna pay if you're just patient. The only hook you had into my buddy was that Glen wasn't supposed to even have the gold in his possession. And you screwed him plenty because of that little indiscretion. But those times are over. Now, get out your checkbook. And don't tell me you're not good for the whole amount, 'cuz I know better."

"Wait a minute," Deluca spluttered. "You can't just—"

Hasso slammed his naked fist through the fragile glass top of an antique display case, sending shards flying. I jumped almost as much as Deluca. Sandralene didn't even flinch.

"Now, are we gonna conduct business like fucking sensible, honest people or not!"

Blood dripped from Hasso's cut hand onto a black velvet tray of silver dollars. He seemed unconcerned.

"Glen, open up the box."

With shaky hands, I dialed the combination and got the box open.

"Count 'em."

I made piles of ten Pandas each atop the wooden counter next to the busted case, for a total of 201.

Hasso's hand still bled onto the antique coins. Sandralene had moved on to page through some sheets of stamps in transparent protectors, showing various Disney characters.

"Do the math, Deluca, and write out the check. Sign it, but leave the name blank for whoever's cashing it."

Deluca scrawled out the sum, over 280,000 dollars, then signed, his hand jittering even more than mine.

"Take the check, Glen."

Only after I had the check did Hasso seem to notice his cuts. "Babe, loan me your handkerchief, okay?"

"Sure, honey. But if you ruin it, you gotta buy me a new one." Sandralene undid her head scarf, loosing a cascade of scented hair, and gave it to Hasso, who tied it around his bloody hand.

"Okay, kids, time to go. Bert, it was nice doing business with you."

At the door, Hasso turned around to regard the stunned coin seller.

"Bert, my friend, in case you're thinking of issuing a stop payment on this check, just remember what I told you I used to do for a living, okay? I'm a little rusty, but hey, it's just like riding a bike."

9

Our day of financial doings was not yet over.

"Okay, head to the Maritime Bank on Hobart. That's a nice branch. I like doing business there."

After we had gone a block, and the immediacy of the tense scene at Deluca's had faded to some tiny degree, I said, "Stan, could you please try not to bleed on the upholstery of my uncle Ralph's car?"

Hasso snorted like a congested bull. "The tender way you treat this piece of shit makes me laugh."

"If it were my car, it wouldn't matter, but it doesn't belong to me."

"Okay, I respect that. But when we're all rich, you can buy your uncle Ralph a half-dozen new cars if you want."

Despite his disdain, Hasso stuck his hand out the window, and the breeze of our passage drew intermittent slow drips from his clumsily wrapped hand as if to mark our path.

The traffic downtown was light, and we were soon approaching the bank. I looked around for curbside parking and found a metered slot.

"Here's the deal," Hasso said. You and Sandralene are going into the bank, and Sandralene will open an account in her name and deposit my fifty money orders for a thousand apiece and also the check, which she is now going to make out to herself. Give her the check, Glen."

I sat frozen, despite the warmth of Sandralene's body laminating my entire right side. The idea of turning over my entire nest egg left me feeling as if I had just been dropped out of a plane, without a parachute.

"C'mon, give it up! This is the only safe way. You can't deposit it in your name—not even cash it—because you're supposed to be broke. Same for me. Paget would have our asses in a sling faster than you can say 'parole violation.' But the cops and the courts and the feds and Nancarrow don't know Sandralene from your Aunt Eudora. She's clean as a whistle. Sure, the bank'll file one of those dumb-ass reports 'cuz the deposit's over ten thousand. But by the time the IRS comes looking, we'll be long gone."

"But … but it's *my* money!"

"It's *our* money now, for the scam! Listen, I knew you'd freak out about this angle, so I thought up a safeguard for you. Once again, neither you or me can buy Bigelow Junction outright. Yes, you're gonna be the public face of the deal, snookering Nancarrow for all you're worth, just like you did that pitiful widow Evangelides and all the rest of your sucker clients. But you can't have your name on the actual papers. Paget, remember? So here's what we're gonna do. We're gonna have your uncle Ralph make the purchase. Sandralene will control the leftover hundred K in the bank—our operating expenses—but your very own uncle will hold the deed that we plan to sell to Nancarrow. That okay by you?"

I thought it over. "If Uncle Ralph agrees, then I'm good with it."

I gave the check over to Sandralene. Her husky voice seemed to intensify the radiance of her body.

"Thank you, Glen," she said. "I knew you'd let me help."

With a cheap racetrack-inscribed pen from the glove compartment, Sandralene filled in the PAY TO designation. Her last name turned out to be Parmalee.

"That's my boy! Now, hustle inside and open that account. I'd come with, but I don't wanna bleed all over the bank's nice carpet."

The customer rep who received us was a studious and personable young black kid, dressed in his best department-store-brand suit and NBA-logo tie. His mustache might amount to something in another couple of years. He looked about nineteen years old to me. Jesus, I was ancient! And I felt even older than my actual age. Nothing like prison to take it out of you.

The kid's nameplate read "Mr. Ed Gerecht," and I don't think he had ever encountered up close as lushly awesome a morsel—make that a platterful—of womanhood as Sandralene. His eyes kept wandering back to her button-straining shirtfront, and I might as well have been invisible. I doubt he could have told an investigator the color of my hair or even my skin. He kept hitting the DELETE key on his computer when he meant to hit ENTER, and vice versa, before we left the bank with a debit card and a checkbook in Sandralene's name.

Hasso was pleased. "Okay, now let's go back to your house, Glen, and wait for your uncle. I can get cleaned up, too."

Back in Uncle Ralph's little house, Sandralene seemed to fill the living room to capacity. She took over as hostess, dishing up beer and sandwiches assembled from stuff in the fridge that I could have sworn wasn't even there. Hasso emerged from the bathroom with a neat bandage on the meaty underside of his palm, and his gray moiré silk shirt dark with water where he had sponged off some blood. His fashion sense might have been strictly Jersey, but he was neat and meticulous.

No one, me included, seemed to feel much like talking about our incipient scheme. I figured there was nothing really to say until we got Uncle Ralph's agreement to act as a beard. I turned on CNN to fill the void as we ate. (Somehow, I could almost hear reports of our not-yet committed crime filling the airwaves.) And I thought about where I stood.

With the reluctant yet irrevocable transfer of my money to this mad enterprise, I was now fully embarked on the scam, and I couldn't hold back. I had to banish all doubts and summon up some of my old mojo from my dope-fiend, land-shark days, when I had been the glibbest, boldest, most self-assured shyster ever employed by the august firm of Ghent, Goolsbee & Saikiri. If our success rested on my blowing smoke up Barnaby Nancarrow's ass, then I was damn well going to blow the most perfect smoke rings ever fashioned. And I was going to have to stand up to Stan Hasso as well. Yes, the original idea had been his. But the planning and execution were going to be shared equally between us, or it wasn't going to happen at all.

Some of my internal debate must have shown on my face or in my body language. Hasso kept casting covert yet amused glances my way, as if to gauge my reactions to the day's undertakings. Finally, he said, "So, Glen, you think your uncle will be cool with this?"

"I can bring him around."

"Well, all right, then! Glen the man!"

Around 6:00 p.m., about the time he finished his seventh beer, Hasso began to droop a little. I was somehow gratified to see he wasn't a total superman after all. The day's events had drained him a little, too. And, come to think of it, he had almost died just eight months ago. I thought again about how a chance encounter that December night had yoked our fates. Life was so weird.

"Where's your room, Glen?" he said. "I'm just gonna grab a little snooze."

I showed him my room. I was still trying to suss out how I felt about being left alone in the parlor with Sandralene when she said, "I'll crash with you, honey."

This was too much. The mental picture of them together in my bed, even just innocently cuddling, was too much for me. And if actual sloppy noises should start to emerge from behind my closed bedroom door ...

"I, uh, I'm just gonna have a little walk around the neighborhood to clear my head."

I stayed away for a couple of hours. That should be enough time to get any savage fornication out of the way. And indeed, when I returned, both my guests were up and around, looking relatively unrumpled.

Shortly after I got back, around eight thirty, Uncle Ralph and Suzy Lam pulled up in her car, home early. They entered the house roisteringly smashed. Uncle Ralph's tall, thin frame seemed puffed up, his white-stubbled cheeks aglow, and Suzy's matronly bulk emanated an earthy vitality.

"We broke the bank, Glen! Suzy had a hunch, and what a hunch! Fifty to one on Johnny Handsome, and she laid down a thousand! We are in the chips, nephew!"

Uncle Ralph noticed Hasso and Sandralene only after he had unleashed his glee. I made introductions all around. Everyone seemed fairly relaxed together. Suzy Lam hoisted up a large paper bag that clinked. "You kids ever had a Bermuda mai tai? Peach schnapps! Winner! I got all the fixings here! Just you wait!"

She left for the kitchen, and soon the blender whirred.

"Uncle Ralph," I said, "I have to ask you for a favor."

I laid out the bare bones of our plan. Not the full extent of the scheme, the name of our victim, or the hoped-for payoff—just the fact that Hasso and I stood to make some real money if Uncle Ralph could act as our front in a certain real estate transaction, for a modest guaranteed recompense. He listened with growing sobriety, then said, "Well, hell, Glen, this sounds like something I would've pulled in my salad days! Count me in!"

Suzy emerged from the kitchen with a tray of colorful drinks, and a cold pitcher holding the rest of the cocktail.

"Why so serious, kids? Time to celebrate!"

Uncle Ralph boiled down my explanation even further for Suzy. She got more excited than before.

"I want to invest! I'll put in a thousand, just like I did for Johnny Handsome!"

I balked. "I don't know—"

Hasso said, "We'll take your money, Suzy. Same payout as your lucky horse if we bring this off."

Uncle Ralph looked a little sheepish. "You can knock a thousand off anything you were gonna pay me. I owe Glen that much already."

"How do you figure that, Uncle Ralph? If anything, I owe you for putting me up in the house all these months."

"Well, you see, Glen, I borrowed one of your gold coins a couple of months ago, when I needed a stake."

My brain stalled out for a moment. "You knew they were down in the basement all along?"

"Why, sure. How dumb do you think I am? You left a trail of ashes every time you dug 'em up. Then one day, you forgot to spin the lock good on the box, and I helped myself. But just to one coin, I swear!"

I shook my head in disbelief.

Hasso's laugh boomed through the house.

"Glen boy, you're gonna have to be a lot slicker with Nancarrow, or we are well and truly fucked!"

10

When I worked for Ghent, Goolsbee & Saikiri, I dressed like a prince. Ermenegildo Zegna suits, Stefano Bemer shoes. The rich fabrics and exquisite tailoring boosted my confidence and assurance. Clients automatically respected me and believed whatever I said, no matter how full of shit I was. Never mind that I was really wearing their stolen money and should have been awash in guilt and remorse. That part never bothered me until I got caught.

Such luxe clothing had long since disappeared from my life, of course. Most days since my release from prison found me wearing a pullover golf shirt from Big Lots and cargo pants or shorts, plus cheap knockoff running shoes in winter, Teva sandals when the weather turned warm. My morale and self-esteem had dwindled under the onslaughts of justice. I had been existing without spirit, one step above tracksuits on the Great Chain of Fashion Consciousness.

That's why today I felt so different, upbeat for the first time in years. Even the lousy J. C. Penney suit and tie I was wearing, augmented by the Dockers oxfords from Famous Footwear, left me feeling more on top of the world than I did in my usual slovenly attire. I had forgotten just how good taking care of my appearance could make me feel.

Stan Hasso looked me up and down approvingly as we stood outside the downtown Licklider Federal Building where Anton Paget, our mutual parole guy, had his office. Freshets of people flowed through the doors and around us.

My sizable partner had chosen not to follow my sartorial lead. "I ain't dressing like no deacon or court clerk," he had informed me. "Never have, never will. That's all right for you. But on me, that look would just shout 'fake.' You can take the boy out of the Gulch, but you can't take the Gulch out of the boy. But never fear, you can count on me to look all proper-like and business ready."

That description manifested now before my astonished eyes in new ankle-peg black jogger pants possessing an unnatural synthetic sheen, black chamois shirt from L. L. Bean, red Kangol bucket hat, and high-top Nikes with Day-Glo detailing. His outsize Italian good-luck horn on its gold chain stood in for more formal neckwear.

Yet Stan was open-minded enough to compliment my own look.

"You're truly styling, Glen boy. I am beginning to see a side of you I never knew. I useta wonder how you conned so many business guys who weren't exactly dumb themselves. But now I can see you got some kinda special charm on you once you clean up. I think we are gonna take Mr. Nancarrow for the ride of his life."

"Well, thanks, Stan," I said. "Your own authentic fashion sense, while not exactly congruent with my standards, renders you bulletproof against criticism. In short, you look totally like you belong in the VIP box at one of the classier strip clubs, swilling directly from the neck of a bottle of Cristal, with several affectionate large-assed women crawling all over you."

"I thank you kindly, pard."

"All right, then. In we go, to brace Paget."

What we intended was a plan we had put the finishing touches on after concluding our business at Aspinwall Realty. There, in the office of agent Martin Bookstaver, a hearty suburban guy with the depth of a birdbath, Uncle Ralph, Hasso, and I had secured the title to Bigelow Junction. Uncle Ralph had played everything at the top of his game.

"Yessir, Mr. Bookstaver, after a lifetime of hard work, I have put a little money by, and now I want to invest it in an enterprise that has long been close to my heart: innkeeper at a fine country establishment. I understand that one of the buildings that accompany the sale of Bigelow Junction is a former hotel."

Bookstaver had the honesty to look slightly uncomfortable. "Well, Mr. Sickert, not so much a hotel as a motel. And I'm afraid it's become a little shabby over several years of idleness."

"No matter. My nephew and his partner are not afraid of good honest hard work, and they intend to help me out every step of the way. We will have those lodgings up and running before you know it. In fact, you'll be our first guest—for free!"

"I'm sure you will succeed, Mr. Sickert. Now, if you'll just sign here, here, and here ..."

Once Uncle Ralph had handed over the cashier's check that Sandralene had drawn, we were the proud owners of five hundred and more acres of upstate scrub forest, which included a pond dubbed Nutbush Lake, as well as the communal properties enfeoffed thereunto.

After closing costs, we were left with just under a hundred thousand in the bank account bearing Sandralene's name.

On the way out the door, Mr. Bookstaver had beamed in a

weird manner at Hasso and me and said a bit too enthusiastically, as if to convey his unreserved benediction, "I'm sure you two lads will be very happy helping Mr. Sickert with his interior decorating."

Outside Aspinwall Realty, Hasso suddenly halted. "Did he think you and me was gay?"

"I believe it was mainly due to Uncle Ralph's calling us 'partners.' But honestly, Stan, there's more to it than that. I'm sorry I didn't tell you this before, but you just give off that unmistakable gay vibe."

"Fuck you, wise guy!"

Uncle Ralph said, "C'mon, now, boys, don't fight. Let's go have a drink to celebrate before I get myself back to the track and Miss Suzy."

At our practically reserved table in Danny's Cavern, while Uncle Ralph chatted up Harriet and a couple of other superannuated bar girls, Hasso laid out his vision for our next few weeks.

"We have to get out of the city and go live at this place. We can't look like we're stalking Nancarrow here on his home turf. Even arranging an 'accidental' meeting would put him on the alert. He may be hoity-toity these days, but he's still got his Gulch radar for scams. No, we gotta make him come to us."

"And you think we can do that with your crooked politician and your computer guy alone?"

"I *know* we can! Then, when we get him on our turf, some place that's unfamiliar to him, you can go to work on him—grease him up for the kill."

* * *

Walking into the Licklider Building, we got ready to face the last hurdle in the way of our leaving town: getting Anton Paget's permission.

We had debated approaching him separately, keeping up the charade that Hasso and I were unacquainted. But our common destination of Bigelow Junction—which, as parolees, we had to reveal to the authorities—would quickly have rendered such a pretense transparent. So we decided to take a chance that he wouldn't find our new friendship suspicious or in violation of some parole technicality. I had figured that, as always, mixing some truth into the stew of lies would help the whole goulash go down easier.

The stumpy, bearded parole officer, today wearing an especially riotous patchwork shirt, regarded us from behind his desk with a gaze that I chose to regard as darkly anticipatory rather than outright jaundiced against us. Paget had heard so many cock-and-bull stories in his career that he had become inoculated against them without losing his ability to appreciate the desperate motives and ingenious creativity behind such tales.

"Gentlemen, take your seats! I am doubly honored today. I never hoped to witness such a slate as McClinton and Hasso. Which of you is running for president, and which for vice president?"

"Anton, you always bust me up. You know damn well how Glen and I hooked up. He saved my fucking life! And now we're amigos."

"Yes, I recall that act of nobility. The cops woke me up at 2:00 a.m. to confirm everything about my client. Okay, so the two of you are the best of chums now. And you plan on leaving town together—if I let you."

I stepped into the conversation. "Yes, Anton, it's to help my uncle out." I explained about Uncle Ralph's purchase of Bigelow Junction, the fulfillment of his lifetime dream, yada, yada, and yada. I could feel myself entering the same kind of hyperverbal fugue state—minus the opioid buzz—that I had so often felt when spieling to clients. And for the length of my talk, I sincerely believed in the truth of what I was saying.

"And so you see, we'd be gainfully employed at last, and actually burnishing the state's reputation by rehabbing a little slice of this rundown region and thus improving the local and even regional economy."

I sat back, spent and sweating, while Paget regarded the two of us in silence.

"C'mon, Anton," said Stan, "cut us a break! We're trying to go straight here and become productive members of society! Just like you want!"

Paget bent to his food-stained keyboard and began typing. "I am transferring your cases to Wilson Schreiber, my counterpart for Bigelow Junction and environs. If you think I'm a hard-ass, you have a surprise coming when you meet Will. If he tells me that either of you so much as looked askance at a meter reader, you will be back here so fast you'll leave your fillings up north. Plus, I'll be expecting to see stubs from regular paychecks, to show you two aren't just on an extended vacation."

Paget suddenly scrutinized us in a fresh manner. "You guys aren't like, I don't know, cohusbands or anything, are you? Because if so—"

Hasso slammed his palm down on Paget's desk. "Jesus Christ! You know I got a woman, dude!"

"Oh, yes, Ms. Parmalee. Will she be accompanying you to Bigelow Junction?"

"Sure, why not? It's a free country."

"No reason. I actually think she's a good influence on you."

We all stood up. I stuck out my hand, radiating sincerity. "Anton, we won't let you down."

"There's always a first time for everything, I figure."

Outside, Hasso unbuttoned the upper half of his shirt to let his stifled chest hair breathe.

"Okay, Glen, now we meet the rest of our merry crew!"

PART TWO

11

The State House looked busy today at lunch hour. Outside the front doors, the broad terrace of frost-heaved brick was thick with conversing politicians, visiting citizens, deliverymen, a security guard or two, a well-behaved gaggle of sign-toting protesters, and a few scavenging gulls slumming from the bay a mile east, on whose less-than-pristine shores our capital sat. Satellite uplink trucks from three local stations and one national network had parked on the sidewalk. This meant diverting pedestrians into the street for a short stretch, which gave rise to much hooting of car horns and angry shouts from walkers and drivers alike. I couldn't guess what newsworthy event had caused the media to converge like buzzards on roadkill. A small herd of visiting elementary-school kids, shepherded by two teachers glowing impossibly young and beautiful in their summer dresses, made their exuberant way across the pavilion from a big faded-yellow bus.

Stan Hasso and I observed all this from the concealing shade of a large copper beech tree in the park across the street. A down-and-outer on the nearest bench was drinking from an iced-tea can the size of a mortar round. No doubt, the "tea" had the color and flavor of fortified wine.

This was our last stop before heading up to Bigelow Junction. Our bags were packed in the trunk of the Impala, and Sandralene awaited us at Uncle Ralph's. She had closed up her apartment for good.

One way or another, none of us were coming back to this town.

"It kinda gets ya, don't it?" said Stan, nodding at the slow procession of cars and pedestrians.

"Like how?"

"Oh, you know, man. Democracy, justice, help the underprivileged, your tax dollars at work, Jimmy Stewart goes to Washington, Martin Luther King—that kinda crap."

"Yes, I suppose I could summon up some misty-eyed sense of patriotism and civic pride—if we weren't here to deliver a thirty-thousand-dollar bribe to a state senator."

The money—a fat wad of well-circulated hundred-dollar bills in an anonymous envelope, cashed out of our bank account by Sandralene, weighed heavily in the side pocket of my light nylon shell.

"Where's the problem?" Stan asked. "Bribes are just as much part of the whole shebang as all them other things. Tradition's gotta be maintained."

"I think you are just better at cognitive dissonance than I, Stan."

"Ya mean keeping two ideas that hate each other's guts in your head at the same time, without letting either of 'em kill the other?"

I looked in wonder at the hulking ex-arsonist. "You know what cognitive dissonance is?"

"Hey, you think I never listened in class? Even back in the Gulch, I knew that the more knowledge you could collect, the more leverage you had against the other guy who maybe didn't know as much. Also, in the jug I got used to reading books again."

"Stan, you are some kind of marvel."

"Believe it!"

As we watched, the figure we had been anticipating made its slow and casual exit from the building.

Senator Flavio Almonte, head of the Regulated Industries Committee, which oversaw the state's nascent gaming business, was shaped roughly like a keg of beer topped by a palm-straw cowboy hat. His lack of any discernible neck made him resemble the legendary enemy of the X-Men, Juggernaut. As if to mimic that villain's costume, today Almonte wore a red shirt with a blue tie and brick-colored pants. His sienna-hued face, beneath a thick mop of dull raven hair, exhibited the wary jollity of someone given to enjoying life's pleasures at the slightest invitation, only to be betrayed by the consequences of such fun.

Senator Almonte ambled across the State House terrace, heading straight toward us on the far side of the intervening avenue with no attempt at subtlety. He had the gait of a peasant carrying a yoke of water buckets.

"Jesus," said Stan, "this guy's about as subtle as a turd on a doorstep. I just hope I didn't read him wrong. He's gotta be able to convince Nancarrow."

Watching him approach, I said, "Well, from what I've seen of him at his press conferences, any attempt he makes at being sly will come across as exactly that. So he might just deliver precisely what this insane scam needs from him."

"Anyhow, we got no choice," Stan said. "It's him or nobody. He's the informer we need—the only guy who might logically have some idea of Steve Prynne's plans that he can 'leak.'" He made air quotes around the word. "Let's head toward the fountain now and let him catch up."

We strolled deeper into the park. The shady grounds were a popular spot on such a nice day: nannies pushing strollers, retirees walking their yappy ornamental dogs. Even accompanied by the unsubtle Almonte, we could count on not standing out. Stan and I had debated meeting with him in a more secluded location but in the end had decided on more of a "Purloined Letter" strategy, right out in the open. Being the sort whose shenanigans had made headlines in the past, the senator was often tracked after hours by newshounds and tipsters. But lunch hour in the park across from the capitol—that seemed entirely too boring a venue for anything scandalous.

The fountain loomed ahead: a big blatant, baroque affair of naked bronze figures, clenched buttocks and proud bosoms thrusting everywhere. The gushing, splashing water conveniently overlaid and obscured any conversation conducted at the edge of the sculpture's stoneware basin.

A nearby food cart was selling arepas, and the delicious smell of the meat- and cheese-stuffed corn fritters wafted our way.

"I could eat about six of those bad boys," Stan said. "You?"

My stomach was a little uneasy. Pulling off cons had been a lot simpler when I was always high. But I was beginning to feel some of that old thrill of getting back into the game, and it made me a lot more confident and a lot less jumpy than when Stan Hasso first rang my doorbell less than a week ago.

"Just get me one," I said, "and something to drink."

Stan went over to the cart and was soon back with the arepas and two bottles of Jarritos pineapple soda. He handed me my fritter and drink, and I regarded the bottle dubiously.

"This stuff has to be the sweetest soda in existence."

"I like it," he said. "You can pick the soda next time, when you're buying lunch."

"That was my money—I *am* buying lunch!"

"Oh, right."

Almonte strolled over to the cart and got his own meal. Hasso and I sat on the damp rim of the basin, and Almonte joined us at a decorous distance.

"So, Flavio," Stan said in a subdued voice, "¿*qué pasa?*"

Almonte took a big bite of arepa, then proceeded to speak through it. "Everything is very *tranquilo*, my friend. Especially with this generous show of appreciation. It is much esteemed, and in return for such a small favor. Do you know what the state pays us? *Fifteen thousand a year.* How can a man survive on such a pittance?"

"You're supposed to be just a part-time pol, *ese.* Citizen statesman. Don't you have a real profession?"

"I help my people with their tax returns, but that is strictly seasonal work."

"You should know better than to count on seasonal stuff, man. That's the trap *la raza* always falls into. Strawberries, lettuce, and apples, one right after the other, until your back is busted."

Almonte laughed with genuine pleasure. "You have me there, Hasso. Anyhow, I think you will agree that I have made a good deal. Some small lies to an obnoxious fellow, and I earn double my salary. You do have the money with you, I hope?"

"It's going in the trash bin when we leave. Make sure you're right behind us. I don't want some can-and-bottle scavenger hitting the jackpot."

I felt I had to add my two cents. "Remember, now, Senator, you need to let the information slip in a way that looks totally accidental. Bigelow Junction is where Prynne wants to build his casino. That's definite. But let Nancarrow weasel it out of you. Feed his image of himself as a master manipulator."

"I understand. The guy is always hanging around the State

House anyhow, digging for this, offering that. He already thinks I know more than I'm saying. It will not be hard to play this part."

"Great."

Stan had finished his six arepas before I got through half of my one. "Gimme your trash, Glen."

Under cover of wiping my hands on a paper napkin, I took out the envelope of cash and slipped it into my greasy paper bag. I handed it to Stan, and he casually crumpled my bag in his, then walked to the nearest waste can, where he deposited the whole expensive wad.

"Don't let us down, Flavio," said Stan, in a tone that implied a causal link between following his advice and preserving one's health.

"You may rely on me *completamente.*"

Some distance from the fountain, I looked back cautiously. Almonte's front pants pocket showed a new bulge as he sauntered along, enjoying the balmy weather.

"Christ, I hate to rely on a weak fish like that," Stan said. "But sometimes you just gotta delegate certain things. Am I right, Glen boy, or am I right?"

The sight of my twenty gold Pandas disappearing into the bowels of the State House left me feeling a little dispirited. Our scam seemed more real and consequential, even more than it had when we purchased the land.

"I sure hope so," I said. "I really do."

12

Sandralene emerged from Uncle Ralph's bathroom, wearing a fresh matrix of makeup and looking runway fine. Her blue and white summer dress, which stopped at midthigh on her bare tan legs, somehow reminded me of a sailor's outfit. If Navy recruiters had used her on a poster, the line of both men and women queued up at the enlistment station door would have wrapped around the block. The leather uppers of her Dolce & Gabbana sandals were festooned with jingling fake gold coins. Whether she had chosen the sandals deliberately, to proclaim her status as custodian of my gold Pandas, or just to complement her dress, I chose to regard the footwear as a good omen for our enterprise.

"C'mon," said Stan, "shake your tush. We gotta hit the road now to get to Bigelow Junction before nightfall. I don't wanna be messing around in the dark, trying to turn on the lights in a shack full o' snakes and grizzly bears."

Bigelow Junction, the domain of Parole Officer Wilson Schreiber, lay some three hundred miles upstate. The trip would be all freeway except for the bumpy, curvy final stretch.

"Maybe snakes and bears frighten you, Stanley, but not me," Sandralene said. "What I've seen in the way of sketchy characters right here in this city is ten times worse. No snake ever tried to slither up my dress, and no bear ever tried digging in my purse with one paw while grabbing my boobs with the other."

The mental images conjured up by Sandralene's colorful descriptions made me weak in the knees. I could not see myself at Bigelow Junction, where the close proximity of her Amazonian presence would be intensified by whatever sexual banter and bedplay she and Stan would get up to, without becoming a neurotic wreck. I had to find a woman soon. Maybe Bigelow Junction boasted a large assortment of easygoing farmers' daughters eager to shack up with an unemployed land speculator.

Uncle Ralph came out of the kitchen, followed by Suzy Lam carrying a brown paper sack.

"Okay, kiddies, sandwiches and drinks for the road. No booze, not even a beer. Just soda! You listen to Aunt Suzy! Cops find ex-cons together in a car, no extra provocations needed! 'Click it or ticket!'"

I took the bag from Suzy while Uncle Ralph looked on with a smile of approval.

As soon as the three of us had cemented our plans to decamp for Bigelow Junction, Suzy had announced her intention to move in with Uncle Ralph. "I love this frosty old tiger. He's so good to little Suzy. And he knows how to have big fun. Besides, only crazy people pay two rents if they don't have to. And your uncle, he don't even pay none!"

True, the old homestead had long been free and clear of any mortgage, and it made no sense for Ralph and Suzy to be subsidizing her landlord when they had grown so close. And Suzy's contribution of her own car to the joint establishment made Ralph feel free to give me the Impala, without my even asking for it. Otherwise, we would have had to spend some of our remaining seventy thousand dollars on alternative transportation.

Now I was glad I had invested my own money to keep the old heap in good running condition.

The first thing Suzy had done upon moving in was to ditch Aunt Gillian's prized parlor set and replace it with stuff from IKEA. Admittedly, the old furniture had been swaybacked and grotty. But the pieces had been there since I was a kid—a remnant token of Aunt Gillian's tastes and a lifetime earnestly endured. And their absence now, along with the presence of alien hipster couches and end tables, rendered the house foreign to me. The changes drove home just how completely I had embarked on this new stage of my life, with no likelihood of return.

"All right, Suzy!" said Stan. "If Ralph didn't have both his hands on your ass already, I might not be able to keep mine off."

Sandralene rolled her eyes. Suzy punched Stan's shoulder hard enough to make him wince authentically.

"Say your goodbyes, Glen boy. Sandy and I'll be in the car."

After my coconspirators had stepped outside, I hugged both Suzy and Ralph. I hadn't expected to feel so emotional about leaving them behind. When I had been flying high (in more ways than one) at Ghent, Goolsbee & Saikiri, Uncle Ralph had seemed merely a nostalgic artifact of my past, inconsequential if considered at all. In prison, I had been too busy surviving and pitying myself to consider his existence. Then he had taken me in to satisfy Paget and the parole board, participated as our front man in the purchase of Bigelow Junction, and, finally, given me his car. That anyone would still love me and invest in me after I so royally fucked up my life had to be some kind of miracle, and it brought tears to my eyes.

"Hey, Glen, don't you forget little Suzy's share! One thousand dollars times fifty, pronto!"

I wiped my cheeks and said, "Okay, Suzy. Pronto."

After shaking Uncle Ralph's hand, I left the house for good.

Miss Sandralene Parmalee insouciantly occupied the shotgun seat, but her man was not behind the wheel of the Impala, where I had assumed he would be. Instead, Mr. Stanley Hasso lay folded at the knees across the back seat, out of view, below the sight lines of the windows.

Without venturing to ask the reason for this unconventional posture, I got into the driver's seat, started the car, and drove slowly off.

"We got one last stop here in the city," Stan said. "I don't think it'll take too long. You know the Verger Building on Newcomen Street?"

"I can find it."

"If there's a parking spot not too close to the front entrance but with a good view, take it. If not, keep circling till one opens up."

Ten minutes of crosstown driving brought us to the Verger Building, an art deco relic still in excellent shape. Luckily, there was an open curbside slot diagonally across the street from the revolving glass door.

"This is perfect," said Stan. "Now we wait."

"For what?"

"Look at the plaque near the door, dummy."

There was the familiar player piano above the legend:

NANCARROW LOGISTICS TRUST MANAGEMENT, LTD.

"It's his HQ," said Stan. "Ol' Algy likes to go to lunch every day about now. I want you to see him, fix him in your mind. Think about how you're gonna take him for that big wad. I'd like to get up in his face and spit in his eye for sending me to the joint. But I'll just stay down here outta sight and contemplate my delayed gratification."

We sat, not speaking, for about fifteen minutes. Sandralene opened her purse and took out a word search booklet and a pencil. She very slowly circled her vocabulary finds. The first time she licked the tip of the pencil, I almost groaned.

As I once told Stan, I had been at a party with Nancarrow before, so I recognized him when he came out.

Shorter than average, his trim build honed by many dedicated gym hours, sporting a thick shock of blond hair that looked unabashedly dyed, Barnaby Nancarrow, née Algy Teague, wore a very nice linen summer-weight suit and expensive brown shoes. The sculpted planes of his salon-tanned face radiated a kind of self-satisfied smugness best captured by that German word *Backpfeifengesicht,* meaning "a face that demands to be slapped."

Two large mooks, one African American, one Caucasian, looking like Secret Service agents fired for moral turpitude, flanked Nancarrow like the bookending New York City Library lions. But instead of being named Patience and Fortitude, they might have been dubbed Suspicious and Hostile.

"He's got his security with him, right?" said a recumbent Hasso. "White guy is Buck Rushlow. Black guy is Needles Digweed. You don't wanna know how Needles got his nickname. Different generation, but both outta the Gulch, just like me and Algy, for built-in reliability and loyalty. I could take either one, but not both at once. Hope you're up to handling whichever one I might have sudden cause to delegate."

"Will it really come to that?"

"Not if we're lucky. But luck's not something you can count on, as we well know."

Sandralene let out a loud squeal then, and across the busy street, both Buck and Needles glanced our way, assessed our threat rating instantly, and, finding it acceptably low, moved on with their boss.

"I just found 'exuberance'!" Sandralene explained.

"You sure did, just like always, honey. Okay, Glen, let's hit the highway. Those goddamn snakes and bears aren't gonna wait on us forever."

13

Despite our best intentions to make good time, darkness and fatigue overtook us as we approached Bigelow Junction. What passed for the center of our nominal town, that densest concentration of miscellaneous communal buildings included in our five-hundred-acre purchase, clustered around Nutbush Lake. Those structures, which we had seen only in some grainy old black-and-white photos at the offices of real estate agent Martin Bookstaver, would serve as our base of operations during the scam.

Scattered across the rest of the unincorporated land were maybe a hundred citizens in forty or fifty isolated private households. They all leased their individual plots of land from whoever owned Bigelow Junction, namely, us.

After being informed of this setup, Stan had declared, "Man, it's just like being an earl or duke or something outta the Knights of the Round Table. King Hasso receives his loyal peasants, lining up with tributes of chickens and cows and potatoes and women. Hey, if we start to run low on operating funds, maybe we can just raise everybody's rent!"

"Listen, Stan," I said, "we are not going to monkey with the existing arrangements and maybe cause a public stink. That's the last thing we need. Besides, you said Nancarrow would approach us with an offer for the land before too long, and then we'll be gone. Our money should hold out till then, so no need to go flogging the serfs."

"Well, that's my *prediction*, not a guarantee. Best to be prepared for anything."

* * *

Our trip north had started off well enough. We had gotten out of the city before rush-hour traffic, with Stan behind the wheel and Sandralene sidled up close to him. I gratefully stretched out in the back seat.

"Sandy, babe, get some tunes going."

From her capacious purse, Sandralene took a sleek cylindrical Bluetooth speaker that fit in her palm and set it on the broad padded ledge under the slope of the front windshield. She turned it on, then took Stan's phone and scrolled through his music app.

I gritted my teeth, expecting the most noxious hardcore hip-hop to emerge, full of gangster boasts and driven by an unrelenting bass beat.

Instead, I was pleasantly surprised to hear down-and-dirty gutbucket blues guitar riffs, followed by a mournful yet energetic male croon.

> If trouble was money, babe, I swear I'd be a millionaire.
> If worries was dollar bills,
> I'd buy the whole world and have money to spare.

I said, "Is that Robert Cray?"

Clearly, Stan had been awaiting my reaction. He looked briefly away from the road and back over his shoulder at me with a broad grin. "Shit, man, Robert Cray is for the Brie-and-Chablis crowd. That is the one and only Albert Collins."

"You like blues?"

"It's all I listen to, man. What, you think just 'cuz I grew up in the Gulch, I got no taste?"

"Stan, my man, you never cease to amaze me."

"That is as it should be, Glen boy."

Stan's phone featured a wide assortment of artists, including some worthy blueswomen.

"Oh, dig this new kid, Samantha Fish. Just in her twenties, but can she play! And a looker, too. Not enough meat on them bones for me, but still pretty foxy."

> Let him go the way I should.
> My heart lies underneath the hood.
> Roadrunner, roadrunner,
> I'm picking up and making tracks.
> When the dust settles I ain't coming back.

Despite the high-intensity soundtrack of soulful lamentations, I soon drifted off to sleep. The events of the past week and a half had really caught up with me. I awoke only when the car was pulling into a shady little picnic grove. I got stiffly out of the car and followed Stan and Sandralene to the pine-sap-sticky wooden table next to a cold fire pit littered with empty beer cans.

The sandwiches Suzy Lam had packed for us turned out to be her specialty: chow mein on a torpedo roll. The bread had softened, soaking up all the liquid, and it was like slurping down a delicious Chinatown dinner, circa 1948.

"Man, the only thing that could've improved that meal woulda been a beer or three. But your uncle's squeeze was right: no sense giving any cops a leg up on us."

Heading back to the car, I said, "Want me to drive?"

"Naw, I'm good for hours. Besides, you drive like an old lady in a full-body cast."

"Thanks."

"Anytime."

Again on the highway, I said, "Tell me more about our fellows in crime."

"You know they're meeting us at the Junction tomorrow. Driving up together from Trinidad Falls. That's where they both live."

"One's a woman."

"Yeah. Varvara Aptekar. I just call her Vee and she don't seem to mind. Vee's folks were from Belarus, part of that wave that came over in the early nineties, after the Commies went under. She was born here, though."

"And her story is?"

"Nancarrow took on her father as an early partner. Unlike a lot of these ex-Commies, Aptekar managed to get some money out of the old country, and he was interested in real estate. The American way to riches, right? That made him just the kind of sucker Nancarrow loved. Aptekar thought he was sly. But he wasn't sharp enough to handle Nancarrow. Algy swindled him dry—left him hanging with a lot of solo debt that was rightfully both of theirs to bear. I wasn't there at the time, but I learned about it later.

"Aptekar took what he thought was the only honorable way out of his troubles. Real Slavic. Shot his wife, then himself. Only reason Vee survived was that she was at a sleepover. She was five years old at the time. Went through a lot of foster homes. When she got old enough to learn what had happened to her family, she worked up the biggest mad-on for Nancarrow that was humanly possible. You think *I'm* pissed at the guy? She's like a goddamn volcano of hate. She's nursed it for ten years now, with no way of getting back at him. When I knew we were gonna need some arm candy to make Nancarrow a little loopy and easier to hook, I looked her up. Of course, Algy has no idea this gal was once the five-year-old orphan he created. She signed up faster'n a shark can take off your leg."

"She sounds like a soured soul."

Sandralene spoke up. "I've met her, Glen, and she's not a bad person. She's just wound pretty tight."

I wondered how easy it would be to work with this woman. But I guessed I should reserve judgment till we met.

"Why didn't you just get Sandralene to act as bait?"

Stan seemed honestly hurt. "Number one, I don't go pimping out my woman, not even for five million. Number two, Sandralene is not Nancarrow's type. I had plenty of occasions to see what kind of broad he favors, and Vee Aptekar is his personal wet dream come true."

"So when Nancarrow comes to visit us looking to buy the land—"

"You are going to befuddle his brain, and Vee is going to tie his gonads in a bow."

"That's some kind of tag team. Now, this computer kid …"

"Ray Zerkin. Vee's ex-student. That's how I got turned on to him. I mentioned to Vee that we needed someone who could finesse the internet, and she brought his name up as a perfect choice."

This new vocational aspect of the woman was unexpected. "She's a teacher?"

"Specializes in the oddball kids—the feebs and simpletons."

"*Staaan*-ley!"

"All right, all right, the differently abled or whatever they wanna be called these days. Special ed. So this Ray Zerkin is some kind of genius with computers, but he's got that wonky brain and personality condition—you know, like Rain Man."

"Asperger's or autism?"

"Yeah, whichever one leaves you mostly functional but still creepy."

"And we're really going to cut him in for a quarter of the take? What's a kid like that going to do with five million dollars?"

"Well, you know, I was thinking along those lines myself. I mighta been talking through my hat earlier. We'll see how it plays out. Maybe Mr. Zerkin can be work for hire, and we'll split the remaining pot three ways."

Talking about the money made it suddenly seem more real. I said, "What are you and Sandralene planning to do after we collect?"

"Well, my first priority is to get someplace Nancarrow can't find us once he catches on. Another country, I figure. And probably one without an extradition treaty with the good ol' USA. I got a few candidates lined up, which I will be happy to share with you."

I hadn't really given much thought to how Nancarrow was going to feel about getting ripped off for twenty million dollars. But it quickly made a lot of sense that the less of a handle he had on who had scammed him, and their whereabouts, the better off our tender hides would be.

"Thanks, I'd appreciate it."

Suddenly, the hideous stench of burning rubber filled the car, and from under the hood emerged noises like those of a robot committing suicide by letting a robot weasel eat out its mechanical guts.

Stan pulled over to the breakdown lane. He got out cautiously as high-speed traffic whizzed past us. He opened the hood, peeked under it, and got back in.

He said, "It's a goddamn belt. I thought you had this heap in good shape."

"Well, I attended to troubles when they popped up, but I

didn't really do preventive maintenance. This wasn't even my car until a couple of days ago!"

Stan retrieved his phone from its wireless hookup with the music speaker and used it to find the nearest mechanic.

Long story short, the repair took five hours. Belts for old Impalas, it seemed, did not grow on trees. At the garage, we consumed endless sodas and chips from two vending machines and perused every grease-fingerprinted issue of *Car and Driver* from 2011 to the present.

And so now, as we pulled into the center of Bigelow Junction—under a black sky with more stars than I had ever seen, and not one source of artificial illumination outside of our car headlights—I contemplated how easily the best-laid plans could go off the rails. A warning for us to have plenty of fallback options to our scheme.

We all got out of the idling car and stood looking at the unknown structures around us. Rustling noises came from the nearby forest undergrowth.

"Fuck it," said Stan. "I ain't up for investigating a bunch of dark moldy rooms at this hour, just to sleep on some old cot full of mouse shit. I'm for spending the night in the car."

Sandralene and I voted likewise.

"I'm gonna take a leak, then go to sleep," said Stan.

"Me too," said Sandralene. She removed some tissues from her purse, then stepped outside the cone of light. I went off in a different direction, but could still hear her pee laving the gravel.

Back in the car, we tried to get comfortable.

I had been assigned the driver's seat, since I was "the dinkiest." Stan hogged the other two-thirds of the front bench seat, while Sandralene's virtue was preserved by her having the whole luxurious back seat to herself.

It turned out she snored louder than Stan.

14

The lineman from the power company was a pudgy, sunburned white guy named Mort Dunkel. He had introduced himself with a hearty handshake and jovial hello when he pulled up in the company truck an hour ago, as if he were a long-lost cousin arriving at a family reunion. Thrown a little off-balance by this cornpone friendliness, I had given my real name before thinking twice, then silently cursed myself. Were we supposed to be using fake names, even among the townspeople? Why hadn't Stan and I discussed this yet? Obviously, Stan could not show his face in the presence of Nancarrow, but the real estate mogul didn't know me or Sandralene or Vee by sight from previous encounters. He would certainly recall the last name Aptekar, though—his old partner he had screwed. So Vee would have to come up with something different. But might my real name possibly be an asset? Maybe my easily obtainable public record of criminality would serve to put Nancarrow at ease. Make him feel that he was dealing with a guy like himself, who wanted to keep everything sub rosa and who, for our mutual benefit, would never snitch on anything shady. Well, I would have to discuss all these options with Stan.

But right now it was too late to withdraw my real name from Dunkel's possession.

Dunkel now perched high atop a ladder leaned against a utility pole that carried the electric cable in from the "main road," as that tiny thoroughfare was called. Squinting, I watched him in the hot sunlight that flooded the tree-fringed clearing. Through the foliage, the silvered waters of Nutbush Lake glimmered like a flattened mirror ball.

Dunkel finished fussing with a box high up on the pole, then climbed down. He wiped sweat off his forehead with a faded blue bandanna and said, "Gotta get in the main building now, Mr. McClinton."

"Okay, sure." I grabbed the ring of keys from the glove compartment, and we headed toward the Bigelow Junction Motor Lodge.

The motel was a long, low wooden structure, two wings of rental rooms connected by a central office. The faded color scheme of forest green and lemon yellow had needed a paint job ten years ago. All the adhesive-letter signage was peeling from too many hot summers and cold winters, curling up along its edges to produce a distinctive postapocalyptic font. The main neon had been shattered by vandals, leaving just the painted, socket-studded outlines of the letters. The office door and the doors of the individual units all faced the gravel parking lot. The office and each rental also had a door on the opposite side, allowing easy access down several paths to the weedy lakeshore. The margin of the lake, I knew from earlier reconnoitering, featured a listing wharf, a ramshackle, boarded-up boathouse, and a short crescent of artificially created beach partially reclaimed by some vigorous aquatic plants. Across the sizable expanse of Nutbush Lake, the shoreline was unbroken but for a couple of waterside houses, each in its clearing and part of our little fiefdom.

A short distance from the lodge, a half-dozen stand-alone "luxury" cabins offered honeymooners a little extra privacy. Another structure had once been a take-out-only food stand. No indoor seating—just a kitchen with window service for burgers, hot dogs, sodas, and ice cream. A second building of similar size had once sold souvenirs and tchotchkes and penny candy, newspapers, and magazines. An equipment garage with several roll-up doors stood discreetly behind a row of pines. It held a fleet of moldering mowers and antiquated utility vehicles, as well as a tool shop equipped with rusting implements.

And that was our little sham empire, the supposed nucleus of what legendary high roller Steve Prynne, Vegas hotshot, saw as his newest casino venture.

Would Nancarrow subscribe to this ridiculous fantasy? Only if I could sell it, bolstered by whatever cyberhoaxing Ray Zerkin could whip up and whatever bullshit our senator for hire, the Honorable Flavio Almonte, could dispense.

Dunkel and I reached the sagging wood-framed screen door of the lodge's office. I had to try several keys to find the right one.

The place smelled of dust, age, and melancholy. Producing a flashlight from his pocket, Dunkel headed knowingly across the gaudy linoleum, toward whatever room held the circuit boxes, while I idled in the spotty half-light coming in through the flyspecked windows. I spun the guest book around on its creaky turntable and looked at the last entry: Mr. and Mrs. Bronislaw Oboyski, from seven years ago. I hoped they had enjoyed their stay.

A lightbulb overhead flashed to life before dying with a sharp *pop*. Dunkel reappeared, grinning. "You're live now, Mr. McClinton. The feed goes from here to all the outbuildings. Now you can start up your water pump. Want me to give you a hand with that?"

"This isn't part of the power company's regular service, is it?" I said. "Will there be any extra charge?"

Dunkel snorted as if I had accused him of being a werewolf. "Shucks, Mr. McClinton, course not. Just want to make you folks feel welcome by lending a hand where I can. People in these parts are mighty glad someone's trying to revive the lodge. I won't pretend you're not gonna get a lot of job-seekers dropping by before long. The employment situation is still pretty grim in these parts."

Oh, great. Along with orchestrating our scam on Nancarrow, we were going to have to deal with hordes of unemployed yokels dropping by. I wondered whether Stan had anticipated this and had some plan in place for dealing with visitors.

"We'll do what we can, Mort, but we've got to take things slow till we get it all sorted out."

"Totally understood, Mr. McClinton."

We found the outbuilding that housed the water pump. The intake came from Nutbush Lake itself, not a well. Under Dunkel's expert ministrations, including liberal applications from an old-fashioned thumb-trigger oilcan, the long-dormant motor began to whir.

"I think you're gonna have to install some new filters, but things look pretty sweet otherwise. Here's a card for Elbert Tighe. Good man. Runs a well-drilling business and can do you right. He'll give everything a better once-over than I can."

Dunkel and I walked back to his truck.

"Don't hesitate to call if you need any more electrical work, Mr. McClinton. I moonlight most evenings."

When the rattle of Dunkel's truck died away, I was truly alone. Suddenly, space seemed to expand around me—too much of it. The nonhuman sounds of the woodlands and the lake felt unnatural to this city boy, making me apprehensive without any good reason.

This would be the third evening since our arrival.

That first morning after our contorted night in the car, we had emerged to size up the place by daylight. Stan claimed one of the stand-alone cabins for himself and Sandralene, while I took the last room in the eastern wing of the lodge. Sandralene had found a broom and some cleanish rags and began a concerted tidying-up campaign on our bedrooms, with water hauled two buckets at a time from the lake. Stan and I perambulated the property, sizing it up and talking about how best to con Nancarrow, fleshing out our still-nebulous attack. By the end of the day, we had better lodgings than the car, although they were still primitive, without electricity, running water, or any sort of bed linens. Luckily, the warmth of the day carried through the night, and although I couldn't speak for Stan or Sandralene, I stayed dressed.

Vee Aptekar and Ray Zerkin had not arrived as planned on that first full day at the camp. Vee called Stan to explain why. Having attained his majority a couple of years ago, Ray Zerkin lived in a group home, under the auspices of some state agency. Getting him signed out for an extended "vacation" under Vee's care involved a bit more paperwork than anticipated. But they hoped to be up at the lodge the next day.

That next day, today, had dawned on a trio of grumpy campers, unwashed and sick of subsisting on snack foods. Having arranged the appointment with the power company representative, I had been tapped to stay at the lodge while Stan and Sandralene took the car to Centerdale for various supplies.

Centerdale, almost an hour north and thus still unseen by any of us, was the nearest town of any size, with stores, restaurants, a movie theater, and other hallmarks of civilization. It was also where our new parole officer, Wilson Schreiber, was headquartered. Stan and I would have to report in to him before much longer.

Around 9:00 a.m., after a breakfast of cookies and warm soda, Stan had gotten behind the wheel of the Impala, with Sandralene sitting close beside him.

"We'll be back by afternoon, Glen. Maybe you can catch a few fish for supper."

"Yeah, right. Just bring back some real groceries, okay?"

"Steaks and champagne, to get us used to living off Nancarrow's millions. Hang tight."

The thought of a real steak had me salivating. I went over to the burger-stand building, where I recalled seeing an old refrigerator inside. Sure enough, it was already chilling down, ready to hold whatever food Stan brought back. I found a can of Ajax, grabbed a rag, and ran some blessedly hot water. (The electric heating element was built in right under the sink.) Soon I had the stove top ready for cooking.

Just as I was finishing, I heard tires on gravel outside.

15

The car was a new royal-blue Volkswagen Beetle, smudged with road dust. As it wheeled to a stop by the office, its retro styling seemed to fit well with the old lodge and this timeless forest. And for a brief moment, standing in the doorway of the little kitchen shack, I had a vivid hallucination, a kind of spontaneous New Frontier fantasy. I was back in the 1960s, long before I was actually born, and the world was a lighter, happier place, with my part in it all solid and safe and certain. It seemed I was running this place for real, just waiting to welcome guests. I half-heard the Beach Boys playing on a tinny transistor radio, and the splashing and joyful cries of children in the lake. I felt happy and at peace.

The driver's door opened, and the daydream blew away in a puff of reality. Still, it had been nice while it lasted—odd and possibly symptomatic of a coming reality breakdown, but nice.

Varvara "Vee" Aptekar was an inch or two shorter than I, trim, and graceful. She wore a demure beige linen shirt, loose black cotton slacks, and flat shoes. Her only jewelry was a small gold cross on a short chain around her slim neck.

I had had some vague notion that all women from Belarus

were blonde. But her shoulder-length hair was chestnut with tawny highlights, artificial or not. Her taut face was all sharp planes, as if various hardships and trials had leached away any sort of padding. The effect was one of stern beauty. Her unpainted lips struck me as severe at first, but then just seemed to fit the general theme of self-discipline and tight constraint.

I crossed the gravel lot. She waited by the open car door, as if ready to dart inside and take off should I prove in any way suspicious.

"You are Glen McClinton," she said in a voice that discouraged any silliness. No accent—right, though her parents were immigrants, she had been born here.

"Yes, that's me. And you must be Varvara."

"You can call me Vee."

"Vee, then." I extended my hand, and she took it with businesslike efficiency. Her nails were unpolished, her grip respectable, her skin cool and soft.

"Welcome to Bigelow Junction," I said, trying for at least a grin. "No cable TV, no heated pool, no nightlife except owls and raccoons. Just what my parole officer ordered as punishment."

Although she didn't actually smile, she didn't seem deliberately frosty. She seemed to accept my lame jest in a kind of tolerant but chastising manner, like an adult waiting for a child to calm down.

"We can't very well expect luxuries when embarked on a mission of revenge, can we? The main reason we're all here is take that goatfucker Barnaby Nancarrow to the cleaners and leave him feeling stupid and broken. Let's not forget that. If we keep our goal always uppermost in our minds, we can't fail. Or so life has taught me."

Man, this was one steely and unswerving gal. I could foresee some strained silences around the breakfast table. How she was going to turn on the sexy charm and seduce Nancarrow, I couldn't quite picture.

"Makes sense, I guess," I said. "Though I have to say, I once had some serious uppermost-in-mind goals that nonetheless landed me behind bars."

"You did something wrong, then. That is obvious."

Well, there was no countering the certainty in that blunt assessment, so I didn't even try.

Vee leaned down to peer inside the car. "It's all right, Ray, you can come out now."

The passenger door swung open, and out stepped our ace hacker.

I doubted that Ray Zerkin weighed much more than 125 pounds, even though he was close to six feet tall. A disordered mop of black hair, a pair of thick prescription lenses in taped-together frames resting on a snub nose. His face was weirdly devoid of affect, but odder still was his attire. He wore the complete uniform of a New York Yankees player.

The kid clutched a top-of-the-line iPad whose screen commanded all his attention.

"Yes, Vee. The signal is still strong. I can do everything from up here."

Vee explained. "He's got a 5G connection on that device. He can do anything online you can do back in the city with your fiber-optics provider."

"Uh, well, great," I said. "That's why he's here, right? So, I guess we need to get you guys set up in a room. Or two rooms."

"No, just one. Ray would freak out if he had to be alone. I've known him since he was twelve, and he trusts and needs me very much. Both his parents died in a car crash back then. It took him forever to recover."

I recalled how Stan had told me of the murder-suicide

involving Vee's own parents. Surely that similarity had helped foster the unlikely bond between her and the kid.

"All right, then, one room. We haven't really cleaned up anything yet for you. You have a preference?"

"Where is everyone else staying?"

I pointed out Stan and Sandralene's cabin, and my room at the east end of the lodge.

"We'll take that one," Vee said, indicating the farthest room of the west wing. Her lack of interest in my company could not have been plainer.

"Let's take a look inside. You got any luggage?"

The VW held a couple of small suitcases, which I took.

Ray followed Vee and me, but his whole attention was fixed on his tablet, which was emitting a familiar sports announcer's voice. "Vee, the game is about to start! The Yankees are playing the San Francisco Giants. I expect the Yankees to do very well today. Perhaps they will equal or improve their historic eighteen-to-four victory over the Giants from October second, 1936!"

"I certainly hope so, Ray." Her voice softened noticeably when she spoke to the kid.

We got the room open and lifted some windows, and it wasn't too bad. The lodge's previous owners had closed things down in a tidy, weather-tight manner, and the intervening seven years had accumulated only dust, leaves, and spider webs.

"Stan's coming back soon with sheets and food and stuff," I said. "I'd offer you a meal, but there's only cookies and soda."

"I love cookies and soda," said Ray.

"Okay! The lodge's first soon-to-be-satisfied customer. I'll be right back."

I left Vee and Ray in their room, with Ray glued to the game and Vee using a paisley scarf from her luggage as a dust mop.

As I was assembling the cookies and soda, the Impala pulled

up, and Stan jumped out. He was eating a juicy peach that I would have killed for.

"Hey, they made it! The whole crew's here! Whaddaya think of our prospects now, Glen boy?" "You have signed on an ice princess as Mata Hari and some kind of sabermetrics idiot savant as our dark-web mastermind. So I need to know, did you bring back any fucking miracles from Centerdale? Because that's what we really need."

Stan slapped me on the back. "Lighten up, dude! We are golden now. C'mon, help Sandralene unload the car. I'm hot, and I'm gonna take a swim."

16

I had to compliment Ray on his ability to work hard and unrelentingly. I had never seen anyone with that kind of focus. Whereas other kids his age would have been bellyaching and bugging off every five minutes, he just powered ahead with the task given him, as if nothing else in the world mattered. If I had been able to marshal that kind of sustained concentration in my own life, I might have gotten rich without resorting to crime. Maybe his weird Asperger's condition had some compensating benefits after all. I suspected that if we provided him with adequate instructions for spoofing Nancarrow, he would not stop until the guy was gaffed and landed. I began to feel a tad more sanguine about our prospects.

Vee was still cleaning her room, with Sandralene's help, and the two of them also planned to install bedding for the rest of us. They had already put away all the groceries, including the promised steaks and champagne. Having donned an exceedingly immodest Speedo swimsuit featuring a green and black abstract motif, Stan was splashing in the weedy waters of Nutbush Lake like a stranded grampus, bellowing snatches of various blues tunes. That left Ray and me to fix up our outdoor dining room.

So he and I went over to the collection of picnic tables that the last owner had stacked under some big shady pines when they closed down the place. It might have seemed like a good storage idea at the time, but seven years later, the tables were rich with moss and pine tar and squirrel scat.

"Think you can lift your end and help me carry this to the cook shack?"

"Mr. McClinton, I expect to try and succeed, if it is at all possible."

"Okay. Let's go."

The kid held up his end fine, though it took some effort, and we waddled back with the table. We positioned it near the shack's side door, which gave easy access to the kitchen area. Then I took Ray to the garage–cum–equipment shed, where we found some industrial cleaner, a wire brush, and a garden hose with a brass spray nozzle. I also noticed a small canopy affair—basically just a colorful tarp with four tall metal poles. We carried all this stuff back to the picnic table, and I located the nearest exterior spigot for the hose. Thank the Lord that Dunkel had gotten the water pump running. I made a mental note to tell Stan about the filters needing changing, and the local guy who could do it.

"Okay, Ray, let's see if you can find any actual wood under all this bird shit."

He eyed the table as if he were a surgeon, and the table his patient. "I believe the structural integrity of the table is uncompromised, Mr. McClinton."

"Have at it, then, kid."

Ray rolled up the sleeves of his jersey, splashed down the table, and began wire-bristling off the years of gunk as if attacking an alien plague intent on the destruction of life on Earth.

"Hey, Ray, slow down!" I said. "You're getting your uniform all wet and dirty."

"I have several more in my suitcase, Mr. McClinton, and I assume there are laundry facilities here. Am I correct in that assumption?"

I had seen an industrial washer and dryer back at the office.

"Yes, Ray, we can do laundry."

"This is awesome news, Mr. McClinton."

"Ray, you gotta start calling me Glen."

"I shall attempt to remember to call you Glen, Mr. McClinton."

I left Ray to his demonic scrubbing and went to see if I could help the women.

Vee was in my room, which, of course, I had left unlocked. I had nothing inside that anyone would want to steal, and there was no one in sight to steal it. She was just tucking in a lightweight blue cotton spread at its upper corners. The bed looked as if it had been made under the eye of a particularly fastidious marine drill instructor.

I had an odd feeling then, watching her fuss with my bed, as if she and I were lovers or married or something. And if she had not already presented herself as unassailably aloof, I might have used the occasion to make some harmless flirtatious innuendo. But her shell of inviolable remoteness around a core of hurt warded me off as effectively as an electrified fence. And yet, I felt somehow that I wanted to say more to her than merely thanks.

"Can I help?"

"No, it's done."

"Where's Sandralene?"

"She decided to go swimming with Stan."

Vee moved to leave. I almost restrained her, as if I needed to communicate a vital message before she walked away. But I simply said, "I appreciate all your help. Not just little stuff like this"—I gestured at the bed—"but with the big plan. It can't be easy, the thought of getting close to Nancarrow after what he did—"

She stopped and looked at me with a stolid expression that felt like the innocuous shell of a roadside bomb.

"Nancarrow ruined the lives of my mother and father. I was five years old. When I was a teenager and learned about my history, I thought he had ruined mine, too. But since then, I've worked hard to make sure he was powerless over me. And that gives me power over him. I'm here because you and Stan can help me exercise that power the way I wish to. No thanks are necessary."

The strength of will that I saw in those dark eyes made me thankful we were on the same side. "You know," I said, "this seems an excellent foundation for a business partnership. As an ex-lawyer, I approve. Good to have all the contractual provisions spelled out."

If she detected any irony, she ignored it.

"I'm glad you see things the same way I do."

"Yes, we have that going for us," I said. "Well, I'm gonna go check out the aquatic ballet."

* * *

Down at the beach, the sight of Sandralene presented such a contrast to Vee that my head spun around like that of a Tex Avery wolf. Stan's girl had poured her bounteous flesh into a crimson two-piece suit that left little to my libidinous imagination. Frolicking in the water with Stan, she uttered a variety of pagan, ecstatic grunts and squeals. Stan picked her up and heaved her into deep water with an outsize splash. Then, incredibly, she did the same to him, although even her exceptional strength could not hoist him very high.

"Glen, you lame-ass motherfucker, get in here and help me! This broad is nuts! It's fucking war! The reputation of all men is at stake!"

"I know when I'm outclassed," I shouted back.

Sandralene grinned lasciviously at me, in an impartial way. "Glen, I will cook you the biggest goddamn steak tonight!"

"Accepted. I bribe very easily."

I had to leave then or go mad with lust.

* * *

Back at the cookhouse, I found Ray, dirty and drenched, sloshing off the table with a final spray from the hose. The planks gleamed golden, as if fresh from the mill.

"Holy crap, Ray," I said, "that is an awesome job! Well done!"

Ray didn't precisely smile, although his expression did change in some indefinable way. "I was not certain it was acceptable until you confirmed it, Glen. Thank you for this confirmation."

"Let's just move it out of this muddy spot."

We established the table in its new location, still close to the kitchen, and I erected the canopy over it.

"Go clean yourself up, Ray. It'll be time to eat soon."

"We will have supper when Mr. Hasso is done playing grab-ass with Miss Parmalee?"

I looked at him closely, but he betrayed not the faintest spark of humor.

"Yes, that's more or less the parameters of the situation, Ray."

"I understand."

17

Eating at the clean picnic table was practical and easy and fun. Ray exhibited a quiet pride at our appreciation for his labors.

I hadn't eaten with such gusto since Stan Hasso entered my life—maybe not even during the long, bored postprison stint before then. Sandralene had broiled the steaks to perfection, and Vee had produced a green salad with a tasty homemade dressing. It had been Stan's idea to get a fire going in the stone ring and roast the potatoes in the coals. They emerged from their foil jackets as lightly charred lumps of pure smoky-earthen goodness, further enhanced by gobs of butter and plenty of salt and pepper.

When Sandralene emerged with the platter of steaks, she made a big show of giving me the largest.

Stan watched the display with a grimace. "You are such a damn pussy-whipped traitor, Glen. Remind me never to count on you against any female opponents in the future."

I put down my fork and said, "When push truly comes to shove, unless Nancarrow has a sex change, you can rely on me as your loyal ally."

Vee didn't participate in any of our banter, using the moments

to cut her steak into precise bite-size pieces of almost machine-pro-
duced uniformity. Ray exhibited a hearty fascination with his
food that verged on animal grossness without quite teetering over
the edge.

Stan had also brought back beer, wine, and spirits from
Centerdale. The ice-cold PBR tasted like pure heaven. Stan drank
three to my one, while Sandralene only doubled my intake. Vee
sipped at a small glass of pinot grigio, making it last for the whole
meal. Ray had several Cokes.

After two days of cookies and soda, we hardly spoke the entire
time. Maybe it was just hunger and the woodsy atmosphere that
made everything taste so wonderful. I felt suspended in a kind of
lost interval between one stage of demanding action and another.
We had set the physical stage for Nancarrow's downfall but hadn't
yet shifted into high gear to bring about that desired outcome.
For now, responsibilities had temporarily ceased to bother us.

Stan and I had raided the rental units and hauled out five
chairs that were comfier than the picnic table's wooden benches,
and now the five of us sat under a night sky glittering with intensely
bright stars. I inhaled the rich primordial tang from the dense leaf
litter beneath the trees and from the black waters of the lake, along
with the wood smoke from the fire before us. The flickering light
was supplemented only by the glow of Ray's iPad shining on his
face. Oblivious of his surroundings, the kid was focused utterly
on what I could only assume were more baseball videos. He was
politely using his earbuds, though, so I couldn't say for sure.

Stan roused himself enough to send Sandralene off to the
cookshack, and she returned with a chilled bottle of champagne
and some tumblers. Stan twisted off the wire, firing the cork
off into the darkness, and poured five glasses and passed them
around. Ray unplugged from his device and studied his drink as
if it were an extract from some alien world.

"Here's to twenty million dollars!" said Stan. "And getting even with a major-league prick!"

We clinked our tumblers and drank. Ray took a tentative sip, then, evidently liking the taste and the fizz, downed the rest. Stan refilled our glasses.

"So, Ray," he said with a slyness that maybe only I caught, "what are you planning to do with your five million?"

Stan had suggested that maybe we could cut Ray a smaller slice of the loot. I figured he was counting on Ray saying something stupid or inconclusive in front of us that he could later use to justify not giving the kid a full share. But Ray did not hesitate in his reply.

"Mr. Hasso, this is a very good question, and I'm glad you asked. I have given a lot of thought to this very good question, ever since Vee told me of this opportunity, and this is what I have decided. I am going to take my money—which is a very lot of money, I know—and I am going to open up a school. It will be a school for people like myself, who have special abilities and special needs. At this school of mine, we will teach people like me how to have a job and how to live on their own. I predict that this will be a big success."

I have to give Stan credit. I could tell that he accepted Ray's answer instantly. He was not a greedy guy and didn't necessarily want more than his cut. I think he was only concerned that the kid wouldn't know what to do with such a huge sum and might waste it on something stupid. He just didn't want to throw five million dollars down the toilet.

"Well, kid, I think that's a swell idea. Maybe you can name the school after your biggest donor, Barnaby Nancarrow."

"Mr. Hasso, that is probably not a good idea, since we are stealing the money from him."

"Noted, kid."

I said, "You and Sandralene still planning to leave the country, Stan?"

"Yeah, and I know just where we're going. I been scoping out a lot of countries before I settled on this one: the Cape Verde islands."

"Cape Verde? What's that all about?"

"Well, number one, they got no extradition treaty with the USA. Number two, they're not some third-world hellhole, even if they are just off the coast of Africa. They're a nice, stable country that's also a beautiful place—a kind of tropical paradise, really. Yeah, their economy sucks—not enough jobs, which has sent a lot of their folks overseas. But that's not gonna bother someone with five million in the bank. It's close to Europe, so we could sneak across for some fun if we don't end up on any watch lists—maybe even if we do. I'm still not counting on Nancarrow pressing any kind of charges against us after we scam him. He's going to be pissed, but too mortified. And the Gulch code of honor don't favor snitches. Anyhow, Cape Verde is looking like my dream spot. Sandy agrees."

Sandralene said, "I'm really sick of winter."

"The only major headache is the language. They speak some kinda weird Portagee dialect. But here's the final thing that pushed me into thinking we should definitely go for Cape Verde. Just a weird kinda coincidence. Turns out there's a bunch of Cape Verdeans living right up in Centerdale! A whole little community. I figure we can use part of our time up here to get tutored in the language. Should help kill the boredom factor while we're waiting for Nancarrow to bite."

Stan's choice of exile sounded pretty good to me. I had no other destination in mind after we brought off our coup, and like Sandralene, I was sick of cold and snow. The thought suddenly recalled to mind that chill December night when I saved Stan's life. It seemed ever so long ago.

"You mind some company?" I said.

"Shit, no! The more the merrier!"

I looked across the flames to Vee, who was sipping thoughtfully at her second glass of champagne. "What about you, Vee?"

"I think I need to stay here, to help Ray with his plans. And for another reason."

"Yeah? What's that?"

"I want to see Nancarrow squirm and hurt up close, once we've screwed him. I want to hear him wail and see him look like an incompetent jerk in front of all his big-shot pals. I want to watch him try to explain how a brilliant operator like him got taken. For me, that's a big part of getting even."

"Jeez, that's stone cold," said Stan. "But I approve. Just make sure he doesn't catch you enjoying his misery. I seen how he lashes out when he thinks people are making fun of him, and it's not pretty."

Vee regarded us with a stern, unflinching gaze. "I'm not pretty, either, when I've got someone I hate down on the ground."

18

I had a long list of chores to tackle.

Get Elbert Tighe, the recommended local well-and-pump expert, on the phone and see about having him come by to give our filtration system a once-over. I didn't care to be drinking any more fish poop or brain-eating amoebas out of Nutbush Lake than I had to, and I suspected the others felt the same.

Sit down with Ray and learn more about what he could do on the internet. I had a bunch of ideas for subtle items that could be planted online to convince Nancarrow of the imaginary reality of Steve Prynne's interest in Bigelow Junction and the desirability of buying us out here. Hooking him and reeling him in was really no different from how I had convinced so many clients at Ghent, Goolsbee & Saikiri to let me invest their funds in projects of dubious merit so I could turn that cash into heroin destined for my arm. But we had to be subtle about this and make sure none of our insertions were traceable back to us.

Call Uncle Ralph and Suzy Lam and see how they are doing. Not only had I discovered that I truly missed them, but they were investors in this scam, on however small a scale, and deserved to be kept abreast of things. Also, as the registered owner of this property, Uncle Ralph had to be reminded to stay alert for anyone approaching him and deflect any inquiries to us. Naturally, Stan's phone could never be referenced, the name Hasso being anathema to Nancarrow and Company, and so my ridiculous antique would have to serve as our switchboard.

In fact, as we got closer to enticing Nancarrow up for a visit, Stan would have to lower his physical profile as well. And considering the force of nature that Stan was, this would require some real self-restraint on his part, and constant reminders on mine. I wondered whether, when the time came, we should perhaps get him lodgings up in Centerdale.

But that raised the next item on my to-do list: contact Parole Officer Wilson Schreiber. I imagined he would want to come out for a visit, to check that we were really living and working here. And he could choose to drop in for further surprise inspections anytime he felt like it. Anton Paget had warned us that Schreiber was a hardnose. How to square that with getting Stan an apartment elsewhere and thus violating his stated residence?

The necessity of keeping up the charade that we were reopening Bigelow Junction for business—a charade that provided Schreiber with the justification for our being here—meant that I had to conduct a lot of other tasks. I would have to contact grocers and laundry companies, employment agencies and tourist bureaus and advertising outlets, letting the news spread that we were serious about starting up the lodge again, and not just squatters sitting on a spec investment. Of course, when dealing with Nancarrow, we would let on that we were here only because we believed Prynne had his eye on the property, and that was how we knew to set such a high value on it. But Nancarrow would also find it quite reasonable that we had maintained such a facade of innocent, suspicion-diverting commercialism in the eyes of the world. After all, that was exactly how he himself, real estate shyster that he was, would have concealed the property's real value to prevent any other speculators from getting wind and horning in.

It was all such a convoluted bluff within a bluff that my head began to ache, trying to keep straight who could be allowed to learn what.

The only thing to do was to approach each task one at a time and make sure we covered each step the best we could. Otherwise, you could get balled up in overthinking.

So I left my room at nine thirty that morning after dissipating a slight champagne hangover with a shower running alternately hot and cold. (The truth came out last night that Stan had brought back not a single bottle of champagne but a case, and we had gone through several more bottles under the stars.) I followed the smell of coffee to the cookshack.

Vee sat under the canopy with a mug of coffee and a piece of toast, a book in her hand. I could hear Stan and Sandralene laughing and chatting inside.

"What are you reading?"

She angled the cover so I could see the title better. A novel by some Italian gal, Elena Ferrante. "Do you know her work?"

"I haven't read a novel since law school," I said, "and that was something by John Grisham."

"I appreciate your honesty." She returned to reading, and I went into the tiny snack-concession building.

The limited space between stove, sink, fridge, and fryer meant that the large bodies of Stan and Sandralene were in intimate proximity—which seemed to suit both of them and their roving hands.

"Hey, get a cabin!" I said. "Preferably at the Bigelow Junction Motor Lodge. I understand they could use the business."

Sandralene disengaged long enough to pour me a mug of coffee. "I hope you like it strong, Glen."

"Nuclear," I said. "Stan, I want to run some things by you if you've got a minute—about Ray's activities and some other stuff."

"Sure." He swatted Sandralene's butt, squeezed past her, and followed me outside. He spoke to Vee first.

"Where's the kid?"

"He always stays up late and sleeps late."

"Well, get him awake pretty soon, if you can. Glen needs to talk to him."

As Vee went to wake our IT guru, I said to Stan, "Don't you want to sit in on this strategy session, too?"

"Glen boy, if I knew how to plant seductive shit on the internet, what would I need you or Ray for? No, you're the expert at these kinda mind games, and I trust you totally. Either you come up with a winning plan that lures Nancarrow into our trap, or we try our best and still fall flat. Either way, I can't contribute anything. I'm just the muscles and motivator and general heavy lifter and watchdog. I thought up the whole get-even scheme, didn't I? That should be plenty."

"Okay, I'm going to take you at your word. Just don't come whining if I fail."

Vee said, "I can help with this, I think."

Stan said, "Way to go, Vee! Two heads, and all that shit. Man, ol' Barnaby doesn't stand a chance now."

"I've got other stuff that needs doing, though. Maybe you could help with that." I outlined my other chores.

Stan took the business card for Elbert Tighe from me. "I'll go visit this well digger and tell him what we need. Size him up and make sure he's not a busybody. Gotta take the car into Centerdale anyhow."

"What for?"

"Oh, coupla things. You'll see."

I regarded Stan dubiously, but he projected an air of innocent cooperativeness. "You'll be back for supper?"

"Sure. Sandralene's coming with me, but she don't mind cooking for us when we get back."

Soon, the Impala had rattled off in a skitter of dry pine needles and gravel. Vee and I, sitting side by side at the picnic table with a pad and two pencils, began to chart Nancarrow's entrapment.

Around noon, Ray joined us, still looking a little sleep-befuddled.

"Hello, Glen. Hello, Vee. This country air is very conducive to drowsiness, I feel."

Armed with a mug of coffee, he turned to his iPad. We wouldn't need him till we had gotten things more nailed down.

Working with Vee proved smooth and efficient. She had a sharp mind yet wasn't attached to her own ideas, and we made good progress. We had ham-and-pickle sandwiches for lunch, then hit it again till midafternoon.

I wanted a swim and almost asked Vee to accompany me. But nothing in our working together had softened the standoffish vibe she radiated, so I decided not to push.

* * *

My first plunge into Nutbush Lake was wonderful. The water was cool and slippery and refreshing and clean. I felt like a kid again and could see how Stan and Sandralene had been so giddy and boisterous in the water yesterday. The shoreline trees laid zones of darkness on the surface, surrounded by glimmers of sunlight. The world seemed complete, with no need for striving. I had a fleeting moment's unease about the elaborate, dicey, probably dangerous scheme we were embarked on. Did we really need more than what we had right here? I floated on my back for a while, luxuriating in the sensation of cool ripples and warm sun. Then the urgency of our dwindling funds, and the allure of a cool five million and all the wonderful stuff it could buy, bestirred me. I swam for a bit, then emerged from the water.

Barefoot, bare-chested, with a towel around my shoulders, I was heading toward my room when the Impala returned.

Stan got out, Sandralene got out, and then a third person got out of the back seat.

The newcomer was a young woman, holding a small duffel bag. Petite, trim figure, explosion of frizzy black hair, mocha skin, with an easy, uncoerced smile. She wore cutoff jeans and a ruffled purple crop top that exposed a smooth midriff.

"Glen boy, this is Nellie! She's gonna teach us Cape Verdean creole, night and day!"

19

Nélida Firmino, age twenty-one, was a nice girl from a nice family. Her father, Ivanildo, was a school custodian in Centerdale, beloved by all the children at Ronald Reagan Elementary. Her mother, Zahira, did not work outside the home but had her hands full raising Nellie's four younger siblings: Adelma, Leidira, Roberto, and Justin. The youngest had apparently been christened after Justin Bieber. *Mãe* Firmino was also kept busy preparing large pots of *cachupa* that simmered more or less continuously on the stove top, filling the Firmino house with enticing scents of garlic, manioc, and plantains. The family had its roots in the city of Praia, on the island of Santiago. Nellie enjoyed the traditional *morna* music of Cape Verde, as typified by the singing of Cesária Évora, but she also favored modern American and K-pop girl bands such as Little Mix, AOA, and Fifth Harmony. Her best friend was another Caboverdeana named Celina, and Nellie would certainly miss their outings together to the mall, where they patronized Popeyes, Hot Topic, Wet Seal, and Hollister while scoping out the hot guys.

We learned all this deluge of information and much more in

the space of forty-five minutes, all of us sitting under the canopy outside the cookshack, sipping drinks in the waning heat of late afternoon. Nellie and Ray favored Cokes, while we four adults had Mike's Hard Lemonade.

Throughout Nellie's impassioned, lilting monologue, Sandralene and Stan beamed with obvious pride at the young woman, who seemed utterly at ease, as if they were her adoptive parents. Vee cast long evaluating gazes her way, with no evident approval or lack of it, impartial as a judge. Ray could not keep his jaw from going slack as he stared unrelentingly at Nellie, who took no offense. The boy seemed to be sweating from more than just the heat. His tape-repaired eyeglasses kept sliding down his nose until, just before they fell off, he absentmindedly pushed them back.

I had not even changed out of my swim trunks, which were now almost dry. The appearance of Nellie and her unanticipated, unconsulted addition to our little gang had left me too gob-smacked to think of dressing. I thought I saw—or imagined I saw—her casting frequent covert glances at my bare chest and legs. If this was really happening, it was flattering, arousing, and disconcerting, in equal measures.

Eventually, Nellie wound down, finishing up a long tale of how she and Celina had once emerged from the mall's cinema to encounter Celina's cousin, Evandro, a male model in New York, who now went by the name "Drew." He had returned home for a short vacation to spread his glamour among the tribe and was outrageously squiring a fellow male model, and wasn't it a shame that such gorgeous guys were both *paneleiro*?

"Uh, yeah, that is a shame," I said. Then I peered with solemn and somewhat miffed entreaty at Hasso and said, "Stan, could you come with me for a minute?"

As we walked away toward the business office, Nellie continued to chatter away like a sports reporter trying to cram every real-time detail into a compressed broadcast.

"All right," I said when we were out of earshot, "what gives?"

"What gives is just what I said. She's gonna teach us the Cape Verde lingo. It ain't straight Portagee, you know; it's a weird mix—*kriolu*. You can't buy language lessons or anything to learn it."

I said, "If she can stop recounting her social life and every errant thought that pops into her head, for one minute, then I admit she might be useful along those lines. But why bring her here?"

"Ah, give her a break, Glen. She's just a little nervous and trying to be friendly and impress her new bosses. As for bringing her here, how else we gonna do it? We can't go into town for regular lessons, can we? We're supposed to be holding down steady jobs here, according to the rules of our parole."

"No, I guess we can't afford to leave this place unattended for long, under the watchful eyes of both Wilson Schreiber and Nancarrow. But how did you meet her? What's she expect?"

"Sandy and I stopped in a Micky Dee's on that first run into town the other day. Nellie was working the counter. I got to talking with her, learned all about her heritage and shit. She ain't shy, opens up real quick."

"Yes, that much is obvious."

"Anyhow, I almost freaked when it turned out she was from Cape Verde—or her folks were. Just the place I had been talking about for our safe haven after the job! What're the odds? It was like getting punched in the gut by Fate. So it turns out Nellie was sick of being a burger slinger and was thinking of getting a new job. I came up with the tutoring gig on the spot. Pretty quick thinking, right? I told her to discuss it with her folks, and I'd come back for her if it was okay. She still lives at home. Gave her my phone number. She called this morning while you were still asleep."

"What are we paying her?"

"Room and board and fifteen dollars an hour for any actual classroom time. But I figure we'll pick up a lot of vocabulary from her just hanging around with us. Look, I already know how to call someone a fag. '*Paneleiro*,' right?"

Stan was fast, and he had a good ear. I don't think I could have repeated that word after just one hearing.

"You know what really cinched the deal, though?" Stan asked. "When she and Mom and Pop learned she'd be living at the Bigelow Junction Motor Lodge and that we were gonna reopen it. Her and her family used to stay here when she was a kid and into her teens. She loves the place. Seems like lots of these hicks have fond memories of the lodge. It was a real favorite resort until it closed. We got a lot of goodwill among the public for rebooting this joint."

"Except that we are not actually rebooting this joint, remember? We're just faking it until we can sell it to Nancarrow."

"I know that! But it don't hurt to be in good with the local yokels."

I considered what Stan had gotten us into. "Of course, we're going to have to keep her in the dark about our real goals here. Can you do that?"

"Hell, yeah!"

I discovered, to my surprise, that I was rather looking forward to Nellie's lively presence around the place, and could not find it in myself to stay annoyed with Stan for not consulting me first. "Then, I guess we're stuck with her. Maybe it'll all work out okay. Let's go back and get her settled."

We returned to find the three women clustered in front of Nellie's phone, watching a video that featured a bevy of Korean girls cavorting on a beach while lip-synching the lyrics to a pop song. Sandralene was gyrating mildly but enthusiastically in place, while Vee wore the look of an anthropologist taking mental notes. Ray maintained his rapt absorption in Nellie's mere presence.

"Nélida," I said, "let's get you set up in a room. There will be some cleaning involved."

Nellie jumped up with a squeal. "Cabin number five! That's where we always stayed!"

Duffel slung over one shoulder, she trotted straight to cabin five as I hastened after her.

Stan called out, "Sandy and I are gonna get supper ready! Shrimps and swordfish on the grill, with coleslaw and sangria!"

I caught up with Nellie at the door of the cabin, found the right key, and unhooked it from the ring and gave it to her.

She looked me in the eye and, without any obvious guile, said, "This your only key? Guess you gotta come see me now if you wanna get in!"

20

The drab, utilitarian outskirts of Centerdale appeared without much preamble. One minute, Stan was powering the old Impala down a narrow, tree-bordered road whose humped and buckled macadam reflected the region's harsh winters and which resembled every other green, leafy mile between here and the lodge. And the next minute, we were out in the open, with a Hess gas station on one side of the newly widening street, a McDonald's on the other, and other small businesses, franchised or mom-and-pop, stretching sparsely ahead. I wondered whether that was the Micky Dee's where Nellie had been discovered. But I didn't ask out loud, and Stan did not volunteer the information.

"No burbs," said Stan. "It's like some kinda magic line in the sand kept them from building out."

I said, "These little burgs had a kind of fortress mentality not so many decades ago. The citizens wanted to huddle together. And they could, because the towns were rich and lively and vibrant and offered everything you needed. And suburbs only came in later, after the heyday of these places. No one's going to build bedroom communities for a town without jobs."

"Wasn't this place called Leatherville way back when?"

Stan's question prodded some ancient memory of my parents talking about our cousins upstate. "Yeah," I said, "I think you're right. 'Shoe and Wallet Capital of the State!'"

"Shit! Might as well've built their future on horse saddles and Roy Rogers holster sets. China's got all our shoe factories, and most of what they make ain't even leather no more!"

We drove by some abandoned factories. I imagined the whir and rush when they were in their prime, as workers came and went by shifts, each man in a respectable fedora, the women stitchers in their knee-length skirts and sensible shoes, everyone jubilant and pleased with their lives. Now the scene could serve as a set for some postapocalyptic movie.

It was really too bad that no casino would be coming here. This place was practically crying out for the kind of economic relief such a project would bring.

We were now in what constituted Centerdale's downtown. Two of every three storefronts in the stately old office and retail buildings were vacant. Still hanging on were a bank, a diner, and a chain hardware store. Improbably, a children's shoe store remained: Lad 'n' Lassie, no doubt coasting on family loyalty. Once the current generation of only child grandkids were outfitted, and their ancient elders who remembered Lad 'n' Lassie finally died, this establishment, too, would go.

Stan parked in front of a sandstone building with elaborate carved ornamentation gracing its upper courses. I almost expected to see one of our mark's signs by the door:

NANCARROW LOGISTICS TRUST MANAGEMENT, LTD.

"FEASTING ON THE CARRION OF FAILED

COMMUNITIES SINCE 1992"

But no, Barnaby Nancarrow had not yet penetrated this far beyond his ancestral territories.

The parole and probation office for Centerdale and the region was on the second floor, reachable by a set of creaky wooden stairs whose metal trim had been worn thin by generations of weary, scuffling shoes. I almost expected to see a door with "Sam Spade, Investigator" etched on the brass nameplate.

It was three days since Nellie had come to the lodge, and her chatty presence there now felt quite natural. It was also the final day we could visit our new do-as-I-say-or-back-to-prison boss without incurring penalties.

A harried young female office manager handled the traffic for three counselors, each with their own cramped cubbyhole. After a longish wait on a hard bench, watching various lowlifes come and go, Stan and I were sent into Wilson Schreiber's work space.

Whereas Anton Paget resembled some dwarf out of the Mines of Moria, our new parole officer reminded me of Rocky Balboa: a big palooka with a beat-up mug and an expression that challenged you to believe he could successfully dial a smartphone. But behind the Clark Kent glasses, his gray eyes shone with intelligence. And when he opened his mouth, any doubts of his mental acuity vanished.

"So, gentlemen, how goes your rustication?"

"My *what*, now?" said Stan.

"He means our exchanging the city for the country."

"Oh, that. Well, Mr. Schreiber, I think it's doing us a shitload of good. Fresh air, hard work, simple meals—all with the goal of making Glen's uncle Ralph's long-standing dream of resort proprietorship come true. Ain't that just how you feel, Glen?"

"Yes, we don't miss the city at all. It was just full of enticements to resume our old bad habits."

Schreiber looked down at our files—I recognized mine from

Paget's office—then glanced at us over the tops of his lenses. "But out here, you two are flying straight. No fooling around. Just busy beavers getting the Bigelow Junction Motor Lodge ready for business."

"Yes sir, that's right."

Schreiber's voice suddenly boomed like a cannon. "Then why the hell, after nearly a week, haven't you contacted any local merchants and suppliers yet? From what I can see—and I can see things pretty damn well—all you've done is loll around on vacation."

I knew I should have made those calls I had considered making earlier. But I had been so busy with Ray, laying out our cybercampaign against Nancarrow, that I kept putting them off. Of course, I could hardly tell Schreiber that. But miraculously, a decent excuse came to mind.

"It's the water, sir. You see, we can't run the lodge without a good source of clean water, and we haven't been able to test the lake yet. We've contacted Mr. Elbert Tighe, and he's promised to help. He knows the staff at the state lab and says he can expedite the test for us. He's coming out tomorrow, in fact. He couldn't make it any sooner. We figure, once he certifies the water as okay, we can move ahead. No sense in committing ourselves to anything before we know that."

Schreiber regarded us both with only half-mollified suspicion. "You've really contacted Tighe already?"

"Yes, sir. You're welcome to call him yourself."

"No, that won't be necessary. All right, take this and go."

Schreiber handed me a single-sheet printout. Looking at it, I saw a timeline for what we had to do to get the lodge up and running. According to Schreiber's itinerary, we had a month till launch date.

"It's almost the end of August now. If you can open in early September, you can still capture a little of the late-summer traffic, plus you'll be ready for the leaf-peepers in October. And if we get some decent snow this winter, the snowmobile clubs'll keep you busy. If you can do all this, I'll know you're serious and not just jerking me off. Understand?"

Stan was practically jolly. "Sure thing, Mr. S, no problem!"

I just said, "We'll try our best."

"You'd better try a little harder than that, McClintock. Your previous best efforts in the business world were not very goddamned impressive."

Schreiber steered us to his office door and shook our hands. "I'll be out to the lodge now and then to check up on things. Try to have a cold beer ready. That's a long, hot drive without AC, and we civil servants don't have it as luxurious as you boys."

Walking out of the building, we were almost run down by a noisy pack of skateboarders—pimply kids, both boys and girls, full of Centerdale's patented anomie and itchy boredom. Back in the car, I said, "So let me get all this straight. We have a lousy hundred grand in the bank—"

"More like a smidgen under ninety-eight thousand, what with the groceries and fronting Vee some travel dough, and Nellie's pay and gas money and such."

"Ninety-eight thousand in the bank, then. And we're running down the clock against Steve Prynne announcing the real place where he intends to invest and thus thoroughly blowing our gaff. And now we suddenly have another deadline of just a month to show some progress we don't even know how to make happen. Does any of this make you feel the least bit pressured or anxious?"

"Yeah, of course," said Stan. "That's why, when we get back to the lodge, I am going to have a long swim followed by several kick-ass drinks and about three cheeseburgers, and then hammer Sandralene until she goes all cross-eyed and drooly. I suggest you do the same—except the part about Sandy, naturally."

PART THREE

21

Back from Centerdale, I decided to have a swim and sort things out in my head. Establish some kind of order, rank our tasks by urgency. We had to satisfy Schreiber's new imperatives, or at least appear to be hitting his marks. Otherwise, he'd be calling fraud on our supposed productive-good-citizen endeavors down here. But it was also nearing time to launch our essential catfishing campaign against Nancarrow. We couldn't wait much longer. I would go over with Ray once more the tricks we had connived, and then let her rip, for better or worse. With so many flaming batons to juggle, I felt that I was losing my focus.

I figured I would have the lakeshore to myself for some contemplative musings. Stan and Sandralene were goofing around in the kitchen shack, making gargantuan sandwiches (there went more of our limited money) and indulging in loud, half-serious, half-comical making out. I might have suggested they get a room, but they already had one. Vee and Ray reclined on lawn chairs under the shade of a big oak, absorbed in their reading. Vee had her Italian novel nearly done, I noticed, wondering fussily whether she had brought another to enjoy, while Ray was scrolling through what I assumed were endless baseball statistics. With everyone accounted for, I should be able to have some quiet time in the water.

But I had forgotten about Nellie. Although she had indeed slipped comfortably into this insane jigsaw puzzle of coconspirators (although without being fully informed about our illicit enterprise), she was still not firmly embedded in my mental chart of figures and forces to keep tabs on.

So when I arrived in my trunks at the unmowed margins of Nutbush Lake, its inviting waters burnished by the downward-bound sun, I found her already there, thigh-deep in the shallows. A melodic bird call resounded as I gawped at her.

She wore a bikini that I would have bet never existed outside a pop song: pale yellow with innocuous white polka-dots, green ribbon at each hip and one between her breasts. While modest, the suit still revealed what seemed, to my woman-starved gaze, a bounty of youthfully taut skin a couple of shades lighter than a freshly hulled horse chestnut. I realized I had stopped short at the sight of her.

Nellie hailed me blithely. "The water, Glen! It's just like I remember from when I was little! So sweet! Come on in!"

I dropped my towel on the beach and entered at a polite distance, still unable to converse normally.

"So, Glen, *modi bu sta?*"

"Huh?"

"I said, 'How you doing?' in Caboverde. Remember, dude? I'm supposed to be teaching you guys *kriolu*. But I only know Santiago style."

"A country that small has dialects?"

"You bet! We got Barlavento, Sal, Boa Vista—so many! But Santiago is the best!"

"Okay. So how do I answer?"

"You say, '*Muitu ben.*' That means you're doing good."

"And what if I'm going crazy?"

Nellie's laugh was a short bark. "*As coisas estão me deixando louco.*"

"*Louco.* So it's like Spanish."

Nellie unleashed a swift torrent of Caboverde whose general tone implied that I was an idiot. "Dude, you *never* say Portuguese and Spanish are the same! That's a big-time insult—to both."

"I'm very sorry. I should have spotted the difference right away. Spanish sounds like singing, whereas Portuguese sounds like you're gargling a mouthful of caterpillars with steel-wool bristles."

Nellie's response was another bark of a laugh, and then two hands on my chest toppling me into the water.

When I came up, I lunged for her, but she was too fast and slippery. She dived away and began freestyling out into the middle of the lake. I followed.

When she finally stopped, it was deep enough that we had to tread water to stay afloat, so there was no possibility of grappling. I was winded, but she wasn't even breathing hard.

"Hey, I got a question. Why you guys want to learn *kriolu,* anyhow? When Stan first laid out this gig, I was so excited I never thought to ask."

I could hardly tell her that we needed her language skills to abet our expatriate lifestyle after ripping off a local real estate baron for several million dollars. But luckily, the old scammer's brain that had served me so well—or maybe not so well—in my lawyerly days kicked in, just as it had in Paget's office, with what I hoped was a convincing explanation.

"We were hoping to staff the lodge totally with minorities. You know, help the underprivileged. And when we learned about the big Cape Verdean population in Centerdale, and their strong work ethic, we thought they would make ideal employees. So we figured if we could communicate better with our future staff—"

"*Oh minha nossa*, this is so awesome! I can't wait to tell my *mamãe* and *papai*! The whole community will be so excited. Glen, I could kiss you!"

Everything happened fast then. She threw her strong, lithe arms around my neck, and I had to churn harder with my legs and arms to keep us both afloat. Her firm, bountiful breasts pushed against my chest, with only that bit of polka-dot fabric intervening. Her lips, with just a hint of tongue protruding, were cool and cushiony and tasted like summer.

When I came out of my swoon, she was already several yards away and swimming to shore.

"I'm going to call them now!"

Whatever was to come of my hasty lie, good or bad, I couldn't regret it—not after that kiss. The years of enforced chastity had almost made me forget what pleasures were involved in such a commonplace act.

Still, I had to alert Stan and the others to my improvised cover story so they could back me up. I suddenly wondered what Nellie made of Vee and Ray. They hardly seemed integral players in any entrepreneurial scheme to reopen the lodge. Maybe we could cast Vee as our silent partner, and Ray as her son or nephew or some such. Ah, well, I could surely invent something plausible if the topic came up.

Meanwhile, I would just float around in the water until my erection subsided.

* * *

That evening, dining again in the cool under the stars, we had corn on the cob, tomato salad, and pork chops as thick as Barnaby Nancarrow's wallet. Everyone but Ray enjoyed a cold sangria that

Nellie had whipped up, rich with brandy, fresh fruit, and red wine. Our cybersavant quietly polished off a liter of Coke with lime slices.

When we all were stuffed, Nellie said, "I'll do dishes."

Sandralene said, "I'll help."

The two women carted everything into the cook shack, leaving us four conspirators to hunker at the scrubbed picnic table around Ray's eerily glowing iPad. Ray sat next to Stan on one fixed bench, and I sat by Vee on the other side.

Vee's palpable body heat and the scent of wood smoke in her hair contrasted with Nellie's cool mermaid aura earlier. Something about Vee's hard shell of angry indifference still made me want to crack it, to see what tenderness might lie hidden within. The clean line of her jaw seemed to be asking to have its tension eased with a touch. But while Vee made no move to inch away from me, neither did she encourage closer proximity. It seemed unlikely she would ever let down her guard—maybe not even at the successful conclusion of our sting.

"I still think bringing Nellie out here was a good move," said Stan. "She brightens up the place, and we're gonna pick up her lingo for our new home. But I gotta tell you, Glen, you might have screwed the pooch with your whacked-out story about hiring all her second cousins."

"I don't think so," I said. "Anyway, I hope not. Once we start contacting local businesses the way Schreiber wants us to, our public profile's going to go large, and if an element of do-gooderism is seen to be involved, that can't hurt."

"Maybe. All right, on to the progress report. Kid, what can you show us?"

"Mr. Stan, Mr. Glen, you will now see some excellent programming. I am not much of a writer. I left that part to Vee and Mr. Glen. They have a way with words. But I am the one who put their words just where they have to be if we wish to lure Mr. Nancarow in. You told me he is always searching online for new business opportunities, for tips and rumors and leads. And he has staff members doing the same thing. Well, I have placed all our disinformation in the best places, where he and his helpers will be sure to see it. But it is not too obvious. He will need to dig a little. But then our stuff will pop up. And it doesn't all sound the same—that is due to Mr. Glen and Vee, of course. But I made sure it doesn't all come from the same place or type of place, either. We have multiple pages that we own, all disguised. And I have managed to get our false information to be carried by legitimate sources as well. For instance, there is an item on the official home page of Senator Flavio Almonte. I understand you have him in your pocket. Additionally, I've employed search-engine optimization—"

Stan cut off Ray's proud recitation. "Okay, okay, I get it. There's a bunch of convincing online shit about how Bigelow Junction Motor Lodge could become the blossoming center of the casino universe, and Nancarrow can't help but see it. But none of it can be traced back to you or to us, right?"

Ray's standard impassive expression listed a bit toward injured. "Mr. Stan, I leave no tracks."

"I assume you gotta do something to bring it all live?"

"It is just a few keystrokes, Mr. Stan."

We all looked at one another by the warm, spooky light of the propane lantern hanging from a nearby tree limb. The step we were about to take seemed more definitive and irrevocable than anything up to now.

"We're good to go?" Stan asked all of us.

Vee said, "Let's hook this big fish, gaff him, gut him, and fillet him good."

22

Elbert Tighe appeared to be constructed of baling wire, hickory, and reinforced canvas. Despite the sticky heat, his gnarled, white-haired wrists protruded from the buttoned cuffs of a blue work shirt, whose sweaty collar gaped around a scrawny, corded neck. And though he seemed all bone and sinew, he had the handshake of a man used to wrestling heavy drill bits and yard after yard of steel casing all day.

Tighe and I were standing in the musty shed that held the old pumps and filtration system. He had spent half an hour in silent inspection while I swatted mosquitoes and tried to duck the cobwebs hanging from the raw planks of the pitched roof.

At last, he concluded his examination, and we stepped outside the cramped structure.

"Well?" I said.

"Let's go back to my truck. I've got some leaflets there."

Parked between the Impala and Vee's Volkswagen was Tighe's battered pickup. From both doors, it proclaimed in faded paint, FIRST-RATE WELL DRILLING AND WATERWORKS, along with his name and phone number.

He retrieved a battered leather portfolio from the cab and brought it over to the table.

"First off, the good news. Your pumps are basically okay. They need an overhaul, but they're up to the job."

"All right," I said. "Great. Now for the rest."

"You know, I told Bill Walters—fella owned this place before you—time and again how the rest of his setup weren't up to code. But he just ignored me. Had a fix in with the inspectors, I reckon, so he needn't bother to upgrade. System was okay when it was just him and his family living here, but when he built the lodge and had guests, different codes came into play. First off, the mouth of your intake pipe is too close to shore. It needs to be extended out farther into the lake. Otherwise, you're gonna get baby pee and goose crap in your drinking water."

"Okay. What else?"

"That cheap-ass filtration unit, if you pardon my language, weren't worth shit to begin with. And sittin' idle all these years ain't helped it none. You try supplying the needs of your guests with that, sooner or later they're all gonna come down with the Tijuana trots, if you take my meaning. Surprised it hasn't bothered you folks yet."

"So what do you recommend?"

Tighe unzipped his portfolio and took out a colorful brochure. "US Water Systems Deluxe Pond and Lake Treatment Unit. This is a damn good company and a damn good product. Never heard a single complaint about 'em in twenty years. Now, look what you get with this. Sediment backwashing filter. Stenner peristaltic proportional chlorine injection. Plus ultraviolet disinfection. And it can handle fifteen gallons per minute. You're just not going to find anything better for this price."

"And that price is?"

"They regularly ask eleven thousand plus. But as a contractor, I can get it for you for seven. I won't tack on any percentage because I want to see you folks make a go of this place. Labor will be about another thousand five, I estimate. And that includes overhauling the pumps and extending the intake pipe. Full five-year warranty on everything."

For a moment, I saw a formless gray void filled with a conga line of golden Panda coins, moving away in a mocking procession that swiftly dwindled to nothing. When my senses returned, I watched Tighe intently, looking for some tell that I was being ripped off. But the retail price of the system was there in black and white in the brochure, and the man radiated old-fashioned hardworking integrity.

"We really need this system in place to run our business effectively?"

"If you plan on keeping your customers out of the emergency room. But maybe you want to try drilling a well. Could end up costing you twice as much."

"Can I talk to my partner a moment about this?"

"Sure."

I found Stan playing catch with Ray, using a big green softball. Stan was bare-handed, while the boy had a top-of-the-line mitt to complement his Yankees uniform. But Ray's awkward stance and ungainly lunges for the ball negated any advantage the glove might have given him. Stan was surprisingly tolerant of the kid's ineptness, lobbing soft and easy throws.

I interrupted the game and explained to Stan everything I had just learned.

"Why the hell are you even bothering me with this, Glen boy? Just do it! We gotta keep up the front, right? What's a few bucks here and there when we're gonna be millionaires?"

"This is almost nine thousand dollars, Stan! A tenth of our capital!"

"Chicken feed! Besides, you don't want the ladies getting sick, do you? They won't put out if they're puking their guts."

"Jesus, Stan, I wish I had your confidence!"

"What's to get all wound about? Either we come out of this filthy rich, or we're just back where we started from."

"Minus all my investment!"

"Glen, you know that the money you plucked from them impoverished orphans and widows during your shyster days could never have been spent in good conscience."

"But we're ripping off Nancarrow!"

"That's different. He deserves it. Now, go back and sign those papers, or whatever you have to do to make it so we're not drinking pond scum and tadpoles."

I returned to Tighe, who was sitting just as peacefully and patiently as Davy Crockett waiting outside a bear's cave.

"Mr. Tighe, my partner agrees that this is the only way to proceed. Let's get the paperwork done."

Tighe stood up. "No paperwork necessary, son, just a hand-shake."

I submitted to having my hand mangled again. Then Tighe said, "Have to go into Centerdale to grab the unit. Be out here tomorrow, have the whole job done the day after that."

"Thank you very much, Mr. Tighe."

"Name's Elbert, son."

Tighe drove off, and I decided I had done enough for the day. I still had to find and call other tradespeople to help us. A roofer, a landscaper, a laundry service, the local media outlets, and a wholesale food supplier—all to satisfy Wilson Schreiber's timetable for the eventual relaunch of the lodge. But I couldn't face the prospect of bleeding more money just yet.

I went looking for whatever cold company Vee might provide, but she was nowhere to be found. I knew she had taken to hiking alone on the local trails, and I wasn't at all sure I could find her.

In the end, I went back to my room for a nap. The warm but nonetheless agreeable space felt like being swaddled in a comforting blanket. A small window fan pushed the air around just enough. I stripped all my clothes off, peeled back the spread, and reclined gratefully on the clean sheets. I dropped right off into the deep end of nowhere.

I had a dream of being back at Ghent, Goolsbee & Saikiri. I was having some kind of important meeting in my luxurious office. Spouting nonsensical legal jargon, I knew that I was impressing the clients—who remained disturbingly faceless—and that I was going to emerge from this case with a huge payoff. It felt good to rake in the big money. I deserved it.

Then the clients were gone and I was alone in the office with one of the legal secretaries—that woman with the strawberry-blond hair and the freckles and the deep white cleavage always on display whose name I could no longer recall, awake or asleep. I was sitting in my nice ergonomic chair with my pants around my ankles and my cock in her mouth.

I emerged from the dream to find Nellie on the bed with me, duplicating the actions of the woman in the dream. When she saw I was awake, she didn't stop for any explanation—just grabbed my hand and put it down her shirt and on her bare breast. Now it was not wet and slippery and buoyant, but warm and heavy in my hand.

My first climax in many months took but little time to arrive. I pulled her up onto me, and somehow, she had her denim shorts off in a flash, bare beneath.

"*Vou meter em você ate você gritar meu nome!*" she said.

She rode me hard and fast until we both came; then she dropped forward, her face in the cradle of my neck and shoulder.

"Oh, Glen," she murmured, "this is how you really learn the language!"

23

Certainly, Wilson Schreiber could not expect us to move forward on other preparations for the lodge relaunch until Tighe had finished installing the new waterworks. And the output of the new filters would still have to be tested by a local lab. So that gave us a day or three without duties—the fake ones, anyway.

Having kicked off the online deception two nights ago, I had been obsessively monitoring the reports that Ray could produce, about who visited what site of ours, or linked to it, and who clicked where, and whether they had actually read the posting, and any associated chatter that his alerts might have triggered. Ray had reluctantly lent me his iPad during the day, as if he were surrendering his firstborn, after showing me how to refresh the various metrics. Like some politician tracking his poll numbers, or an author obsessing over his sales figures at Amazon, I checked every ten minutes, waiting for Nancarrow's IP address to show up. But there was nothing so far.

We had a standing order to Senator Almonte to call us if Nancarrow put out direct feelers to him. But no such call had yet come.

After about eight hours of driving myself crazy this way,

around four in the afternoon I returned Ray's iPad to him with instructions to call me at the first sign of activity.

"Mr. Glen," he said, "I have several bots running that will inform me immediately of developments of this nature. I could have told you earlier, but you seemed too nervous to listen."

"Yes, well, your instincts were correct. I probably wouldn't have listened. But in the future, try me anyway."

"People are not very logical, Mr. Glen, are they?"

"Ray, you are wise beyond your years."

The kid smiled, then got busy with his gleefully reclaimed tablet. "The Yankees are playing the Red Sox tonight at Fenway, Mr. Glen. I'm extremely excited. Their rivalry is long-standing and intense."

Concentrating on the computer all day, I had slighted Nellie, and now I sought her out.

Yesterday's late-afternoon sex had not led directly to our sleeping together throughout the night. At the end of our post-coital cuddling, needing to get up for our communal supper, she had seemed just as relieved as I when I suggested that we keep our new intimacy to ourselves for a little while, until we could figure out how to introduce the development to Stan and Sandralene and Vee. Not that what Nellie and I chose to do together would normally have been any of their business. But under these clois-tered circumstances so fraught with tension, expectations, and anxiety, we all owed each other a certain degree of transparency. Too much was riding on our functioning as a tight unit, and any uncertainty could be divisive. But we had to deliver the news in the way least disruptive to our social dynamics.

I found Nellie sitting with Sandralene and Stan outdoors. They all were laughing uproariously. When Nellie recovered herself, she said, "No, dude, try again. 'What's happening?' *Kuzé ki sta fladu?*"

Stan's mangled repetition of the phrase sounded like "Cozy keister flew-do."

"Oh, man, you ever visit Cabo Verde, you are going to get eaten alive! You will pay twice as much as any other tourist, just for butchering *kriolu* like that!"

"Fuck it! I'm always happy to let my money talk for me."

Nellie jumped up when she saw me. "Glen! You finally done with that stupid computer? Let's go for a swim."

"Sure. In a little while. But I want to check in with Tighe, see how he's coming along."

"Okay, I'll go get my suit on!"

Nellie trotted off to her room. I watched her go, admiring the sweet, swaying symmetry of her walk. When she was out of sight and I turned back to Stan, he was grinning like a bettor who just cashed in winning tickets on all the Triple Crown trifectas. Sandralene's smile was more restrained and enigmatic. Buddha-like.

"So, you finally took my advice," Stan said.

"What advice?"

"The advice I gave you on the drive back from Schreiber's: if you wanna relax, loosen up and bust a nut in some warm cooze."

I felt my face flushing, though apparently I needn't have bothered about Sandralene, who registered no embarrassment whatever. I could hardly imagine the even filthier things she heard when she and Stan were alone. The notion of their bedroom talk actually began to get me aroused. Nellie was sexy, but Sandralene was sex itself. Nevertheless, I should at least sound offended.

"Jesus, Stan, have you no shame or dignity, no sense of decorum?"

"Oh, come off it. There's no harm in boning that girl. She's all right. And you were never gonna get in Vee's pants anyhow."

This lateral swerve knocked me right off my pins. "Me and *Vee*? What the hell are you talking about? I never ..."

"Christ, Glen, do you ever even take a look around inside your own head? Or is it too fulla fog? I thought prison mighta taught you something. Lots of time for contemplation in a cell. You been hot for Vee since the day she got here. Don't know why you'd fall for a cold fish like her, but damn if you didn't. It's a losing cause, though. You're a shitload better off with Nell."

I found I couldn't contradict Stan with any semblance of honesty. "Okay. Maybe you're right. Let me ask you something, then. If you knew I was interested in Vee, she probably did, too. How do you think she'll react to me and Nellie being together?"

"Oh, on the outside, she won't show a thing. Inside, who the hell knows? That woman is a puzzle wrapped up in a mind-fuck inside a Secret Santa present."

I looked at Stan with befuddlement. "Are you actually paraphrasing Churchill?"

"Who's that, now?"

"Never mind. So you think Nellie and I can show, like, public displays of affection and it won't freak Vee out? She's got a big part to play, after all, once Nancarrow shows up here—if he ever does. She's got to be totally focused."

"Nothing you can do will tip that iceberg. So quitcha worrying."

Nellie was walking up, a yellow terry-cloth robe over her bikini.

"C'mon, Glen! I want to swim!"

She linked her arm in mine, and we headed toward my room to get my suit.

I looked back at Stan and Sandralene, and they were grinning like parents who had just succeeded in marrying off the homely daughter.

Me.

24

The old filtration unit stood in the grass outside the shed, looking more antique, punier, and more corroded than it had in the cobwebbed shadows indoors. Elbert Tighe's truck was parked nearby, its tailgate down and packing materials strewn about. Sounds of activity came from inside the pump house.

I went inside. Tighe had rigged up a utility light, turning the already broiling interior into a sauna and filling my nostrils with the smell of creosote. The fancy new equipment filled the place to bursting, but somehow Tighe had made it all fit. Flat on his back and half concealed by the machinery, he stuck out his hand and said, "Pass me that nine-sixteenths box-end, Kirwan."

A wiry young black man in a green FIRST-RATE WELL DRILLING T-shirt quickly found the proper tool and put it in Tighe's outstretched hand. After a few moments of muttered profanity, Tighe emerged from the tangle of pipes, dripping with sweat. He stood up and brushed himself off.

"What do you think, Glen? Told you it would take most of a day to install, and I was right. Hope you folks were okay using bottled water all day. Same thing tomorrow—I still have to extend that intake pipe."

"Elbert, you've done the impossible," I said. "This job would have taken me six months and I'd still get it wrong."

Tighe's sober face showed no obvious pleasure, but I got a sense he was proud of his skills and didn't mind the praise.

"Oh, by the way, meet my assistant, Kirwan Allen. Still got a lot to learn, but smart as a whip. Kirwan's brother married my niece, so he's practically a nephew."

Kirwan grinned. "Uncle Elbert, right. From the plantation side of the family."

I said, "Looks like you two could use a break. Kirwan, you think the boss can get by on his own while you go up to the lodge and bring back some drinks and a snack?"

Tighe gave a nod, and Kirwan said, "Absolutely."

I left them and joined Nellie down at the water's edge. She had dropped her robe and was sitting on a mossy fallen log. This beach was going to take a lot of restoring to be ready for customers. But then I caught myself and thought, *Yeah, if we were staying to do what we pretend to be doing.*

When I came near, Nellie sprang up effortlessly and splashed out into the Lake.

"Catch me, *você preguiçoso!*"

"What did you call me?"

"You slowpoke!"

I dashed after her, into the welcoming waters. She outpaced me, hurling herself under, surfacing, and stroking for the center. I caught up with her eventually, but probably only because she let me.

Having a younger girlfriend was either going to leave me in fine physical condition or kill me with pleasure.

We hugged and kissed and felt each other up, treading water

longer than I would have thought possible. Then Nellie broke off the fun and pulled away a little. Droplets glimmered in her long lashes, and she looked so gorgeous that if I could manage without drowning us both, I would have jumped her bones right then and there.

"I told my folks all about your plans," she said. "How you want to hire some of our people to work here. They're so excited, you will not believe it! They're spreading the news in the community. When do you think you'll start with the interviews?"

Holy shit. Things were moving too fast. Sure, I could conduct fake interviews and then stall the applicants. But I suddenly realized that our instant and unannounced departure upon selling this fake gold mine to Nancarrow would be the ultimate betrayal of Nellie. Somehow, I had assumed, even if only subconsciously over the past twenty-four hours, that when it came time to split, if we were still together, I could just tell her the truth and get her to run away with me to Cape Verde. It was her ancestral home, after all. But now that happy outcome seemed a lot less likely.

Nellie kept looking at me with those dark, luminous eyes, her beautiful lips that I had just been kissing quirked in expectation. What could I say? Once again, I had to rely on the same capacity for on-demand plausible bullshit that had been such a mainstay of my misbegotten career.

"We need to get all the other vendors in place first. Then, in about a week, we can start interviewing for staff. We won't need a huge workforce, don't forget—say, seven, eight, ten people. And that's counting all the shifts."

She beamed. "That's ten more jobs than exist now! Oh, Glen, this is so great!" She grabbed me by both shoulders. "Let's go back to your room and celebrate. I'll teach you a couple of new phrases, very handy." She stuck her hot little tongue in my ear, then whispered, "*Mas dibagar* and *mas dipresa.*"

My swim trunks were rapidly becoming a pup tent. "What's that mean?"

"Slower—and faster!"

We got out of the water, and Nellie put her robe back on, leaving me wishing I had one to hide my current condition. To my relief, Kirwan and Tighe had ended their break and were busy again in the shed, so I had no immediate cause for embarrassment. Not that it required much explanation, given Nellie's luscious appearance.

I could hardly believe that I was about to have sex for the second time in twenty-four hours—well, third time, depending on one's definition. Not bad for a guy who had resigned himself to never making love again.

My door on the lake side of the lodge was still locked, as was Nellie's, so we came around the corner—and stopped dead.

Parked next to the other vehicles was a black-and-white police car. And standing by the front fender was a cop, talking to Stan.

25

I tried to keep my voice level and unbroken. Any thoughts of sex had evaporated like spit on the sunny side of Mercury.

"Nellie, I think you should go change clothes and check with Sandy about getting supper ready. I'll see what Stan and the officer are talking about."

Nellie's face showed concern. "You don't need me to help you, maybe? I don't think anything can be wrong. I recognize that cop, and he's okay. Not a jerk. Sheriff Broadstairs, from Centerdale. He coached my brother's basketball team."

Duh. I hadn't fastened on to the fact that Nellie's being a local might help ingratiate us. Also, the way she was dressed, any straight male cop would have a difficult time concentrating.

"All right, thanks. Let's see what he wants."

We approached slow and easy, although it had to be obvious that neither of us was concealing any weapons.

Sheriff Broadstairs continued talking to Stan but was eminently aware of our presence. In his late forties, he was nearly as tall as Stan, but less massive, with a face as blandly unpretentious as tapioca pudding. He wore a regulation uniform of khaki shirt and olive-green trousers, and the usual range of gear and weaponry on his belt. The only personal touch was the decidedly nonregulation leather Aussie digger hat with a band of silver conchos.

When we drew up next to Stan, Sheriff Broadstairs politely doffed that unconventional lid to Nellie. His Gary Cooper-ish voice had the same old-shoe affability as his face. I instantly pegged him as a dab hand at putting suspects off their guard. All those reruns of *Columbo* in the prison common room were not for nothing.

"Is that little Nélida Firmino? My cats, but you have gotten to be a real lady now! I recall when you weighed about sixty-five pounds and had no more curves than the baseline from home to first. How's your brother Roberto doing? Still got that wicked layup?"

So much for Nellie's disarming looks. For all the sexual tension on display, Broadstairs might have been her dad.

Nellie smiled with broad sincerity. "*Nossa Senhora!* At least you didn't claim you used to change my diapers! Yes, Sheriff, Roberto still plays well. He's away at the community college this year."

"That's good to hear. And what about you, kid? Last I heard, you were working in town. Some fast-food place, I think."

I knew without a doubt that Sheriff Broadstairs was already fully informed of Nellie's change in occupation. He had probably learned about it within hours after it happened. And he knew that I knew. And all that unspoken knowingness between the two of us meant, *I may be a cop from the sticks, but you boys have got to get up pretty early to put one over on me, and you'd be wise to remember that.*

"Not anymore, Sheriff! I got something way better! I'm here to help these new friends of mine get the lodge open for business again. They're going to hire all Caboverde people, you know!"

"Well, now, that is pretty spectacular. I think you might have hitched your wagon to a rich star, Nélida. That is, if it's not just one of those burn-up-quick shooting stars."

Stan spoke up for the first time since I arrived. I was relieved to see he looked unworried. "We're here to stay, Sheriff. You can bet your last bullet in a gunfight."

Nellie asked the question I had been dying to ask. "But what brings you out here, Sheriff? Not just to check on me, I hope. Like you said, I'm a big girl now."

Sheriff Broadstairs lifted his hat just enough to scratch his scalp, then snugged it back down. "Well, even though this might be a tad embarrassing to speak of in front of your new employers, Nélida, I have to admit I'm here—officially, that is—just to convey a certain message from a friend of theirs in town. That would be Wilson Schreiber, their parole officer."

If Nellie was disconcerted by the sudden revelation that we were ex-cons, she didn't let on. "And what does he say, Sheriff?"

"He wants to congratulate these two entrepreneurs on such a speedy installation of their new water system. Elbert Tighe has handily kept us abreast of progress. But Will also wants to remind them that this stage has to proceed swiftly to the next—namely, lining up all their suppliers and employees. And that brings me to the *un*official reason for my visit."

Stan said, "If you can handle a Frialator, Chief, we estimate we'll be going through about two hundred pounds of potatoes a day, once all the cabins are rented. Nice after-hours part-time work for a man in your position."

The look Broadstairs gave Stan could not be construed as vicious or hateful in even the mildest sense of those words. But neither was his look jovial or humorous or harmless. I settled on *coldly calculating* as the proper description.

"Well, I surely appreciate that offer, Mr. Hasso, though I fear I must decline. These old flat feet would not take stand-up duty without complaining. But your willingness to consider me for employment makes me hope you'll be agreeable to what I have to say. Why don't we get out of this sun, though?"

We went to the picnic table. Under the canopy, the air seemed much cooler. Without being asked, Nellie said, "I'll get some cold drinks. Is beer okay?"

"Well, Nélida, I see now that you learned from your mama how to be a fine hostess."

We sat. With Nellie gone, Stan leaned in aggressively closer to the sheriff. "All right, let's have it. What's the shakedown gonna cost us?"

"Mr. Hasso, that is the worst possible interpretation you could put on my words—which I haven't even spoken yet. Maybe you'll do me the honor of listening. After all, you two wouldn't be happy if I jumped to a lot of conclusions about your actions here, based just on some superficial observations, would you?"

Stan huffed, then sat back ostentatiously, folding his arms across his chest.

"Are you boys familiar with the Centerdale Chamber of Commerce? As strangers to these parts, you could not find a better guide to commercial enterprises in the region. All our members are certified to be honest and talented experts in their fields. Now, it just so happens that, what with sheriff being a quiet and underpaid job hereabouts, yours truly has time also to serve as president of the Centerdale C of C. And as such, I feel it is my duty to present you two with some friendly guidance on hiring."

The sheriff unbuttoned a shirt pocket and withdrew a folded sheet of paper. He laid it flat on the table and smoothed it out. "Now, here we have a handy list of the best businesses in the area—just the types of firms which your enterprise will be requiring. Any name you pick off this list will offer total satisfaction at modest prices. Not rock-bottom prices necessarily, but totally fair. I think you'll agree that you get what you pay for and that the tradesman is worthy of his hire. I can vouch personally for each and every one of these folks—especially this gent, who happens to be my brother-in-law."

The sheriff's finger indicated Golden Touch Roofers.

"Now, I hope you realize just how much time and effort this list is going to save you two. There's no need to waste hours conducting your own research, making a million phone calls, and such. Instead, you can plunge right ahead, just the way Will wants you to, without worrying about getting stuck with some loser or incompetent or fly-by-night. So what do you say?"

I took the paper from the table before Stan could erupt. "Sheriff, we really appreciate this guidance, and we will start calling these fine tradesmen as soon as we get back the lab results on our drinking water."

"Excellent! I knew you'd appreciate the offer of honest help."

Nellie came up then with our beers, and we lifted them in a toast to the success of the lodge.

"And to lifting the bottom lines of so many fine local businesses," Sheriff Broadstairs added.

26

The sheriff had gone. Elbert Tighe and Kirwan had gone, with a promise to return early tomorrow and finish the job. A muted greenish-purple dusk was turning the treetop canopy into dark, mysterious vaults and bringing with it a refreshing coolness. Birds were making their settling-down noises. Savory smells emanated from the cook shack, where Sandralene and Nellie labored. Vee was setting the picnic table with the paper plates and plastic utensils and paper cups that we were using tonight to avoid trying to wash dishes without running water. (The lodge had been sold to us with much of the kitchenware, including large quantities of clunky old-fashioned china and flatware.) Surprisingly, she was actually humming something, though it sounded like one of Wagner's more melancholy passages. Ray was half reclined in a lawn chair with his iPad, listening to the quintessentially American sounds of a sportscaster narrating a baseball game. During this timeless summer moment, the play-by-play might have been coming to us through an old cathedral-style Philco.

And Stan Hasso was swearing mightily as he kicked a rusting industrial-size vegetable-oil can around the clearing.

"Goddamn greedy goatfucker! Coming up here with his list of shit-weasel goombahs all set to bleed us dry. I will hang him up by those brass balls of his if he shows his ugly mug around here again! Let him try and squeeze a nickel out of us!"

I followed Stan at a respectful distance, waiting for him to run down of his own accord. As the tirade dwindled, his kicks at the can got less and less enthusiastic. I suspected that the lightweight boat shoes he wore, while perfectly stylish and congruous with the rest of his casual, sporty outfit, did not provide the sort of protection that such a futile endeavor called for.

Stan eventually ceased abusing the empty can and walked with a slight limp over to the table. He plopped down just as Vee finished her setup. She made no reference to Stan's rant, but only said, "I'll be resting in my room. Call me when the food's ready."

Stan grunted, then yelled out, "Sandy! Bring me a beer!"

Sandralene's voice belled out from the kitchen. "Get it yourself, you lazy shit! The chefs are busy!"

I said, "Let me get it, Stan."

Another grunt.

I came back with two beers and sat next to my partner in crime.

"You know, of course, that we have to hire the people he wants us to hire."

"Goddamn it, of course I know it! What kind of frigging idiot do you take me for? I had to blow off steam, though—that or let you all watch my fucking head explode! Or maybe stick a spike in my arm again. I could go to Centerdale and find the dealers in five minutes flat."

For one fleeting second, I could almost taste the brilliant heroin sliding through my veins and feel the warm, all-embracing relief it brought.

"Don't even joke about that shit," I said.

"All right, all right, don't worry about me. You want me to kiss my one-year coin from Narcotics Anonymous for you? It just slays me that this putz feels he can waltz in here with his demands and we have to accept them."

"I would say he was perfectly rational in making such an assumption."

"Sure he was. Because that's how this lousy fucking world works! Ever since I was a kid in the Gulch, I've been getting pushed around like this. And let me tell you, it never feels any better, no matter how often it happens. Even good old Algy— Nancarrow, that is—who grew up side by side with me, turned around and screwed me good. Him telling me to burn down every other building he owned, then letting me take the rap! I can't wait until we make our big score. He'll learn what it feels like to get reamed up the ass, and I'll finally be the guy doing the reaming."

"I hear you," I said. "But we've got a certain hard distance to cover before then, and everything has to go smoothly. We can't afford to antagonize anyone, especially the law. Besides, I doubt that his people will charge much more than anyone else around here—maybe even the same or less. And he did save us time looking up contractors."

Stan lowered his beer and regarded me as if I were a rainbow unicorn with dreadlocks. "You are truly like some ten-year-old Campfire Girl who is buried in horseshit and says, 'There's got to be a pony here someplace!' I have never seen anyone so determined to put a positive spin on things. Are you really the same evil crooked lawyer who ripped off all those people?"

"That was the drugs."

Stan snorted. "Drugs always need a willing partner, buddy. They don't work on Mother Teresa."

A bell rang. Nellie stood in the doorway of the cookshack,

yanking with one hand on the cord of what, in her other hand, looked like a ship's bell. Where she had dug that up, I couldn't even hazard a guess.

"Dinnertime! Come quick, or we throw your share to the ducks!"

Everyone assembled at the table, beneath the lantern light. Out of the kitchen came a mouthwatering array of swordfish, mashed potatoes, and asparagus. Tonight, the sangria used white wine. Dessert was strawberries over store-bought pound cake with Cool Whip.

After the main meal, I had spun around on the picnic-table bench with my legs outward, to uncramp them. When Nellie served me cake, she—impulsively, I believe—sat down on my lap and made a big deal of sharing my plate. It felt honest and good, though a little showy, and I could hardly dump her from my lap. Not that I wanted to unburden myself of that firm, soft warmth. But the display still made me a little uneasy. I kept darting cautious glances at Vee to gauge her reaction. She had her nose buried in a new book.

Eventually, the party broke up and Nellie came back with me to my room.

After bone-rattling sex (to me, anyway; I hoped it was for her, too), she said, "So, who did you murder?" She was trying hard to keep her voice light, but I could tell she was concerned.

So over the next hour, I told her all about my past. I didn't hide anything, though I tried to put the best face on it all—even if Stan would have called me a Pollyanna.

I glossed over how Stan and I had hooked up, letting her think it was through prison and rehab connections. And I certainly didn't reveal our true scam. I stuck to the cover story about Uncle Ralph investing in this place and sending us up here as his representatives.

Nellie had listened silently and attentively throughout. When I finished, she didn't say anything for a minute or so.

"And Stan. What's his story?"

"I can't responsibly tell you that. His biography is his own matter to share. You'll have to ask him."

"Okay, I see." Another short silence. "A lawyer! Huh! You could earn so much so easy. Not like anyone I ever knew. But the temptations must be so big, too. Drugs are bad. I blame the drugs. You're just lucky you didn't pick up anything nasty from the needles."

She hastily levered herself up off me, her beautiful breasts pendulous in the gloom, and I could sense, even in the dark, that she was suddenly scared.

"Tell me, Glen, please. You did not pick up anything nasty from the needles, did you?"

I pulled her back down and hugged her tight. "Nélida, Nélida, I would cut off my right arm rather than hurt you."

She accepted that, and I thanked God it was the truth.

She fell asleep then, leaving me to wonder how I was ever going to tell her the rest.

27

As I sat at the desk in the lodge's office, dreaming of a swim while studying invoices and work orders and punch lists and paint and textile samples, I felt a little crazy and uprooted. Lulled by the sounds of construction under way and trucks rumbling by and people coming and going, I felt almost as if an out-of-body experience was coming on. I'd had one of those during my addict days. Floating above your own unconscious body as some kind of ectoplasmic spirit, looking down at a temporarily untenanted vessel. Feeling vaguely baffled at the dislocation (or bilocation), but mostly peaceful and accepting—although today's version of that hallucination threatened to reverse the ratio of those emotions: more bafflement, less peace.

What the hell was I doing here? How had we gotten into this current fix? The trail up to this point seemed too convoluted to trace backward by the breadcrumbs, even though each individual step had been easy and comprehensible and seemingly a smart and necessary move.

Stan and I had started out to work a simple scam, just two mooks out to rip off a bigger bastard. Our scheme involved a low-effort real estate subterfuge and some online hacking; therefore, we had acquired two coconspirators: Vee Aptekar and Ray Zerkin. So far, so logical. Then I had lucked into a girlfriend, Nellie Firmino. Not a predictable happening, but totally acceptable even as it complicated matters. But this latest development? Suddenly, I had a real managerial-type job, with all the attendant headaches and responsibilities. This was nothing I had foreseen or desired. If I had wanted, I could have gotten a grunt job like this back at home, living with Uncle Ralph, and held on to my stash of golden Pandas.

And now, two weeks into our residency here at the bucolic Bigelow Junction Motor Lodge, thanks to the implacable dictates of our parole officer, the place was a hive of activity.

Golden Touch Roofers, under the aegis of Lonnie Griffin (Sheriff Broadstairs' cheery brother-in-law), was busy replacing all our shabby shingles on the main building, the cabins, and the several outbuildings. Instead of just defaulting to some standard shingle, I had been forced to examine several choices, listening to Lonnie extol their various qualities, and only then decide.

Aphrodite Fabric Creations, helmed by the excitable and talkative Jennifer Brosseau, who struck me as someone who should have her own show on HGTV, was redoing all the furniture fabrics as well as selecting new curtains, bedspreads, and towels. This had required long consultations between us. The old bedsheets had been deemed barely acceptable, but only after a thorough laundering by Redcliff Linen Services, owned by the dour, disheveled, and taciturn Leon Redcliff. Thank God for at least one contractor who didn't care to gab!

The staff at Gonsalves Provisions, from the ancient Valdo Gonsalves himself (still working ten-hour days at age eighty-five) down to his innumerable sons, daughters, nieces, and nephews, was busy compiling and refining a standing order for foodstuffs that we would need once we opened to hypothetical hordes of ravenous vacationers. Nellie was delighted that we had chosen Gonsalves instead of the Anglo-run firm that was the other option on Broadstairs' list.

"They are the best!" Nellie gushed. "They carry everything. The spiciest linguiça for your *jagacida*. The freshest octopus for your *polvo a modo ze de lino!*"

"We're going to serve a Caboverdean menu here?"

"Oh, not exclusively! But some special dishes—*por que não?*"

And, of course, all those expensive perishables had to be stored under the proper Board of Health conditions. (I'd had no idea how many inspectors considered us their responsibility.) Which meant large new fridges and freezers. We could count on Pyrtle Restaurant Supplies for that. The salesman in charge of our account, Ron Peppler, had taken one look at the little concession shack where we had been cooking all our meals, and pronounced it woefully insufficient to hold the new equipment. And since we were going to have to expand and rewire the structure (under the capable hands of DiPippo Construction), we might as well add a big new gas range to our purchase list. Oh, yes, and the propane dealer was Cobb & Sons. The elder Cobb, Doug, was so youthful that he and his twin sons, Ben and Rich, looked more like triplets.

Did I mention that a new window-rich, medium-size dining room was part of the expansion? That meant more work on fabric coordination for Jennifer Brosseau, but she had to bring on board Brenda Bethune from Green Radiance Furniture. Listening to the two women together was like putting your head between two massive speakers while Stevie Nicks and Kate Bush sang two different songs.

All these vendors and contractors demanded infinite amounts of my finite time, from sunup to sundown. Scheduled meetings were bad enough, but once decisions were made, nothing ever went precisely as planned. I was kept running from one minicrisis to the next.

Of course, I had tried to get Stan to take up some of the slack, but he just scoffed.

"Do I look like I got your brains or patience, Glen boy? First time one of these delivery guys mouths off to me or tells me about some kinda delay or hang-up, I'd probably haul off and belt him. No, this is your shtick. But I know you can handle it."

The only chore I was spared was writing the numerous checks. Sandralene Parmalee still held the purse strings of the Maritime Bank account that safeguarded our rapidly dwindling funds.

I recalled the first check she wrote, to Elbert Tighe. At the end of their second day on the filtration job, Tighe and Kirwan had been sitting under the canopy, each with a cold beer.

"Now that you're up and running," Tighe said, "we got that water sample for the lab. But it's just a formality. I've never seen a US Water Systems rig that failed a test. You can use that feed from the lake now with total confidence."

At the time, I hadn't foreseen the chaos and duties yet to come, and so I felt a naive relief at the end of this process and was eager to pay Tighe off and see the end of him. Knowing he had informed Sheriff Broadstairs of our progress here had taken some of the shine off his integrity in my eyes.

"Thanks, Elbert. Uh, I suppose we need to settle up now."

Tighe nodded and handed over his bill.

I went to find Sandralene.

She was sunbathing on a towel on the ground out back of her and Stan's cabin. Stan was fishing, having found some old rods and tackle in the garage.

Sandralene's incredible bikini had not expanded to cover any more skin since its first appearance before my startled eyes.

In fact, it seemed to have shrunk a bit—possibly because all the large meals had added a nondetrimental pound or two to Sandralene's prodigious physique.

"Sandralene?" I said softly. "Sandralene?"

She came awake like a lazy tiger.

"Sandralene, could you come write a check for Elbert?"

"Of course, Glen."

The high-heeled sandals she stepped into added only about three inches to her height, but now she seemed to tower over me more than ever before.

At the picnic table, Elbert and Kirwan might as well have seen Medusa. I don't think they would have moved if I had tossed a lit stick of dynamite between them. Sandralene remained standing as she wrote the check with slow and deliberate movements. When she had finished, her solemn and intent expression blossomed into one of pride at fulfilling her duties.

"There you are, gentlemen! Thank you both so very much!"

That initial majestic dispensation of my funds had set the pattern for all the other occasions. We got the fastest work and quickest deliveries that Bigelow Junction had ever seen, just so the owners could present their invoices and bask in Sandralene's presence. Even Jennifer Brosseau and Brenda Bethune were not immune. Not that either of them was gay, I was willing to bet, but just that they, too, wanted to experience the powerful juju of this Amazon Who Held the Checkbook.

But while Sandralene disbursed our funds, I was the guy who monitored the shrinking balance in our account. Using Ray's iPad, I could log on to Maritime's system and watch as our money steadily evaporated.

When we had gotten down to a truly scary low number, with many bills still outstanding, I buttonholed Stan.

Of course, Nancarrow had not yet taken one nibble at our

bait, putting our future tenure here in question. If he had bitten, I could have been more sanguine.

"Stan, I don't want to be the bearer of bad news, but we are rapidly heading toward insolvency. What are we going to do about it?"

"What about those rents from the serfs?"

We were now into September. At the end of the month, the quarterly rents from the families who leased lots on our five hundred acres would be due. A couple thousand bucks.

"It's not much. And I don't think we can even last till then."

Stan thought a while, then said, "I got it. We're going to open a line of credit."

"With Maritime? They won't give us a penny."

"Not with them, with some Centerdale bank. They're the ones who want us to make a go of this place. We're the fucking cash cow for the whole community."

"I don't know …"

"Gimme your phone."

I handed over my phone, and Stan whizzed through my contacts before finding the one he wanted.

"Hey, Uncle Ralph! How's it hanging?"

28

I was never sure whose idea the bonfire was. True, we had a lot of nontoxic construction debris piled around the lodge: plywood scraps, short lengths of two-by-fours, large cardboard boxes, pallets, a couple of busted chairs that Brenda Bethune and Jennifer Brosseau deemed unworthy of rehabbing. Perhaps a case could have been made up front for burning the stuff rather than paying someone to cart it away. After all, we were not in an urban situation here, but out in God's country—unincorporated lands not subject to crown or church, where a man could burn up as much damn trash as he wanted. Or at least as much trash as he could afford to make. Also, plenty of dead timber was available just at the edge of our cleared property. So a bonfire was a pretty natural idea.

I suspected Stan's hand in this. It seemed just the kind of ostentatious, macho display that he would naturally imagine. But somehow, assembly of the pile of burnables—in a spot safely distant from all buildings and vehicles—had begun while Stan was still out on the road with Nellie, using the Impala to pick up her immediate family in Centerdale—*Mamãe, Papai,* and three of her sibs—for the celebration. And really, there were too many people bustling about for me to fasten correctly on any individual as the instigator. Maybe the idea had arisen spontaneously among several brains. By the time I took notice of the bonfire's construction, it was well under way and many hands were involved. Besides the six of us who normally lived at the lodge, the place was swarming with all our contractors, their crews, and, for all I knew, the former spouses and adopted kids of their various office staffs, whom I had never met. It was four in the afternoon on the late-September day when all the work was officially considered done. The last task remaining before we would be able to open for business was to hire our on-site workers.

I had deliberately put off interviewing people till now, despite Nellie's quite logical assertion that interviews could go on concurrently with construction. I figured that the longer I stalled this farce, the closer we might get to hooking Nancarrow and succeeding with our scam, all without actually having to conduct a motel business. But still, all these many days after Ray had launched our seductive disinformation online, we had nary a bite. So now I had to pretend to be interested in hiring cooks and busboys and lifeguards and housekeepers.

Nellie, of course, was wildly enthusiastic. "Glen, you know I want our place to take off, so I'm only going to steer the best people to you. No slackers, just good workers. They only don't have jobs because there are no jobs around. You don't mind if some of the applicants are my cousins, do you?"

I tried to get my head out of its funk. Nellie's earnest excitement didn't deserve a cold dousing.

"No, of course not. But if any of the women are as sexy as you, I can't be responsible for my actions."

"*Você palhaço!* I'll show you who's the sexiest of all!"

That interchange had led to an agreeable afternoon interlude during which, for a short time, I could forget my troubles.

I gave up watching construction of the towering stack of flammable stuff. It had too many associations with a funeral pyre—mine.

The former cookshack and concession stand was unrecognizable now. Despite wincing at what it had cost, I had to admit, it looked nice. One large room, done up in old-fashioned knotty-pine paneling, opened off the enlarged kitchen. Its floor-to-ceiling windows cantilevered outward so that in good weather—as, for instance, now—the place could seem like an open-air pavilion. There was even a small dais for a live band. Inside, all the tables bore sparkling white tablecloths. They were not set with real plates and silverware, because tonight's meal would employ paper plates and plasticware, all of which awaited on long side tables, along with paper cups and paper napkins.

Tonight's meal was to be prepared outdoors. Two homemade grills—the kind raised high on angle-iron cradles and fashioned from fifty-five-gallon drums split down the middle and hinged— now held glowing coals that were reaching the perfect cooking temperature. The chefs were a couple of young guys supplied by Valdo Gonsalves, who hovered over his protégés like some ancient deity of the hearth. Alongside the grills were folding tables bearing what looked like enough meat to satisfy a modest-size pack of velociraptors. Some distance off, an array of galvanized tubs full of ice and bottled drinks glittered like the Great Lakes in midwinter.

I tried not to tot up all the costs in my head. After all, we were supposed to be celebrating the completion of construction, and the imminent relaunch of the lodge.

And also the new line of credit from Midland Trust Bank.

* * *

Once Stan had clicked off the connection to Uncle Ralph and handed me back my phone, I had found my voice.

"You realize this is insane, right? How can we justify pumping more money into this scheme? We've blown through all my stash after you promised me it would last for the duration."

Stan had sounded genuinely wounded. "How the fuck was I to anticipate Schreiber holding our feet to the fire about making this place actually work? I thought we'd just sit here and have ourselves a little vacation until Nancarrow came sniffing around. Your money woulda covered all that, no problem."

"Well, we should have anticipated that there'd be some officious bastard looking over our shoulders and demanding results. That mistake's on us. But now you're dragging my uncle deeper into fraud. When he agreed to act as our beard and purchase the place, he was committing no crime. But now, when you ask him to take out a loan under false pretenses—"

"What false pretenses? Haven't we shown our good intentions by pumping all our hard-earned dough into this shithole? Now we just need some more funding to bring it off. Happens to legit businesspeople all the time. They run short. When we finally bail outta here, nobody's gonna say anything except we tried and failed and got discouraged. Boo-hoo-hoo, another victim of the bad economy."

"And what about leaving Uncle Ralph stuck with the loan?"

"He's not gonna be stuck with no loan, because we are going to repay it first thing, outta the dough we rake in from Nancarrow. Then we split for Cape Verde."

"I don't know. It sounds dicey. I counted on us moving fast once we ripped off Nancarrow, before he could take any action against us."

"Yeah, you're right about that. We are gonna move fast—we have to. Can't let old Algy cook up some revenge. He'll be hurting, and there's no telling what he won't stop at to get his money back. But we'll have plane tickets in our hands the minute the check clears. Plenty of daily flights to Cape Verde, never totally booked. I did the research. We'll pay a premium for quick tickets, but who cares? Chicken feed. Ray can get them online in thirty seconds. Then we're outta here with five million apiece in our hands. We can leave the loan repayment with Ralph, along with some sweetener, and let him deal with the bank. And that reminds me, if you're bringing Nellie with you, you'd better make sure she's got her passport up to date."

I didn't reply right away.

"What's the matter? Getting cold feet about taking her? How could you kick her to the curb? I thought she was hot stuff in bed, given all the time you two spend there."

"No. It's just ... we haven't really discussed it yet. You see, she doesn't know about what we're actually doing here. She thinks we're into the lodge reopening for real. And she's kinda heavily invested in the idea."

"Holy shit, Glen! I thought for sure you woulda told her the truth by now!"

"Well, I haven't. And don't you spill the beans, either. I'll do it my own way, in my own time. Warn Sandralene, too. And I'll see Vee and Ray about it."

"Putting off the hard stuff never works in the end, you know."

"Gee, where were you with this sage advice when I was running my Ponzi scheme? I might never have gone to jail!"

Stan clapped me on the shoulder. "And then we never woulda met and ended up here today!"

"Wouldn't that be a crying shame."

* * *

Uncle Ralph had arrived two days after the phone call, in Suzy Lam's maroon Kia, now dusted with road dirt, with Suzy herself behind the wheel, of course. He jumped out of the car like a spry, excited kid, albeit one with wrinkles, gray hair, and a three-day beard. Suzy, weary from doing all the driving, got out a little slower. But after a short rest and refreshment, she was back to her old lively self.

"You introduce me now to everybody, Glen. We know Stan and Sandy; they're righteous folks. But we need to see your other friends before Ralph puts his good name on the line again. Your people are the real crystal ball for your success, Glen. Don't you ever forget it!"

I did the honors for Vee, Ray, and Nellie. Suzy quickly registered her approval of them all, though she had her usual no-nonsense observations to make as well—right to everyone's face, naturally—regarding Vee's "excessive soberness," Ray's quietness, and Nellie's untested youth. Uncle Ralph had weighed in positively as well. His endorsement of Nellie was particularly enthusiastic, consisting of lots of winks and semilecherous leers in my direction when he supposed no one was looking though everyone really was. Jesus, was I that transparent in everything? I didn't rate my chances of conning Nancarrow very highly, unless I got my game face on.

The day after Uncle Ralph and Suzy's arrival, we were in Centerdale, in the office of the loan manager at Midland Trust Bank, one Harriet Kilmer, who surely had a nickname among her coworkers, along the lines of "Iron Maiden" or "Miss Hardnose." But we came with recommendations from Schreiber, Sheriff Broadstairs, and all our vendors. Moreover, there was something about Uncle Ralph's naive, elfin enthusiasm that seemed to awaken Kilmer's atrophied sense of empathy.

"So, Mr. Sickert, exactly how big a line of credit do you feel you need to fully capitalize your investment?"

We had coached Uncle Ralph on this. "Well, Harriet, the way I figure it, we can't really get by with less than a quarter of a million. Might never touch the bulk of it, but it's better to have it and not need it than the other way around."

Stan regarded the polished tips of his shoes as if they might help him divine Harriet's answer. I pretended to be working sums on Harriet's borrowed calculator. Only Uncle Ralph had directly engaged Harriet's gaze.

She said nothing for what seemed an eternity. I almost got up to leave.

"Well, Mr. Sickert, given your good faith in investing so much in our community already, I think that figure is only reasonable. There's no sense in dooming such an important project to failure by taking half measures."

Out in the car, with the papers all signed, Stan said, "You goddamn magnificent horndog, Ralph, why'd you stop at a quarter of a million? You coulda got into the old girl's pants, too, if you wanted."

Ralph said, "Suzy's woman enough for me, Stan. Keeps me plumb tuckered out, every single night."

I sank back in the passenger seat, wishing there were some way to selectively unhear things.

29

Work on the bonfire had ceased. The damn wobbly pile was about fourteen feet high. It wouldn't be lit, I assumed, until the climax of the evening. Burning Man East. God help this place when the enormous thing was torched. Maybe the whole lodge would catch fire and disappear, preferably with no lives lost. We could still sell the land to Nancarrow. That was all he was interested in: the theoretical footprint for Steve Prynne's casino dreams. Was it right to pray for such an act of destruction, and the shattered hopes of so many innocent locals, Nellie foremost among them?

I was debating the ethics of sending my prayer for an inferno heavenward when I noticed Elbert Tighe and Kirwan running two garden hoses toward the pyre. Of course. Tighe's frontier efficiency would have considered all dangers and immediately conjured up defenses.

"Glen," said Tighe, "you're probably happy now that we put in that reserve tank. Fifteen gallons a minute is good, but sometimes you need to draw down faster."

Indeed, once we had secured our line of credit, I let Tighe

convince me to bump up our water capacity with a large reserve tank that filled itself when the system was being underutilized. Couldn't let the patrons run out of water for their hot showers, now, could we?

I gave up on the feasibility of asking God for help. He was obviously against me, too.

Freed from toting wood, the partygoers now turned their attention noisily to refreshments. Bottle caps popped off into the grass; beverages gurgled into red plastic cups. Behind a table all her own, with a blender at the end of an extension cord, Suzy Lam was mixing and dispensing Bermuda mai tais. A ghost of the too-sweet taste of peach schnapps filled my mouth. Uncle Ralph, glass in hand, stood proudly at her side. It was hard to tell whether he was already plastered or just joyful.

Outdoor floodlights—on the main building, on the dining room, on stanchions in the gravel parking lot—cast zones of near-daylight radiance in the deepening nightfall. And any holdout islands of darkness were banished by lighted tiki torches.

The savory smell of roasting meat filled the soon-to-be-autumnal air.

I thought I should see how Ray Zerkin was getting along, for he had assumed a certain important duty for the evening.

Ray sat behind a bank of electronic equipment, including several large speakers. He wore big, nerdy headphones and was busy scrolling through screens on his iPad. When he saw me, he took the headphones off.

"I'm almost ready, Mr. Glen. I was just integrating Mr. Stan's files with mine. I've never really attempted to listen to the music he calls the blues, so I will just insert some of his songs at random intervals. But, of course, I have a very good playlist of my own material, which is very logically arranged."

One day, I had discovered in conversation with Ray that in

addition to baseball, he had a passion for one particular musical genre: classic disco.

At first, I thought he was pulling my leg; then I remembered that pranks were not really his thing. But I should have known that Ray's sincerity was unwavering. This gangly kid, who would never in a million years come near a dance floor, found something in the quintessential dance music that resonated with him. Maybe it was just the glamour or the frequency of beats per minute, but something clicked deeply.

And he knew everything, not just the recognizable hits. He played stuff for me I had never heard: Anita Ward, Vicki Sue Robinson, the Dazz Band—I can't remember them all.

Once I learned this, putting Ray in charge of the music for the party was a no-brainer. He wasn't going to mingle otherwise. His seat behind the equipment represented a safe refuge.

"Are we ready, Mr. Glen?"

"Hit it, maestro."

"Bad Girls" by Donna Summer began to pump from the speakers. The reaction from the crowd was instantaneously positive and electric.

Several women of various ages came up to Ray's perch.

"Great choice, Ray!"

"Ray, you rock!"

"Can I get you a drink, Ray?"

"Ray, you taking requests?"

Ray's emotionless demeanor barely concealed a trembling nervous pleasure, reminding me of a wild animal consenting to be petted. "I wouldn't mind a Pepsi, please."

Turning away from Ray, I saw the Impala pulling in, its headlights sweeping the scene. I hastened over.

It looked like a clown car unloading as the big old beater disgorged seven people. From behind the wheel, Stan, of course, emerged. Nellie and her mother slid out from the front seat, passenger-side. (Nellie had been in the middle, next to Stan, and I wasn't sure I liked that, but I supposed they had enough of a chaperone with Mom.) The youngest boy, Justin, had been sitting on his father's lap in back, with the girls Adelma and Leidira taking up the rest of the rear. Standing self-consciously by the rear fender, those two adolescents exhibited the same nascent beauty that Nellie had in full bloom, and I had to mentally shake myself not to ogle them. Little brother Justin possessed a preternatural air of wisdom. He was utterly unlike most of the Anglo kids his age I knew, who tended to be spoiled and bratty.

Nellie raced up to me, grabbed my arm, and pulled me over.

"Here are my sisters and brother, Glen. And this is my *mamãe*, Zahira, and my *papai*, Ivanildo. You have to all like each other, or I'll die!"

In the next three seconds, Nellie's parents ran about ten thousand instinctive calculations on my character and net personhood, and thankfully, I emerged with a positive rating. Ivanildo's handshake was a fraction less powerful than Stan's or Elbert Tighe's. And hugging the plump Zahira was like sinking into a fragrant feather mattress.

"Glen, you don't mind if I show my family all around, do you? You can keep busy for a while?"

I wanted Nellie by my side for comfort and reassurance that tonight and all the rest of our time here was going to go right, but I could see that she really wanted to show off the place and her new friends.

"No, of course not," I said. "We'll hook up later."

Nellie trotted off, jabbering in Caboverde at about a thousand words a minute.

Stan came up to me. "Jesus Christ, that girl can yap!" he said. "I don't think she shut up for one minute, coming or going. Thank

Christ Sandy is a lady of few words. Where is she, anyhow?"

Stan's intolerance of Nellie's chatter, whether manufactured for my benefit or not, made me forget how close they had sat in the car. "I think I saw her in the kitchen, stirring a pot of tomato sauce."

"Quiet as a mouse, and a hell of a great cook. That's a winning combo right there, without even getting into how she fucks like a bunny on steroids. Sandralene! Your man is back!"

Stan made a beeline for the kitchen, and after getting myself a beer, I began to wander about the festive scene. But watching people have so much fun when I wasn't having any myself proved strenuous, so I drifted away from the center of things.

A giant smooth-skinned beech tree on the edge of the property cast a cone of darkness below itself. Something inside that penumbra glinted with the light from a distant tiki torch. I went over to look.

Varvara "Vee" Aptekar, her back against the tree trunk, was weeping softly in the night.

30

I didn't want to intrude, but it was too late to become invisible. Vee had seen me through the tears and disarrayed hair, so I stepped deeper into the well of shade and seclusion. The raucous party noises seemed to recede, drowned out by the katydids and crickets and frogs in their urgent, endless calls for sex.

My eyes were adjusting to the gloom. Vee's hands were balled tight, and she used each fist to wipe away tears and snot. The plain silver bracelet that had caught the torchlight glinted again. From a hunched-over posture, as if reacting to a gut punch, she straightened her spine firmly against the tree trunk, like someone facing a firing squad and determined to be brave.

"Take a picture, why don't you? Capture the exact moment when the female freak shattered. Trust me, it won't last long."

"Vee, come on, get honest with yourself. You're no freak show, and I'm not some gawking rube in the audience. I'm your friend."

"My friend. That's rich. I haven't had a friend since I was five. That's when I learned how fast things can turn to shit."

This was the first time in all these weeks that she had ever talked about her past, and I wanted to tread cautiously so she wouldn't change her mind about opening up. But at the same time, I sensed she wouldn't buy any euphemistic rose-tinted crap.

"Listen, Vee, I know you had a rough break. Losing both parents had to be horrible, especially in a murder-suicide. But it's happened to lots of people before, and some of them recover."

"Yeah, I thought I was recovering okay, too, for a few years. And then when I was fourteen, I found out why my mother and father had to die. When I learned what a fucking bastard Nancarrow was and how he had gone on to live his life happily after he ruined mine, something shriveled up inside me. That's when I realized there is no justice, and what slime people really are. Not one decent soul in a million. And certainly no saints in my world. That's when I knew I had to be as hard as I could if I was ever going to get even with Nancarrow."

I stepped closer to her. She didn't flinch away.

"Okay, so you developed some real hatred for humanity, and a mission of revenge. Me, I'm just in it for the money. I can't really grok the getting-even part. But Stan's out to get even, too. Nancarrow screwed him over pretty bad—a couple of years in jail. But you don't see Stan hating life because of a bum break. Just the opposite. This mission has made him even more stoked for success. How are you even going to appreciate getting even if you can't take joy in anything else?"

She shook her head and squeezed out the last tears. "Stan took the hit when he was all grown up. It's different for kids. But happiness is not part of the plan, Glen. I just want revenge, pure and simple. To hurt Nancarrow bad. I can't hurt him as much as he hurt me, but maybe hurting him even a little will help me feel better."

I got a little disgusted then. I wasn't going to change Vee's mind or disposition, dispel her monomania, or heal the wounds of a lifetime. I couldn't even start, because she wouldn't let me or anyone else inside her fortress. Maybe some of my disdain for her willfully self-punishing stance came through in my tone.

"All right, then. You tell me that's how things stand, so I have to accept it. You're like some unfeeling robot bomb with one purpose—a heat-seeking missile with one target. What the hell are you crying for, then? Cowgirl up, for Christ's sake, and let's get the goddamn job done!"

Vee stood silently for a moment. "But that's just it. My part is finally coming up. I've got to whore myself out to Nancarrow. Make him want me. Seduce him and get him off his guard. Help convince him that buying this place is the best deal he'll ever make. That's how I'm going to earn my share of the money."

"Right. So?"

"So, I'm not sure I can do it."

I thought I saw where she was heading, but I had to pretend not to understand. "What do you mean? You're morally opposed to acting like a whore?"

"No. I don't think I can fake it well enough. I—I haven't slept with anyone in three years. I've forgotten how."

"It'll come back to you," I said. "I didn't think I remembered how to con anyone, after getting caught and sitting in jail for a while. But so far, I've managed to fool two parole officers, several bank managers, and practically the whole town of Centerdale. I believe I can fake out Nancarrow, and so can you."

"I just don't know—"

I laid both hands on her shoulders. "Look, Vee, you are a beautiful, sexy woman. You can do this. Nancarrow will be all over you. Trust me."

"But I—"

I pulled her against me, and my hands slid down her back and onto her ass. I smelled her unperfumed animal scent. She clamped her arms around me, and her slick, salty lips mashed mine hard against my teeth. Her tongue drove against mine, and I shifted my right hand under her cotton shirt, onto her breast. Everything went fast from there.

Bent forward with her palms and left cheekbone against the rough bark of the pine, her capri pants and underwear around her ankles, Vee took me inside her with a sharp cry that I prayed no one else could hear—a visceral sound full of mingled exultation and despair, rage and resignation, satisfaction and resentment.

If Nellie hadn't been pumping the urgency out of me for weeks now, I would have lasted about ten seconds. But I managed to bring Vee to an evidently satisfactory climax before abandoning all control.

Enervated, I sagged forward onto her for a few moments before I recovered and realized how uncomfortable this must be for her, braced against the hard, unyielding surface. But as she had done all her life, she bore the weight without complaint.

Disengaged, we put our clothes back on in silence. I was realistic enough not to expect some momentous realignment or epiphany on her part. I didn't imagine myself that spectacular a lover. But I did imagine us going forward on some new and friendlier basis. So I was unprepared for what Vee next said, in her old familiar tones of inviolable self-assurance.

"That helped. It really did. I think I can do it now. Congratulations. You've ensured the success of the plan—or at least removed one roadblock. But if anyone ever hears a single word about our little refresher course, well, just remember this."

The tip of something sharp pricked the skin of my belly. I looked down and saw a thin blade in Vee's hand—a stiletto, perhaps.

"I have this in case Nancarrow gets wise. I'll have my revenge one way or another. But I can use it on anyone."

"I, uh … kiss and tell? *Moi?*"

The blade vanished as if it had never been there. Vee ran her fingers through her hair to straighten it. "You leave first. I'll see you around."

The well-lighted grounds, full of revelers, seemed like some other dimension—an alternate reality where everyone was well adjusted and understood how to enjoy life. I tried to fit in.

I met Nellie, who had left her family at a picnic table with plenty to eat and drink. The happy Firmino clan quickly became the nexus of an ever-changing swirl of partygoers, all of whom seemed intimate friends of the family. I suspected that they would be partying deep into the night before settling down into the several rooms of the lodge we had reserved for them. I put away plenty of booze, until all the lights acquired a soft nimbus. At intervals, I saw Vee, being social in her own formal way, never giving off the faintest clue to what had just happened.

The party accelerated, and I witnessed things I never anticipated. Or did I only imagine, for instance, bank officer Harriet Kilmer twerking with Kirwan Allen?

When the bonfire was finally ignited, I found myself hollering wordlessly with the rest of the spectators, as if we were pagans at some turning of the seasons.

The next thing I knew, someone was shaking me awake in the warm daylight on the other side of my closed eyelids. For a startled moment, I had a delusion that it was Vee, come to slit my throat.

But when I opened my eyes, with Nellie snoring softly beside me, I discerned, of all people, Ray Zerkin, who had entered our room with all the naive impropriety that was his nature.

"Mr. Glen, you have to look now. Mr. Nancarrow—he's all over our honeypots!"

PART FOUR

31

The following week brought us all together to discuss the crux of our plan one last time before it was set in motion.

Nellie, of course, was not privy to this crucial meeting. Just the five of us coconspirators sat crammed into the efficient but comfy stand-alone cabin that Stan and Sandralene had chosen all those weeks ago when we first got here. That day seemed an eternity ago, on the far side of a welter of crazy activity. And now, with the imminent arrival of Nancarrow's scouting party, that vanished day also seemed a time of uncomplicated ease. I would have liked to go back there, before meeting Vee and Nellie set me up for such a storm of feelings. Before the actual moment when testing our harebrained scheme against our opponent would surely reveal all its flaws. I recalled a favorite saying of the professor in my trial practice course: "No plan survives contact with the enemy." But returning to that innocent time was no more possible than running my whole criminal life in reverse, spinning the clock back to the day I passed the bar exam and my folks took me to dinner at the fanciest restaurant they knew. (It was a place I would sneer at only a few years later, in the midst of my new high-rolling lifestyle.) And now here I was, in a cabin with four people I had known for barely a month, about to set in motion an intrigue there would be no coming back from.

Stan and Sandralene sat side by side on their bed. Vee and Ray had taken the only two chairs (upholstered in the tasteful burnt orange selected by Aphrodite Fabric Creations). That left me to park my butt on the corner of the tiny writing desk that Brenda Bethune had cloned for each cabin.

Stan said, "Okay, I'm gonna go over this once more just to be sure everyone knows what's what. We can't fuck up. Everyone has to do their special thing perfect the first time, because we ain't gonna get no do-overs. Understand?"

We all nodded.

"Okay, let's hit the high points again. That sucker Nancarrow took the bait. All them big-ass graphs and numbers on the computer prove it. Thanks to Ray and Glen for bringing that off. And that phone call we got from Senator Almonte clinched it. Algy's rarin' to ride—thinks this deal will earn him some serious dough and get him in good with major-league players like Prynne. But despite him being so hot to trot, you're not gonna see the big dog himself up here right away. I know him, and he's always mighty cautious. First, he's going to send some guys to scope things out. I'm betting he sends Rushlow and Digweed, 'cuz they're his best men, but it could be someone we don't know."

I thought back to that distant-recent day when we left the city for the mystery lodge, watching Nancarrow leave his office building, flanked by the two toughs named Buck Rushlow and Needles Digweed. I didn't relish the thought of them on the premises.

"Whoever he sends, you'll be able to spot him, because he'll stand out like a nun in a cathouse. He'll be asking his questions all subtle-like and scoping everything out, so's he can report back whether things are like they appeared online. Your job is to give the impression that you're just trying to earn an honest buck with this place. Nobody knows nothing about Steve Prynne and his casino plans. That part comes later. We'll tip our hand at just the right moment. But for now, you all have to look like you're living out your life's dream by investing in this place and catering to a bunch of squalling families and boozy fishermen."

Vee said, "Having Little Miss Sunshine at the front desk will bring that off."

I bit my tongue not to respond to Vee's gibe. I knew she didn't really take to Nellie. I couldn't call it jealousy, because nothing existed between Vee and me after that one anomalous incident under the beech tree. Vee's disdain was merely part of her soured take on life, her attitude toward everyone in general. I only felt sorry she had to express it, and wished I could make her see life in a different light.

"Yes," I said, "Nellie is totally into her new position and doing a bang-up job."

That morning nine days ago, when Ray barged into my hungover sleep with his news, things had instantly kicked into high gear.

Once Nellie was awake and sensible, I told her to start the wheels going for hiring staff. She was stoked, and got out her phone right away. The applicants, many more than we could actually hire, arrived in a borrowed school bus twenty-four hours after getting the call. It took just a day to vet them, and another couple of days to bring them on board with paperwork. Luckily, though I had never done any payroll or bookkeeping before this, I could decipher the government requirements easily enough. Withholding forms and immigration checks and all that. My law school professors would have winced to see me using my expensive education for such menial tasks.

The Bigelow Junction Motor Lodge now had a staff of twelve: six in the kitchen and dining room, a groundskeeper, a handyman, two registration clerks (one for a twelve-hour day shift, one for the twelve-hour night shift), and two housekeepers. We avoided hiring a lifeguard, because swimming season was all but over, and we posted the newly graded and resanded beach with several SWIM AT YOUR OWN RISK signs. I had to memorize a lot of oddball Caboverdean names to go along with a set of happy faces, and was still trying to keep my Nouhailas straight from my Evandros.

Since our workers could not feasibly make the long commute between here and Centerdale every day, I had engaged in some illegal discriminatory policies and hired all young unmarried people. Then we had bought two used double-wide trailers, set them up with water and electrical connections (Tighe and DiPippo, happily at your service), and dubbed them the male and female dorms.

Ray had cooked up a homepage for the lodge, advertising our relaunch, with booking apps and rates. I had contacted local media outlets—radio and newspapers, no television—and placed several ads. We quickly hit 70 percent occupancy (ten of our fifteen rooms and cabins, thanks to the residual goodwill and happy memories of the lodge). With three units taken by us, that left only two open, and I planned to keep them empty for Nancarrow's scouts.

The lodge now had a payroll of about sixteen thousand per week, offset somewhat by our paying guests. The rents from our year-round tenants had come in. All in all, figuring in utilities and other purchases, we were operating splendidly at a substantial loss. Uncle Ralph's line of credit was getting its workout. But who cared? The facade was in place for Nancarrow's inspection, and that was all that mattered.

Once all this was in place, I went to Nellie and told her I was making her the manager of everything.

"Oh, *minha nossa!* I can't believe it, Glen! This is my most important job ever! I'll do such good work! You will be so proud of me, and the lodge will earn us all such big money!"

She'd thrown her arms around me and planted a few dozen kisses all over my face. I felt like the worst jerk alive. *Yes, the lodge will earn us big money, and you'll share the loot, Nellie. But it won't come the way you think.*

Interrupting my reverie, Stan continued with his coaching. "Great. Everything's running smooth, and this part of the deal will be a piece of cake. We just have to look innocent to draw the rat into the trap. Then, *bang-o!* Everyone has to look innocent except for you, Vee. If I know Algy—and I do—his boys will be keeping their eyes open for local trim, as part of their regular marching orders. Nancarrow's got no main squeeze back home, so far as the grapevine tells me. But even if he did, he's always on nooky lookout whenever he's on the road. So you've got to impress his scouts. Come off sexy and available. Not like no hooker or bargirl. More like the bored-widow type."

Vee did not seem upset by these instructions. "I understand perfectly."

Stan turned to Ray. "You dig what this is all about, how you gotta not let anything slip? I just want you to stay in the background and work on those assignments we gave you."

Ray had three tasks before him. He had a certain document he had to fake up, using some dark-web resources if necessary to create an air of authenticity. He had to establish for us a secure, untouchable foreign bank account that could accept without question the large wire transfer that we expected Nancarrow to pay us with when he took over the property. And he had to work up a watertight bill of sale for the lodge and get Uncle Ralph's signature on it, via FedEx. (Uncle Ralph and a tearfully happy Suzy Lam had bidden us goodbye a couple of days after the night of the bonfire.)

"Mr. Stan, you know I don't like talking to strangers, especially bad ones. And with the postseason games coming up, I am highly engaged most of the time."

"Okay, Ray for the win! I guess if we got all our ducks in a row, it's time for me to take a hike."

Stan stood up and hefted a loaded backpack from the floor at the foot of the bed. A small tent and sleeping bag were strapped to the outside.

He couldn't stay here and risk being seen by Nancarrow or his hired guys. Neither could he relocate to Centerdale, because then Schreiber would have to be informed, and with what excuse? So the plan was for him to camp out, unseen and alone, not too distant from the lodge, on the far shore of Nutbush Lake.

We all trooped outside.

"Remember," Stan said, "I'm just fifteen minutes away. Send Sandy for me if you need me. Don't phone me, because people get careless with their phone talk, and you could get overheard saying something compromising. She knows the spot. Send her even if you don't need me, with some hot food. She can make it a goddamn conjugal visit, too, just like in minimum security."

Stan grabbed Sandy and kissed her extravagantly. Then, with no warning, he hugged me! It was like being grabbed by a bear that had bitten into a can of body spray.

Setting me down, he said, "Thank Christ that goddamn Paget ain't here to see us hugging, Glen boy, or he'd think we was queer after all! All right, good luck to us all. We'll be spending Algy's dough before he even knows he's been screwed."

Stan strode off like some ghetto Johnny Appleseed, and the rest of us went to work.

32

Nellie looked quizzically at me, and I had to remind myself of her sharp native intelligence. She might be unschooled, but she was far from dumb.

"Stan wants to *meditate*? What's he gonna meditate about: his stomach or his dick? Or both? Don't get me wrong, I love the guy. But he doesn't seem like Buddha material to me."

"Maybe 'meditate' is the wrong word. He told me he just wants some quiet time." I ransacked my mind for something convincing. "Prison does strange things to your head. Sometimes, you get used to being in a cell by yourself, and crowds make you crazy. This has been a stressful ordeal, getting the business off the ground. You have to admit that. I think he just needs some Stan time." Inspiration struck. "Also, I think he and Sandy had a little argument. Maybe he figures he can make her miss him this way."

This bit of gossip intrigued Nellie. "An argument? What about?"

"I don't really know. I keep my distance from that relationship. It could be like *Clash of the Titans*, where the mortals get squashed. You'll have to ask her."

I knew that with Nellie tied up, hour by busy hour, with managing the lodge, I could get to Sandy first and warn her about my invention of an argument between her and Stan. Let her come up with some likely theme.

"Okay," Nellie said, "whatever you men gotta do, you gotta do. I don't understand it, but I know I'd be missing you if you ever took off."

We kissed—the sensation was as sweet as ever, never losing its thrill—and I left her trying to reckon how we could go through six dozen eggs so fast serving only twenty-four separate breakfasts.

I prowled around the grounds for a while, trying to walk off my nerves. We hadn't had any new arrivals in the past twenty-four hours, and I was pretty sure none of the older renters were spies from Nancarrow. So that meant his boys had yet to show up. What was keeping them?

All our workers bustled industriously about, grateful for their jobs. The lake had quite a few swimmers of all ages, enjoying the unseasonably hot weather. Although the lodge had no dock yet, we had bought two used skiffs that could be beached on the sand. Anglers had both of them rented for the afternoon.

Forgetting for the moment the deceitful nature of this enterprise, I felt a surge of pride at the way the business had taken off. But the emotion only left me feeling worse because it was all a house of cards, a Potemkin village.

I decided to look in on Ray and make sure he was on task. But on the grass outside the room he shared with Vee, I encountered a startling sight.

There, reclining on a lawn chair, was a woman I didn't recognize at first. It took me a moment to register that it was Vee, in her role as Mata Hari.

She had ditched the usual drab blouse and loose linen pants in favor of denim short shorts that revealed long, lovely legs.

She wore gold sandals that laced up her calves, and a men's shirt tied off to exhibit her taut stomach, and unbuttoned enough to reveal a rim of lacy bra. She had put her hair up, and her makeup conveyed a wanton sophistication. The designer sunglasses added an air of inscrutability.

I couldn't see where she might be carrying the blade, but I wasn't willing to bet she had left it in the room.

I stopped beside her chair. Maybe my jaw hung open a little as I began to feel aroused all over again.

Even her voice had changed. No longer indifferent or harsh, now it dripped with a juicy indolence. "Did you want something, Mr. McClinton? I believe my rent's paid up for the next week."

"Holy Christ, Vee."

She reached up and tilted her sunglasses down. Her face suddenly lost the sultry tramp look and reverted to her standard mask of aloof stoicism. The contrast with the rest of her appearance was unsettling.

"Motivation can work wonders, Glen. Ask any actress. When you want something bad enough, you figure out how to get it." The sunglasses went back into place, and the new personality kicked seamlessly back in. "Please be sure to let me know if I can do you again—I mean, do anything *for* you again—Mr. McClinton."

I turned away, forgetting I had intended to check on Ray. And that's when I saw a black Cadillac Escalade come up the drive.

33

The big SUV pulled into an empty spot in the gravel lot. The doors opened, and two men got out. White thug Buck Rushlow and black thug Needles Digweed, each in boots and camo and looking like a linebacker with a chip on his shoulder.

I began to miss Stan a great deal.

My stomach felt heavy, the way it had the day I first saw Sheriff Broadstairs from across the lawn. But along with the sense of dread, this time I felt a kind of pleasurable excitement—exaltation, even.

All the waiting and preparation was finally over. Win or lose, the game was afoot. At the end, we'd be rich, or ... I couldn't bring myself to guess. Alive, I hoped, even if stone busted. But the potential thrill of skinning these morons, of helping Stan and Vee pull off their big get-even, revived the glee I had felt when reeling in yet another sucker of a client back in my lawyering days. Their money was about to become mine, and they were actually stupid enough to have bought my spiel and practically forced their dough on me of their own accord. All I ever had to do was ask for it with innocent enthusiasm.

So as I walked over to the new arrivals, I put a bounce in my step and a broad innkeeper's smile on my yokel's face. Nothing too overdone, just a faintly dimwitted hospitality and eagerness for their patronage. I could feel myself believing the reality of my guise, inhabiting the role fully: the key to any successful con. I would soon show Vee she wasn't the only method actor around here.

"Howdy!" I said. "Welcome to the Bigelow Junction Motor Lodge. My name's Glen McClinton, and I own this place. Beautiful day, isn't it? Hope you had a pleasant drive, wherever you hail from. You fellows looking to stay with us, I hope?"

Both men wore sunglasses, which made them a little hard to read. Buck Rushlow's thick wheat-straw hair covered a bucket-shaped head with features spaced a little too far apart. Needles Digweed sported tight, short cornrows, scraggly facial hair, and an astonishingly artificial-looking nose that surely had seen serious plastic surgery after a run-in with a razor, broken bottle, or length of rebar.

Digweed said, "Yeah, boss, that's why we're here. Aim to get us in a little huntin'." He opened the rear hatch on the Escalade, and I saw two black fabric rifle or shotgun cases, along with camp stools, blaze-orange jackets, tree stands, and a tarp.

The sight of the guns amped up my unease, but I didn't let it show. After all, hunters were supposedly part of our bread and butter.

"Well, sir, we own five hundred acres, and there's no hunting on lodge grounds, of course. But everything after that's national forest, and long as you got your license, you're good to go. Just have to be careful of the locals, and maybe a few hikers. Any land that's not posted, you can assume you're good. People in these parts understand hunting. Now, the season at the moment is only on for turkeys, geese, and deer. You're a little early for bear or moose."

"That's fine," said Rushlow. "We're not fussy, long's we get to shoot something."

I had to interpret that comment innocently, of course. There could be no hint of suspicion that I knew who they were and why they were here.

Both men had a perceptible but not overwhelming south-of-the-Mason-Dixon-Line accent. I had supposed that Barnaby Nancarrow would hire locals, former or current, from the Gulch, just as he had with Stan Hasso, out of childhood loyalties and pride in having transcended his roots and appearing as a patron to his left-behind homeboys. Then again, maybe hiring out-of-towners made more sense. No conflicts of interest with relatives, their records unknown to the authorities (at least initially), greater dispassion when it came to breaking legs and busting heads, and so forth. Nancarrow had probably used his connections to import these goons from Atlanta or the Carolinas.

"All right, then, sounds like you fellows are primed for some fun. I assume you got your licenses in order? Local sheriff's kind of a hardnose about rules and regs."

I was giving the dodgy Broadstairs more credit for dutifulness than he deserved, but they couldn't realize that.

"Right here," said Digweed, patting one of his many pockets.

"Fine, fine! Let's get you settled in, then. We have two rooms open. You each need one?"

I tried to put all the expected local businessman's greed into the question, and was rewarded by seeing Rushlow and Digweed exchange a look that plainly said, *What the hell kind of suckers does he take us for?*

"No thanks, we'll manage with one," said Rushlow. "Long's it's got double beds. Won't be spending much time in the room, anyhow."

"Think you'll be here a week or so? I can give you a special rate."

"Naw, just a couple of days. This is kind of a sneaky short vacation. Gotta get back to work soon."

Rushlow was lifting the gun cases from the back of the SUV.

"Here, let me give you a hand with those," I said. "I can get one of our staff to carry any other bags."

Rushlow hesitated a moment, then handed the guns over to me. "Thanks. We'll unload the rest of our stuff later."

The alien weight of the rifles felt disturbing. I shuffled them awkwardly before I could get a grip on the handles, and began leading the way to the office.

Of course, I made certain to pass as close as possible to the sunbathing Vee.

"Your room's down this end of the building. Just take a gander before we register you, to see if it's to your liking."

The two hoods were so poleaxed by Vee, they would have made happy noises if I had shown them two cots on a compost heap in the middle of a junkyard.

Looking over the top of her shade at the admiring newcomers, Vee lifted her cocktail and proceeded to turn the simple act of drinking through a straw into an obscene performance illegal in several of the more conservative states.

"Gee, Mr. McClinton, you shouldn't ought to sneak up on a girl that way. What if I had been on my tummy with my top down? I could've gotten spooked and jumped right up!"

That mental image left both me and the new guests a little light-headed. They leered wordlessly at Vee, who accepted their horndog eyeballing as pure appreciation.

Once they had inspected their room for a full three seconds, we all headed to the office.

The registration desk was manned by Anildo Pereira, who could usually be found reading some fantasy novel on his phone when not occupied by his sparse duties. Technically, he was supposed to help out in the dining room if things were dead up front, but I didn't press the issue. Now, seeing new guests, he hopped to it.

Nellie's desk was off in a corner of the room, behind a folding screen we had erected. I said, "Okay, then, see you gents later," and, leaving Nancarrow's boys with Anildo, I went to check on her. She was banging away at a calculator. Seeing me, she immediately complained, "Glen, we have to do something about this damn electric bill. It's killing us!"

"Okay, don't worry about it. I have something more important to tell you. Come take a walk with me."

We stepped around the divider and past Rushlow and Digweed, who were bent over their paper registration forms, looking as if they had never held a pen before. (We had no computer system.) I gave Nellie a look that plainly said, *Note these guys.*

Once we were halfway to the lake, I told her the story that Stan and I had cobbled together.

"Nellie, I was hoping I wouldn't have to burden you with this, but those two men are looking for Stan. We hoped they'd never find him, but it seems as if they know he was here. They're ex-cons with a grudge. He heard through the grapevine that they might have gotten on his trail. That's the real reason he headed for the woods. We can't let on that we even know him, or there could be trouble."

Nellie's normal ebullience transmuted to grave concern. She was genuinely worried for Stan. "Ay, *seguro*. I won't say a thing. I'll make sure none of *meus compatriotas* say anything, either. We know how to hang together, *verdade*. But won't these guys recognize you and Sandy?"

"No, neither of us. Never met 'em. So we can help watch Stan's back and keep him safe."

"Me, too, then! We can't let anything happen to Stan—or to the lodge!"

34

Nellie had been wondering how we managed to burn through so many eggs in the dining room. But that mystery would never have come up if Digweed and Rushlow had been our guests earlier. At breakfast the morning after their arrival, they wolfed down a dozen eggs and a pound of bacon between them, along with a stack of blueberry buttermilk pancakes. (Jenise Rezende, our young female chef, had gotten her degree from the Culinary Institute of America and was decidedly overqualified for the job. But she had been forced to return to Centerdale after graduation to care for sick parents and, after their recent deaths, was still deciding what to do with her life, which is how we had nabbed her skills for the lodge.) I was rethinking the wisdom of having the "Hungry Man's All-You-Can-Eat Breakfast Special" on the menu.

Stuffed at last, they had departed with rifles and packs for a day of "hunting"—that is, a recon of the place. They weren't scoping out the territory for its suitability as a casino site—that was far beyond their skills—but for its permeability and defensibility. If their boss was going to come here—as he must for our plan to succeed—then he would have to be assured of being able to provide for his personal safety.

I didn't worry about them encountering Stan by accident. His campsite, though close by, was well off the beaten track, obscured by dense undergrowth, and best accessible by water. He had moored a kayak there beforehand, hidden in the reeds, for a quick exit. And last night at dusk, I had sent Sandralene out in one of the skiffs to alert him to our new arrivals. Watching her pull effortlessly on the oars with her strong arms and broad back, I had sighed. In a more perfect world, I would surely be entitled to a harem. But that night, in bed with Nellie, I forgot all about my whimsical longing for Stan's woman.

While the two goons were out poking around, I mentally rehearsed the sort of questions they were bound to ask about the business, and my best answers. I had to present the enterprise in the most appealing light to make it look as if we were rubes, and Nancarrow could just barge in and scoop us up for some "generous" multiple of what we had paid—a sales figure in the public records—but still a tiny fraction of what Steve Prynne would soon be offering him. Little did that bastard Nancarrow know that he was going to the wall for twenty million cold.

I left my breakfast in the dining room. Nellie had risen and eaten a couple of hours before me, so eager was she to start the day's work. I relished both her tender goodbye kiss as I lay abed, and the extra sleep, since I suspected that once things began to heat up, lazing around would be a forgone luxury.

A FedEx truck pulled up. This had to be the stuff Ray had created: two documents essential to our scheme.

I approached the delivery guy, but he wouldn't turn the two envelopes over to anyone but Ray. Just as well. I ushered him to the room Ray and Vee cohabited. Vee was out somewhere—her Volkswagen was gone—but Ray answered the door. He accepted the envelopes and left an illegible scrawl on the FedEx driver's computer screen. I followed him inside his room.

Vee's bed, alongside a nightstand full of books, had a military neatness about it, while Ray's looked as if an army of feral teenagers had camped there, leaving it full of crumbs and snack wrappers and dirty baseball shirts.

Ray studied the two envelopes intently, then said, "This one is from Uncle Ralph."

I took it and opened it.

Inside was the perfect, watertight sales agreement for the lodge, vetted by good lawyers and a real estate agent back in the city. Ralph's formally old-fashioned signature awaited Nancarrow's to complete the contract. The buyer's name and selling price had been left blank.

Ray had slit open the second envelope and withdrawn its contents: an unsealed business-size envelope containing a single folded piece of stationery.

The letterhead, on thick, expensive stock, displayed the famous gold-embossed, hand-scripted Prynne name, with its terminal decorative dot. Prynne's trademark floral motif embellished both the paper and the envelope. The name and address of Prynne's lawyer headed the salutation, with the lawyer's signature affirmed underneath by Steve Prynne's own scrawl.

And the body of the letter offered the owners of Bigelow Junction Motor Lodge twenty million dollars for all rights to the property.

The date on the letter was still several days in the future.

When Nancarrow arrived to buy us out, we would be eager, after a little confusion and hesitation. After all, we were just some Podunk businessmen sitting on an unexceptional property, and the business was losing money. Who wouldn't be eager to sell under those conditions? Nancarrow would be hooked, steepling his fingers and crooning, "Excellent!" He would consider the deal as good as done, the land already his.

But then, after we had dithered for a while, once the date on the letter arrived, we would turn into incorrigible holdouts. Because now we knew what the land was really worth, thanks to Prynne's newly disclosed offer.

So why would we then take Nancarrow's twenty-million-dollar matching deal, when he proposed it, without asking more from him for bypassing Prynne's bid? Because we would let Nancarrow convince us—as Stan and I were confident he would try to do—that only his business savvy could get more from Prynne. That we were small-time duffers who had no negotiating skills and were not operating from a position of strength. We might even screw up the deal entirely, whereas Nancarrow was a genius deal maker and had leverage. He could threaten to build his own casino on the land if Prynne did not come through with more money.

And thus, the deal would wrap up nicely. Nancarrow would assume he had snookered us, getting the truly worthless property at a bargain price. And we would walk away with his twenty million.

I handed the letter back to Ray and said, "Good job. Keep this hidden in a safe place."

"Yes, Mr. Glen. I will hide it inside the most valuable book I own. I could never lose it then."

Ray picked up a massive worn paperback with a picture of a baseball batter on the cover: *The Bill James Handbook.*

"Good choice, Ray. How's that banking business coming?"

"We now have a very private account that will hold our money safely here and overseas, Mr. Glen. Do you know, I think financial matters are really pretty interesting. If my time were not all taken up with baseball and my disco music, I might have gotten really involved in that field."

I made a mental note not to invest in the stock market without consulting Ray, should his priorities ever shift.

Outside, I thought of tracking down Nellie to see what she was doing for lunch. But several niggling chores intervened as workers found me. And I had to help one family find their car keys, lost somewhere between the beach and the lodge. So lunch kept getting postponed until about two o'clock, when Sheriff Broadstairs drove up as I stood outside a unit, helping Bethinho Fonseca, our handyman, rehang a door.

The sheriff had a passenger with him: our parole officer, Wilson Schreiber.

I left Bethinho and walked over to the visitors.

"Gentlemen," I said, "welcome to our exclusive resort. Romance under the pines, and all the Caboverde stew you can inhale."

This was Schreiber's first visit, and he looked around appreciatively at the activity. "McClinton, I might have misjudged you and Hasso. This place actually looks like a serious and well-run enterprise. I guess my faith in you two was not misplaced. Where is your partner, anyhow? I'd like to congratulate him, too."

"He's out fishing. Should I send someone for him?"

"No, don't bother. But I have to remind you that you two are both due for a visit in my office. I can't be running out here every week—got other bad boys to mentor. I only managed to get here today because Sheriff Broadstairs was coming this way."

With any luck, Stan and I would be lolling with our women on the tropical beaches of Cape Verde in a week. "I understand," I said. "You can count on us." I turned to Broadstairs. "You had an errand here, too, Sheriff?"

"I heard you got your first hunters. I need to check their licenses."

"They're out in the woods right now. But we can provide a

nice little snack for you if you want to wait. Just tell Angelita at the register that it's on the house."

"Well, now," said Broadstairs, "I wouldn't mind that at all. Heard tell you turn out a fine meal here. C'mon, Will."

Bethinho and I were just finishing the door repair when Vee returned in her Volkswagen.

Getting out of the car in her short skirt, she managed to flash her panties at me and anyone else who happened to be watching. She grinned as I came over.

"Mr. McClinton, you look all hot and sweaty."

"Nothing a little swim won't cure. Care to join me?"

"Oh, I couldn't. I expect to be very busy soon."

She opened a plastic CVS bag, and I looked inside.

The bag held nothing but a box of condoms and some lube.

"Gotta seal the deal," she said, with a wink and leer that could have been mistaken for a brokenhearted spasm of pain. She had so emptied her heart that all the universe's cold, aching darkness had flooded in.

35

I was still distressed by the crude implications of what Vee had so blithely shown me (How could she accept her filthy part in this scheme with such unconcern?) when Rushlow and Digweed returned, bearing one scrawny turkey carcass between them. I "happened" to cross their path before they could get to their room. Maybe now they would pump me for info on the lodge. But they must have been too beat to bother.

The two men looked exhausted, with smudged faces and briar scratches on the backs of their hands. It seemed that following their arsonist playboy boss around from restaurant to office to nightclub in a plush urban environment took less effort than bushwhacking all day in thick woods.

Rushlow held out the dead bird. "Hey, man, you think your kitchen grunts could dress this for us and put it on ice?"

I took the turkey by its limp neck. "Of course. I only wish you'd bagged a few more. Maybe better luck tomorrow."

"Yeah, well, that's the thing. We weren't so thrilled with the hunting. Kinda tough terrain. And that interstate running through your land pretty much scares all the critters off. Only way it could be worse is if there was an exit onto your place. Be pretty easy then for just about anyone to come and go. But that don't matter. I think we're gonna split tomorrow. We've seen enough."

I tried to convey that I would miss their money more than I would miss them personally. "Oh, that's really too bad. Well, don't judge us too harshly. Might just have been your lousy fortune not to run across any game today. I hope you'll tell your friends how well we treat our guests. Business is really booming. And you might have better luck with the bears in the upcoming season."

Digweed seemed disgusted. "I don't need to think about tussling with no motherfuckin' bears right now. All's I want's a hot shower."

"I hear you," I said. "But you need to see the sheriff first. He's over in the dining hall. Came to check your hunting licenses. I told you he was a stickler for regulations and such."

I was pleased to see Rushlow and Digweed exchange a small look of tense alertness. Let them feel uneasy. Nerves never sharpened anyone's perceptions or planning ability. If you could get your opponent riled or nervous, in the courtroom or elsewhere, you had an advantage.

I conducted my guests over to the dining hall. Schreiber and Broadstairs were enjoying their draft beers and playing the pinball machine we had installed a few days ago (Adkins Gaming Supplies had been another name on the list Broadstairs gave us). The lodge's former owners had held a beer-and-wine license, and once we chose the distributor on the sheriff's list, reactivating the license was a cinch.

Sheriff Broadstairs played until the ball finally sneaked past the flippers, before turning his attention to the two out-of-towners. He scrutinized their hunting licenses with frustrating slowness, then asked for their driver's licenses for comparison. At last, he pronounced himself satisfied, and Messrs. Digweed and Rushlow hastened off.

Broadstairs regarded me with an inscrutable attitude. "Those boys come an awful long way for just a day or two of turkey shooting. But city folks can be peculiar. Anyhow, they helped you pay your bills, right?"

"I suppose."

"Will, let's hit the road. I could enjoy the hospitality a while longer, but I got malefactors to upbraid. You, too, I expect."

I was happy to watch the sheriff's car depart.

By now it was late afternoon, and I hadn't seen Nellie since she kissed me goodbye in bed early this morning. That was too long to be apart.

I found her at her desk with her feet up, having an iced coffee. She had insisted we stock this Caboverde brand, Pico do Fogo, which Gonsalves Provisions carried. More expensive than other brands, but the taste was worth it. I was hooked now myself.

She looked weary. I borrowed her cup and had a sip.

"Christ, how many sugars did you use?"

"I got to keep extra sweet for you, *verdade*?"

"*Seguro* times ten."

She smiled, but without her usual bright enthusiasm. "Oh, *minha nossa,* am I beat. I been going almost twelve hours now. When I came here as a kid, I never knew all the work that went into running this place. Kids never know nothing adults gotta go through. I think it's gonna be a quick supper, then early bedtime for me tonight, if you don't mind."

She looked so sweet and so vulnerable, gorgeous, and dedicated that I ached for her. I wanted to tell her that her hard work would pay off soon, that all her worries and striving would be over. But I couldn't bring her into the scheme without the consent of all. And I didn't even think it would be a wise move. Nellie might be too conflicted about it, given her obvious attachment to the lodge. But once I presented her with the fait accompli of the sale to Nancarrow, she would have no choice but to hop aboard the gravy train. It wasn't as if I were doing her some disservice by offering to split five million dollars with her in exchange for abandoning this two-bit operation, was it?

"Nélida, I could never mind anything you do. You want me to bring you dinner in our room?"

"No, I like to see how the customers are enjoying themselves. I get feedback on how to improve things." She drained her coffee, then swung her feet off the desk. "Let's move it, *você preguiçoso!*"

Dinner was simple but delicious: fried chicken and sweet potato fries and homemade coleslaw. But Nellie could barely keep her eyes open. I saw her off to bed around seven thirty.

As I was leaving our room to make a last circuit of the property, Sandralene found me.

She put her lips close to my ear, bending to do so, and I almost got dizzy at her hot, scented whisper.

"Stan wants to see you."

"Where is he?"

"In his kayak, in that little cove to the east. Come on, I'll row you out."

In the skiff, I considered offering to take the oars, then realized the futility of trying to be more capable than Sandralene.

Stan floated in his kayak like a large cork in a small bottle. Gentle wavelets lapped at the grassy bank as he stirred his paddle just enough to stay in place. The dense canopy over the cove cut down on even the dwindling remnants of daylight from the darkening sky, but I could still see well enough to admire Stan's thick blond beard. I suddenly realized how much I missed having him around.

"Jesus, how long you been out there in the woods, big guy? You look like you haven't shaved in six months."

"Yeah, well, I got nothing better to do with all that testosterone, since Sandy ain't using it. But we ain't here to admire my rugged good looks. Get me up to speed."

When I was done, Stan nodded sagely and said, "Everything's working out perfect, just like I planned. Send Sandy for me when Digweed and Rushlow leave, and I'll slip back into the lodge for a few hots and a bath and some mattress time—and I don't mean sleeping."

Stan paddled over to our craft and leaned in to kiss Sandralene. She leaned, too, nearly dunking all of us in the process. Then we split up.

Back on land, I continued my patrol of the property. I wasn't even sure why I bothered, but it was a habit by now and made me feel that I was accomplishing something.

In the room occupied by Nancarrow's boys, the lights were on and the curtains were drawn. But the unmistakable noises from within painted a clear enough picture of what was going on.

Vee's laughter held a manic edge that no one but me would notice.

36

Following Rushlow and Digweed's departure, Stan came back to the lodge for a hedonistic twenty-four hours. He scraped the yellow hedge off his face, tanked up on hot food to dispel the bitter memories of his cold canned meals under the stars, and monopolized Sandralene's ardent ministrations for a good eight of those hours.

When Nellie eventually got a chance to talk with him, she took one of his big hands in both of hers, gazing at him with those liquid brown eyes. "Stan," she said, "nobody's gonna find you or hurt you if I have anything to say about it."

He seemed genuinely touched. "Well, thanks, kid. But it seems like *I* should be protecting *you*. I hear you're working yourself down to the bone, managing this joint. Ain't that partner of mine a righteous enough dude to make your life easier? He should be shouldering all the work."

"Oh, no! *Verdade*, Glen works as hard as me. It's just that the lodge takes so much effort and attention. That's why I'm glad you're back. We can really use your help."

Stan looked guilty and a little nervous. "Uh, well, you see,

I ain't rightly returned full-time yet. Those boys, Dickwad and Rashblow—I got a feeling they ain't gonna give up so easy. They'll be back, and I can't let 'em catch me. So you guys are still gonna have to soldier on without me. But just for a little while longer, I promise. Then everything'll be jake. No more worries."

"You truly promise?"

"On my sister's virginity."

Nellie's phone rang then, and she left on one of her endless problem-solving missions.

I said to Stan, "You don't even have a sister."

"I do, but she's the champion mattressback of State U. Once, in a generous mood, she took on *both* teams in the big Thanksgiving Day game, then went home to her boyfriend and complained she wasn't getting enough!"

I was drinking an iced coffee at the time and snorted a few ounces of it out my nose. "You are such a bullshitter."

"I totally agree. But hey, I always keep you on your toes and laughing, right? Life's too short, bro. I'm just glad to see you loosening up a little."

"That's only because I have abandoned all hope that we're going to come out of this with our skins intact, never mind a profit. And also, maybe because I'm getting more sex. So what's the truth? Do you have a sister or not?"

"Let's just say that birth control was not a big priority in the Gulch that my folks lived in. Not many families with just one kid. And it's safe to figure that any sister of mine has probably got to fall *somewhere* on the spectrum between virgin and slut."

Hearing about the sex life of Stan's sister, whether real or imaginary, made the specter of Vee's interlude with Rushlow and Digweed burst into my mind again. After that dutifully orgiastic night, she had retreated from their quarters to the room she shared with Ray, and had not emerged since. I tried to get some sense of how she was doing from Ray, when he came out to fetch her meals. But he just looked at me without a trace of guile or irony, and said, "Vee is my teacher, Mr. Glen. She has always been good to me. I like to see her happy."

I couldn't take that as anything but a reproach, intended or not.

Finally, I came up with a way to learn how she was doing, without looking overly worried. I called for another late-night meeting in Stan's cabin, before he went back into hiding.

Ahead of the meeting, I told Stan of my concerns: how Vee might be traumatized by what she had felt obliged to put herself through. Stan was worried only about her ability to bring off the seduction of Nancarrow.

"You think she's losing her taste for what she's gotta do? Is she gonna crack or maybe pull out?"

"I doubt it. I get the impression that if she ever breaks, it will be a sudden and complete collapse."

Stan pondered this. "Well, like I told you way back when, she is one tough broad with a giant-size hate for Nancarrow. I think she can drive herself through anything, right through to the end."

"Okay," I said, "but at what cost?"

"Everything she's got to give, probably. But sometimes that's the price you gotta pay for whatever you gotta have."

My own lousy sacrifice of a quarter-million dollars and a few weeks of my time began to look meager by comparison.

Dressed demurely again, Vee Aptekar was the last to arrive. Although I had never seen her smoke before, she had a smoldering cigarette pasted between her unpainted lips and otherwise exhibited a wan indifference.

I tried to fill my voice with kindness. "Hi, Vee. Good to see you up and around."

She exhaled a plume of smoke. "Yeah, thanks. I was just taking a short vacation from all the good times, but I'm okay now."

Stan shot me a look as if to say, *You see? Everything's cool.* I wasn't so sure, but I had to take Vee at her own self-appraisal.

"Well, just let us know how we can help."

"You all do your part, and let me do mine. I'm all right."

Stan took over the discussion. "Now that we got that settled, there's not really much else to lay out. The plan is working like a dream. Expect Nancarrow any day. He ain't gonna send no lawyer, no front man. He likes to scope out new properties himself. Always has. Just remember, glory means as much to him as dough. And since he stands to make a whole lot of both, he's gonna be all over the scene."

Apparently reassured by Vee's stoicism, Stan addressed her contribution forthrightly, without any euphemistic crap.

"Vee, you know I didn't ask you to ball those two slimy shit-for-brains. But that's only because I didn't think of it. I figure your instincts were rock solid. You sent them back to the city with their heads spinning. And the way they love to gloat about chicks they've banged, Nancarrow is gonna arrive here practically with his dick in his hand. With Glen's bullshit and your, um, assets, Algy's gonna get so twisted around, he might offer us *more'n* twenty million!"

Vee lit a new cigarette off the butt of the old one. "Wow, thanks, Stan. A girl likes to be appreciated for her talents."

"I'll settle for the original twenty," I said, trying to divert the discussion back to money.

Ray spoke up. "Now that I have been looking into banks and similar things, I believe I could increase my share by making some smart financial investments. If anyone else cares to trust me with a portion of their share, I will try to do the same for you. I think more money is always better than less money."

Stan clapped Ray on the back. "You're too generous, kid. Thanks, but no thanks. I figure straight interest on five million will carry me and Sandy a long way."

"I'll consider it," I said.

Stan said, "Is that FedEx envelope from Vegas all set?"

Ray had arranged, through his dark-web pals, for an empty FedEx envelope bearing the originating address of Prynne Resorts, Inc., to be sent from Las Vegas once Nancarrow was here to see it arrive. When he later saw the letter on Prynne's stationery, offering to buy our property for twenty million, he would assume it had been delivered that day by FedEx, thus tipping us off to the property's value.

"Yes, Mr. Stan, all set."

"Okay, then. High fives all around!"

Vee gave all hands a bored slap. Ray, evidently seeing the opportunity to emulate his baseball heroes, jumped up awkwardly with each salute. Each of Sandralene's hearty slaps traveled down her arm to give her breast a mesmerizing jiggle.

"I gotta go away again now," Stan said. "I wish I could be here to see that peerless turd Algy swallow the hook, but it just can't happen. So I'm counting on all of you to etch in your brains how dumb he looks, and share it with me when I get back. Before we go our separate ways, anyhow."

The meeting dissolved. Outside the cabin, as Stan was snugging into his pack, he said, "So, you're still coming with me and Sandy to the islands, right?"

"Sure. Of course."

"And you want to bring Nellie with you?"

"Yes."

Stan thought a while. "We're gonna have to figure out how to clue her in to the real deal then. It has to be handled just right. Let me think about it while I'm sittin' in the woods with nothing else to do."

Stan walked off to where his kayak was beached, and I tried to imagine him as a rough-hewn Thoreau, mining philosophical gems in his isolation by the shore.

But such a fantasy evidently required a bolder imagination than mine.

37

It was just around noon on a bright Friday, with the weather holding unseasonably warm. Walking out of the office, I wondered idly how climate change might affect our resort. Would the lake remain full all summer? Would the high season get extended? Wet kids dashed around, yelling and ignoring their mothers' calls to get out and dry off for lunch. A party of six nonresident hikers emerged from the woods, heading for the dining hall as if beckoned by the enticing smells that wafted from its open windows.

I was expecting the arrival of our band. For the first time, we were trying live music. It was just a local jazz trio, but one with a good statewide rep. The Lucky Graves Group, featuring a slightly unorthodox combo of sax, keyboard, and drums. Nellie had thought they might draw people from Centerdale, nonguests who would make the drive and drop some much-needed dollars. Dubious at first, I soon caved under the force of her enthusiasm.

"Glen, you got to take a chance!" she said. "Spend money to make money. You'll see! Why'd we ever build that little stage in the dining room if we aren't ever going to use it?"

"I dunno, maybe because DiPippo forced it on us to jack

up his bill, and we had to agree if we wanted to keep him and Broadstairs happy?"

"Ay, you cynic! Always with the downers. Trust me, this is gonna be great. Besides, maybe I can get these guys to play some *batuque*—after midnight, when all the kids have gone to bed. I think I heard they know how. You watch me dance *batuque*, you are gonna explode in your pants!"

With a promise like that, it was hard to refuse.

But Nellie and her *batuque* prowess were nowhere around at this crucial moment, as I heard the sound of tires on gravel and looked up.

Like some infernal harbinger of doom, the black Escalade rolled onto the grounds of the Bigelow Junction Motor Lodge as smoothly and inexorably as a storm cloud. I tried to see it as a talisman of our imminent good fortune, but the vibe it gave off was not amenable to any optimistic spin.

I went back inside the office and told our clerk, Anildo Pereira, to go to Vee's unit and deliver a message.

"Tell her the fish has arrived and is ready to be gutted and filleted."

Anildo seemed puzzled. He and the rest of the new staff knew Vee only in her role as the motel tramp. "I didn't know Ms. Aptekar helped in the kitchen."

"Just run and tell her, okay? But don't make a big deal out of your errand, right?"

I supposed I should have gone out and boldly greeted Nancarrow and company at their car, putting on my Mr. Greedy Hospitality Guy hat just as I had a few days ago for Digweed and Rushlow. But instead, trying to master my emotions and nerves, I pretended not to notice the SUV's arrival and stepped back inside the office and waited for them to come to me. I double-checked the registrations to make sure the two units reserved for our trophy fish were still vacant. And, of course, they were.

The screen door of the office opened outward under the hand of someone hazed by the sunlight into a white glare.

It proved to be Buck Rushlow, followed closely by Needles Digweed. They swept in like the king's advance guard, looking left and right. And behind them, an impeccably put together Barnaby Nancarrow. Dapper, self-assured, radiant from Pilates and the tanning salon. A true master of the universe, even though that universe had been born in the white-hot big bang of many arson events.

Now or never, do or die. Into the valley of death rode the lonely ex-junkie disbarred lawyer ...

My smile radiated game-show-host wattage. "Why, Mr. Digweed and Mr. Rushlow! Very nice to see you. Though frankly, I am surprised to have a chance to greet you again so soon. I thought we had disappointed you."

"Naw," said Rushlow. "We didn't mean half that shit we said. Just woke up on the wrong side of the bed that morning."

"In fact," Digweed chimed in, "when we got home we told our boss about what a great place you had, and he insisted on coming up for the weekend. No hunting, though—just relaxing. He even brought us along, since we had to cut our vacation short before. He's a pretty great guy."

"This is him," said Rushlow. "Glen McClinton, Barnaby Nancarrow."

The way Rushlow intoned Nancarrow's name, you might have thought I was being introduced to a hybrid of Prince Charles, the Koch brothers, and George Clooney.

I shook hands with Nancarrow. He had a decent grip that was obviously doled out according to some kind of internal meter that registered the importance and net worth of the recipient. I moved the needle a tad past halfway. I had something he wanted, but I didn't possess much status or value on my own.

"Pleased to meet you, Mr. Nancarrow."

His plummy voice betrayed none of his underclass roots.

"Barnaby, of course. And I'll call you Glen."

Although I had met Nancarrow that one time at a party, during my respectable days, and had seen him at a distance on our way out of the city, this was my first real chance to take him in up close. I had to admit, he was a handsome bastard. Tall, sandy-haired, eyes the color of windshield-washer fluid. His clean-shaven profile might have allowed him to serve capably as the TV-commercial spokesman for a pricey brand of liquor that didn't taste very good compared to less-famous beverages, but which coasted along on chic patrons and astute product placement. He kept himself in top shape with what must have amounted to twelve hours a week in the gym. His determinedly casual outfit must have run him somewhere north of two thousand dollars, not counting the shoes. As a former fan of male finery, I recognized Paul Stuart tailoring. A cashmere and silk zip-neck sweater in forest green, gray houndstooth wool trousers, blue suede hiking boots. The final touch would have looked ridiculous if Stan or I or most other guys had tried it, but somehow, he managed to carry it off: a light-as-air silk scarf printed with ancient Persian warriors on horseback, in a palette of golds and browns. I figured the warrior motif was meant as subtle intimidation.

I don't think I was too obvious in my appraisal, or took too long in making it. Nonetheless, he seemed to register my scanning for what it was, generously permitting it, even basking in it, as if he were accustomed to such admiration wherever he went. It was his way of silently saying, *Admire me all you wish; you will never measure up.*

But despite his flawless dress, his manicure and epidermal exfoliation, his intelligent gaze and lofty air of superiority, and his name on all those elegant plaques outside so many doors, there remained about him an ineradicable nimbus of Gulch alum Algy Teague—an oily exudate compounded of coarse avarice, desperate striving, and a carefully masked sense of inferiority. I could easily believe that here was the man who had ordered Stan Hasso to torch so many of his holdings.

Or maybe I was just projecting onto him the insecurities I wanted him to bear. Maybe I couldn't stand the thought that he had succeeded in transforming himself from his rough origins into something better, while I had taken the opposite course.

Nancarrow's next words were a little disconcerting.

"Glen, my associates and I took an awful chance in coming up here unannounced."

"Oh?"

"Yes. In our spontaneous excitement, we neglected to book ahead. Now we can only pray that you have lodgings for us at your fine establishment, and on such a busy weekend."

"Well, it seems you're in luck, Barnaby. We do have two rooms, thanks to an unexpected cancellation. I assume that Mr. Rushlow and Mr. Digweed won't mind doubling up again?"

"Boys? Any objections?"

The smarmy duo, no doubt recalling the fun they had as bunkmates with their casual motel tramp earlier, registered no complaints.

Anildo returned just then and eyed me significantly, as if to say, *Message delivered.* Leaving him to handle the paperwork, I took the unit keys.

"Let me show you to your rooms. We can pick up your luggage as well."

The bodyguards went through the door first. But despite their precautionary vigil, as Nancarrow exited, he was nearly bowled over by someone hurtling into him.

38

Vee had outdone herself in come-fuck-me allure, without actually teetering over into hookerwear. She wore a little flowing, flouncy white summer dress with spaghetti straps, revealing much and hinting at the rest. Her tanned legs fairly glowed. Platform sandals with straw uppers added statuesque inches to her height, and the classic seductive arch to her posture.

Bouncing back off Nancarrow, Vee fell against the willing arms of Rushlow and Digweed. She righted herself with a hand on each man's chest. They looked both flustered and titillated, with a veneer of embarrassment at their failure to catch Vee before she had caromed into their boss.

"Oh, boys, thank you so much!"

Nancarrow rapidly regained his aplomb and adjusted the minor kinks in his attire. He regarded Vee with unabashed desire modulated only by the immense number of women he had possessed.

"Oh, Mr. McClinton, I am *so* sorry! You know I don't generally run around knocking people down—especially impressive strangers! It's just that I was so upset, I had to hurry over to get your help. When I stepped out of my room, there was a *snake* on my doorstep! And he was huge!"

"I don't believe we've had a single snake sighting around the lodge before this, Miss Pomestu."

Since Vee could not very well go by her real last name—the surname of Nancarrow's betrayed partner of yore—she had coined this one.

Vee scowled now at my judgmental attitude about her snake sighting, and put fire in her tone and eyes, making her all the sexier. "Are you saying I *imagined* the snake, Mr. McClinton?"

"No, no, of course not. It's just that—"

Nancarrow graciously but firmly interrupted. "This could all be handled so much more efficiently by simply going over to the young lady's room and checking for any slithering trespassers. May I offer my services, Miss ..."

"Pomestu. But you can call me Vee. Oh, and I haven't said sorry yet for bumping into you. I'm so sorry!"

"The encounter was actually quite pleasant, Vee. I'm Barnaby Nancarrow, by the way."

Vee accepted Nancarrow's hand and held on to it a beat longer than etiquette demanded. Rushlow and Digweed were smirking behind her back until they caught the steely look in Nancarrow's eyes and shifted to more formal demeanor.

"Pomestu—that's an unusual last name."

"It was originally Estonian. That's where my grandparents came from. But I'm afraid it got messed up when they came to America."

"Well, I have to say that based on what I have seen, Vee, Estonia must be home to some of the most gorgeous women in the world."

"That is so sweet of you to say, Barnaby!" Vee huffed at me. "At least *some* people know how to treat a lady."

"Shall we go and investigate now?"

"Please. I'd be ever so grateful."

I accompanied all four to Vee's doorstep, just a few yards from the office. Of course, no snake was to be seen.

Nancarrow was pure solicitude. "Do you suppose it could have gotten inside, Vee? Perhaps we should check."

"Oh, would you, please?"

She unlocked her door, and Nancarrow and I followed her through while his two muscle heads stood guard outside.

The room represented the essence of bachelorette existence: a bit of whimsy in the stuffed animals and decorative pillows, some hard-edged practicality in the stockings and slip drying over the back of a chair, and some desperate touches in the overflowing ashtray and stack of *Cosmo* magazines. There was no trace of Ray Zerkin, of course. He was now bunking with me, and Nellie was sharing Sandralene's cabin.

Explaining these new arrangements to Nellie without revealing the scam had taken some delicate footwork. Luckily, we had never gotten too specific about why Vee and Ray were here at the lodge in the first place. We had just let Nellie assume they were friends of Stan's who needed a place to stay.

I eventually boiled down my lies to a new and fictitious incompatibility between Vee and Ray.

* * *

"Ay, I can see that," Nellie had said. "That Vee, she's really gone off the rails. I don't understand it. Those first few days after I came here, she seemed okay. *Talvez um poku frio.* Maybe kind of distant, you know? And all those weeks when the workmen were here, she kept a low profile. She could have been hitting on them, but nothing. Then, once we go into operation, *bam!* She turns into some kind of *mulher de vida fácil.* It's hard to figure."

"People are strange," I said.

"*Verdade!*" At the time, we were behind the screen in the office, and Nellie snuggled into me, all soft, firm curves and pleasant scents. "But, Glen, this is going to make sleeping together impossible for us!"

I had been so engrossed in carrying out our entrapment of Nancarrow, I completely failed to consider this. "It's just for a little while," I said. "Bookings will tail off when the high season's over, and we'll get Ray set up in his own room. Meanwhile, we can always steal an hour here or there when he or Sandy is out."

"Oh, I hope so, Glen!" she had said, with a kiss full of fleshly promise.

* * *

Now Vee said, "I don't see any snake. Oh, my God, maybe it's under the bed! Mr. McClinton, would you look? I think you should be able to ensure that your guests are safe!"

I got down on my hands and knees and scoped out the dust kitties under the bed. When I got back on my feet, Vee was just pulling back from whispering in Nancarrow's ear. He did not seem displeased.

I tried to sound suitably annoyed yet deferential to a paying customer. "Miss Pomestu, if you're done with us now, I have to get Mr. Nancarrow set up."

"Oh, of course. Sorry to be such trouble!"

Vee stood in her doorway and watched us proceed a few yards away to the two adjacent units that would accommodate Nancarrow and his lunks. Nancarrow looked back at her before going inside. Vee waved happily at him.

If there was ever a man who did not think with his gonads, I hadn't met him.

39

I thought I could spare a few minutes from supervising everything at the lodge to go see Stan and not get caught doing it. I missed his reassuring presence more than I had expected. And maybe I still felt he was the senior partner, and just needed some attaboys from him, and another pair of shoulders to bear the angst. Also, he might have some thoughts about how to bring Nellie up to speed on what was really going on. Contemplating the moment when I had to disclose everything to her was giving me the heebie-jeebies.

The hired band, the Lucky Graves Group, scheduled to go on at eight, had shown up around five in a hard-used white Ford van with some amateurishly drawn musical notes adorning its sides. Nellie introduced me to the ebullient Lothar "Lucky" Graves, the leader and sax man. The skinny, plain-faced woman on drums was Maxie Trimmer, and the keyboardist was a chunky bearded guy named Ledger Danielson. Once they had inspected the room and the stage, they settled down in the shade of a chestnut tree for a noodling rehearsal. Lodge patrons, attracted by the music, came and went. Ms. Trimmer had only part of her kit set up, and Danielson was fooling around with what looked like a child's toy keyboard, but they sounded pretty good, and I hoped their reputation would draw in the Centerdale crowd that Nellie anticipated.

I checked out the kitchen, then headed to my room to get into my swim trunks. Nellie intercepted me halfway there.

"Glen, this new guest—who is he? He came with those hunter jerks who were here before, and I had him figured for just another *olho do cu* like them. But he seems more high class. Pretty nice, in fact. You know what he just asked me to do?"

It flashed through my mind that Nancarrow had decided to hit on Nellie as backup, just in case he crapped out with Vee, and I started to get mad. I also felt a little nervous that she might say something to him that would unsettle our scam, or that he would say something about a possible sale of the lodge—he hadn't broached the matter with me yet. I really didn't want the two of them getting chatty.

"I don't know anything about him, really," I said. "The hunter boys said he was their boss. Boss of what kind of business, I can't say. Maybe he runs a club and they're his bouncers. I have to admit, he does have better manners than those two mooks. But he's also a lech. He'd like nothing better than to perv on a sweet young thing like you."

"Ay, you're jealous! It's so cute! No, believe me, I didn't get those vibes from him. He just wanted me to arrange a favor. He brought his own champagne with him. Two cases of Dom Pérignon—I seen the labels. You know what that juice costs? About two hundred dollars a bottle! He just wanted to know if we had room to chill it down, and I told him *seguro*."

I felt myself relax. "Oh. That's all right, then."

"Maybe he'll share it with us if we ask nice. I never tasted stuff that good before!"

"Well, let's just concentrate on showing him a good time, and maybe he'll feel generous. Don't go bugging him."

"Bugging him? I got too much to do!"

She kissed me quick and scurried off.

I unlocked the door to my room. The shades were drawn, and the Ray Zerkin fug of spilled snack foods and teenage sweat was thick but not terrible. As an adolescent, I had no doubt generated just such a musty atmosphere back in my hooked-on-video-games days. I thought of how my parents had indulged me back then, and a pang of regret and nostalgia shot through me.

Looking up from his iPad, the first thing Ray said was, "I miss Vee. When can I go back with her, Mr. Glen?"

"Well, Ray, you probably won't be sharing a room with Vee again up here at the lodge. You know that our scheme is in its end stages, right? In large part, thanks to you. And so, with any luck, we're all going to get rich and go our separate ways. Now, you should be safe in your old stomping grounds, just so long as you don't go spending your money too fast and too loud. Nancarrow doesn't even know you exist. And you have to keep it that way by staying hidden while he's here, even though it's boring and a pain."

"I have covered my online trail so no one can find it, Mr. Glen."

I leaned back against the closed door of our quarters, suddenly feeling a little sapped. "Good, good, I expected nothing less. So you're going home soon, and I suspect you'll see Vee there as much as you ever did." A thought crossed my mind. "Has she told you what she intends to do after we pull this off?"

"Vee has said to me that she would like to change her name and start a new life somewhere. But I always hoped it would not be too far away from me, so I could still see her. I assume she would tell me her new name." Ray grew contemplative. "But you know, there is always Skype."

Change her name and start a new life. She'd be hard to locate after that. For a moment, I fantasized that she would come to the Cape Verde Islands with the rest of us. Although I had a hard time imagining what kind of ménage would suit her, Nellie, and me.

"Well, Ray, there's no point worrying about the future. We can't always know how things will work themselves out."

"That is pretty much how I feel, too, Mr. Glen."

* * *

I changed into my trunks, grabbed a towel, and headed to the beach.

This late in the day, no other swimmers were around to see me enter the water and start stroking east, close to shore. I hadn't had a chance to take a swim for too many days, and the water, still holding the unseasonable warmth, felt wonderful.

I reached the little cove where Sandralene and I had met Stan a few nights ago. His camp had to be some distance in from the water, and I watched for his beached kayak as marker.

My arms and legs were tiring—I must have swum half a mile—and I almost didn't spot the unnaturally straight line amid the surrounding organic shapes and contours. I swam to the mossy bank and rested a minute. The earth smelled rich and loamy. Then, with my bare feet feeling every pebble and my bare calves feeling every twig and briar, I went deeper into the under- brush until I came upon Stan's tent.

I poked my head inside the tent flap. "Stan?"

I was immediately grabbed from behind in a viselike hold and lifted off the ground, then swung around and plopped down.

Stan Hasso grinned. "I heard you coming for about the last ten minutes, even while you were still in the water. Just wanted to show you it's hard to catch me unaware-like."

"My aching ribs are a testament to your Natty Bumppo tradecraft."

"All right, then! What brings you out here, anyhow?"

Still rubbing my side, I said, "I wanted to fill you in on today." I gave Stan the rundown on Nancarrow's arrival and Vee's setting of the hook. Then I said, "I was also wondering if you had any great ideas on how to break the news to Nellie when the shit goes down."

"Yeah, it came to me, and it's simple. Once Nancarrow signs the bill of sale, we have to move fast. We don't tell your girl how much we sold the place for, and we damn sure don't tell her that Nancarrow bought what he figures is casino land and that he's bound to shut the lodge down. We let her think the place will keep running under new ownership as a gravy train for all her cousins. And we get her sympathy by saying we just couldn't run at a loss anymore and had to make a deal. Poor Uncle Ralph, his life savings gone, boo-hoo-hoo. But everything's hunky-dory now, because we even turned a little profit. Then you say, 'Nellie, you sweet piece of ass, I am totes in love with you and your ancestral rock pile, and now I want to go live the simple life in Cape Verde. Will you come with me?' Once she says yes and you're safely overseas, then you can give her the full story. But not till then."

"And you think she'll buy it?"

"Glen, that is up to your smooth tongue—in more ways than one!"

40

Nellie was ecstatic.

"Oh, *minha nossa*! This is just like I remember from the old days, when I was little! Happy crowds under the stars! People are gonna be talking the lodge up so big after this, we are bound to have so much success!"

Nellie's business instincts had proved spot-on. The hoped-for crowds from Centerdale and the surrounding area had indeed shown up for this Friday night performance by the Lucky Graves Group. There had to be close to seventy jazz fans present, in addition to the lodge residents. We should have posted a cover charge.

Arriving back at the lodge after my clandestine visit with Stan, my arms and legs felt rubbery from the long swim. I changed into the nice linen slacks and sports shirt befitting the host of such a popular venue and dived right into my duties, earning a grateful smile from Nellie as she bossed her crew.

The tables and chairs nearest the stage were pulled back and squeezed together to make space for dancing. Seating quickly filled up, and since the night was warm and cloudless, we could leave the tall hinged windows open for a pavilion effect. Moreno and Jaaziel had raided the garage and come back with thirty cheap folding chairs gifted to us by the happy-to-be-gone former owners. They were cobwebbed and grimy, and I had to enlist some of the off-duty staff to hose them down and dry them off. We went through all our week's utility towels, and I made a mental note to call the laundry service first thing tomorrow.

In surprisingly short time, we had ranks of chairs set up on the grass around the dining hall, most with a view of the stage.

The regular dining hall staff of six included only two waitresses and four workers in the kitchen. That was enough during the days, but not tonight. So I enlisted our housekeepers, Rosa and Simonica, to circulate and serve drinks and food. The prospect of overtime pay plus tips put fresh spring in their tired step.

By the time the band launched into their first number, drinks were flowing, dancers were swaying, and bowls of spicy goat stew were sliding onto tabletops just as smoothly as if we did this sort of thing every night.

Finally free of duties, I could zero in on Vee and Nancarrow.

Somehow, Nancarrow had secured the best table, centered perfectly across the dance area from the stage. Only he and Vee sat there; Rushlow and Digweed stood at opposite points across the room. Allowed to nurse a cold beer apiece, they also seemed to appreciate the music—as well as the lovely figures of our waitresses and any other women in sight.

I sauntered over to Nancarrow's table. One of his bottles of Dom Pérignon nestled in a makeshift cooler: a plastic bucket that had held shucked clams, now decoratively swaddled in a cloth napkin and filled with ice. In the absence of real champagne flutes, two narrow wineglasses sparkled with bubbly.

"Barnaby, Miss Pomestu, I hope you're enjoying yourselves."

Vee wore a black cocktail dress, black stockings, and heels, and Nancarrow had broken out a different two-thousand-dollar getup.

"You bet we are," said Vee. "This is the most fun this old joint has shown me since I got here."

Nancarrow seemed genuinely relaxed. No one would ever have surmised by his genial, laid-back attitude that he was here on a mission: to use his insider knowledge to bilk the lodge's unsuspecting owners of Steve Prynne's yet-unannounced opportunity. He just seemed like a nice, albeit pompous and self-satisfied, guy on vacation.

His easygoing demeanor suddenly hit me as postcoital bliss. But surely he and Vee could not have gotten down to it so quickly, just a couple of hours after meeting. The kind of woman Vee was representing herself to be would surely hold out—and be expected to hold out by the man eager to get in her pants—for at least a little extravagant courtship, some champagne and dancing, before she came across. I looked more intently at Nancarrow and decided that no, he hadn't closed the deal with Vee yet. He was just this good at what he did. Somehow, he was able to segregate his hedonism from his avarice, his personal life from his business dealings, in a way that I could not. It seemed to speak of a Zen-like in-the-moment ease with whatever life brought. Or maybe just a high-functioning sociopathy. Paradoxically, this ability to compartmentalize made him seem all the more formidable an opponent, and I reminded myself not to underestimate him. When he was focused on business, he would be just as intent on winning as he now was on enjoying himself.

"Indeed, Glen," said Nancarrow, "this is truly remarkable. Such a simple, almost primitive setup. No glitter, no glitz, but just look at how people are enjoying themselves. You know, I can see now why my boys insisted I come up here for the weekend. This place of yours has a lot of potential."

"Why, thanks, Barnaby. I take it you have some experience with operations like this one."

"Oh, I dabble in a lot of things to earn a living."

"Well, I have to circulate now. You folks enjoy yourselves!"

"Perhaps you'll join us a little later, Glen, when your duties permit. I have altogether too much champagne for just two people to consume. And by the way, thanks for letting me ice it down in your facilities."

"No trouble at all, really."

Nellie was in the kitchen, transferring warm beers from a case into the fridge. I mentally tried out the dialogue with her that Stan had outlined—suitably rephrased, of course—and in my dreamscape it all went smoothly. I began to relax a little more.

"Hey, girl," I said, "you've got to take it easy. Let the others do that."

Straightening up, Nellie suddenly looked weary, and she wiped sweat from her brow. "Maybe you got something there. I been running flat-out all day."

"Go sit in the corner over there, and I'll get you a drink and a bite."

I was happy to wait on her at the chopping block, where she had pulled up a stool. Watching her eat and drink like the young, healthy animal she was, I got the feeling that we could overcome any barriers arising from the sale of the lodge.

The food and drink had a tonic effect on Nellie. "Okay, *velho,* now I think you owe me a dance. I gotta loosen up for that *batuque* later that I promised you."

Out on the dance floor, Nellie felt good in my arms. Lucky Graves' sax was spinning out such a dense, elaborate sequence of notes that it took me a while to recognize that he was playing "All or Nothing at All."

Pivoting, I saw Nancarrow dancing with Vee, his hands low

down on the upper slope of her ass. The sight made me feel something, but I couldn't say exactly what.

The band's generous first set went till ten thirty. They came back on at a little past eleven, looking fresh and ready to rock.

The crowd thinned out around one a.m., most of them to make the long, twisty drive back to Centerdale. By two thirty, only a handful of outsiders and residents were hanging in. The place was a shambles of empty bottles, dirty dishes, and overturned folding chairs.

Nellie and I had been sitting with Vee and Nancarrow for an hour or so, not saying much. That Dom Pérignon had gone down like nectar, leaving us pleasantly stupefied.

Then, at the end of a number, Nellie jumped up. "It's *batuque* time! Lothar, you know what to do!"

Lothar nodded to the drummer, and she began laying down pure loping, looping Afro-Caribbean percussion, subtly underpinned by the sax and keyboard.

Nellie dashed out onto the emptying dance floor, and all the other Caboverdean girls followed her. They began chanting along with the drumming, repetitive phrases that seemed to invoke sultry tropical deities as black as interstellar space. It suddenly dawned on me just how close the Cape Verde Islands are to Africa, geographically and culturally.

Apparently, Caboverdean women were capable of completely untethering the lower half of their lithe bodies from the upper half, and moving their hips in mind-bogglingly intricate patterns that contained all the carnality in the universe, while gently waving their hands in a vaguely hula pattern. The effect was hypnotic.

Suddenly, an anomalous figure joined the dancers.

Sandralene.

She had been absent, I realized, from the earlier festivities. Maybe she had been moping over Stan's absence, or just wanted to steer clear of Nancarrow for fear of giving him some inadvertent entrée into stuff he shouldn't learn. Whatever the reason, she had been nowhere around till now, drawn out of seclusion, perhaps, by the change in music.

Sandralene tried her best to fit in. The other girls made space for her and tolerated her, trying to bring her into their rapturous dervish trance. But she just couldn't bring it off. Under any other circumstances, her dancing would have been appreciated, I was sure. She was adequately graceful and beyond sexy. But her Anglo-Amazon presence, her contrasting moves and attitude, came off as jarring and stiff. A bison among gazelles.

To give Sandralene credit, she didn't take long to realize her incongruousness, and she bowed herself off the dance floor and out of the hall with as much good spirits and panache as she could muster. But underneath the smiles, I thought I detected a wounded soul.

I excused myself to Nancarrow and Vee, who barely seemed to notice my departure. She had one leg draped over his lap and was leaning in to breathe in his ear.

I noticed that Rushlow and Digweed had made themselves scarce as well. Had they hooked up with some of our staff? There was nothing I could do about it if they had. I wasn't acting in loco parentis for our female employees. And despite the dormitory trailers being segregated by gender, I had good reason to suspect that there had already been plenty of liaisons among the workers—perhaps even between workers and guests. You could not confine a bunch of young people to a remote locale like this and not expect them to make out with each other.

I caught up with Sandralene as she approached her stand-alone cabin. The attenuated strains of the *batuque* still mocked her at this distance.

I put a hand on her shoulder. "Sandy? Sandralene? You okay?"

THE BIG GET-EVEN

In the shadows, I couldn't see whether she was crying. "Yeah, I'm fine. Thanks for asking."

"I liked your dancing."

She snorted. "I looked like a bumbling spaz next to those hot little things. I guess I'm getting old."

"Aw, c'mon, don't make me laugh. You are the sexiest woman at the lodge."

"It's awfully nice of you to say that, Glen. I could kiss you."

And so she did.

My head spun with booze and that incredible kiss. It was every bit as ripe and lush as I had ever imagined. For weeks now, since she first climbed into my car, this untouchable woman had inspired nothing but lust in my brain. And suddenly, it seemed as if the whole universe had inverted and my fantasies and reality had exchanged places.

Although it killed me to do so, I pushed her away.

"No, Sandy, Stan—"

She pulled me into her, grabbed me by one wrist, and put my hand on her ass.

"I know all about Stan, Glen. And he knows all about me. That's why he told me I could have you if he wasn't around. And now I'm gonna."

I really had assumed that my life was as complicated as it could ever get.

Ha.

PART FIVE

41

As the shadows paled into dawn, I was still wide awake. I hadn't slept one second of the past three and a half hours. The intimate and thrilling revelations of Sandralene's exotic bodily landscape, augmented by my own desire to match her ardor, had kept me going despite all the possible hindrances of too much liquor, free-floating anxiety, residual guilt over having sex with Stan's woman, and my long swim in the waters of Nutbush Lake. Sandy and I had rutted like the last two members of a dying species intent on repopulating the entire planet, and now I was satisfied, sore, and generally insentient. But not asleep.

Sandralene, by contrast, was snoring with the same less-than-ladylike gusto I had encountered that first night of our arrival at the lodge, when the three of us sacked out in the Impala.

Before she dropped off—as reliably sated, I hoped, as I was—I had whispered one question to her. "Why?"

"That's an easy one, Glen: I like you. And you saved Stan's life."

As she dropped off into deep sleep, her words ignited something like the explosion of an atomic bomb—all radiance and heat that lit up the inside of my skull. The whole past ten months, from that December night when I blasted a shot of Narcan up Stan Hasso's hairy nostrils, right down to the present moment, assailed me like a lifetime of memories compressed into a giant writhing, spiky organic mass and hurtled straight into my gut. I apprehended the whole insane yet seemingly predestined sequence of events not so much intellectually as with my entire nervous system. My bones and blood vessels resonated with the cosmic vibrations of the whole universe—or at least my minuscule portion of it.

It was as if someone had invented the most perfect virtual-reality device ever and I had been allowed to immerse myself, as an observer, into some stranger's existence before being ejected back into my own limited mental shell.

Of course I couldn't fall asleep after such an epiphany! It left me feeling somehow that no matter what came of it, every step of my path so far, even back to my misdeeds at the law firm, had been integral to my existence, the only possible expression of who I was and where I was going.

Nobody ever counts on getting such a moment of revelation. That's what makes it a revelation! Most of the time, we go our whole lives without any such windfall of grace and insight, dying as unaware as when we were born. And if such awakenings do come, we can never predict the circumstances surrounding them. I realized it was up to me to do something with this moment of clarity. But how?

One second, I was lying next to the whipsaw-emulating Sandralene, and the next instant I was on my feet, scrabbling for my clothes.

This was now Nellie's cabin, too! Where the hell was she? Had she maybe quietly opened the door while Sandralene and I were going at it, taken in the scene, and slunk away?

After shucking on my clothes, I cracked open the cabin door onto the dawn-lit estate. Not a soul in sight.

I slipped out. Where could Nellie be? Where had she spent the night? Maybe she, too, had given in to temptation and found another partner. That orgiastic dancing would surely have inflamed any woman's libido.

I thought of making my way back to the room I shared with Ray, and establishing an alibi for the night. But could I count on Ray backing up any story I manufactured? His sense of honesty was inhuman. Unlike the rest of us, he wasn't primed to utter white lies in most circumstances—another reason why we were keeping him sequestered. Not just for his own safety, but also because he might let slip a whole host of inconvenient truths.

A mild burst of laughter, male and female, issued from the direction of the dining hall. I went to investigate the source.

Amid the debris of the concert, the members of the Lucky Graves Group sat around a table with steaming mugs of coffee and plates of breakfast food half demolished. With them were Nellie and our chef, Jenise Rezende. The musicians had stopped playing last night sometime after I left with Sandralene, and they were still decompressing, having gotten no more sleep than I had.

Nellie jumped up when she saw me. She had dark crescents under her eyes and was disheveled from the dancing, but showed no sign of participation in any other vigorous recreational activity. Without knowing it, she stood on higher moral ground than I could lay claim to.

"*Ai*, Glen, that champagne! It made me a little nuts. And then with the dancing! Well, sometimes you just gotta cut loose, *verdade*? I been working so hard, I needed that."

She hugged me, and I had to pray that the liquor and my own sweat overwhelm the scent of Sandralene. "You got a little sleep, I hope? But how you like my dancing, huh? Was it everything I promised? It make you real *com tesão*, I bet!"

"Nellie, I … You mean so much to me."

I meant it. But of course, that declaration, while true enough, left out a lot.

She kissed me, then turned back to the musicians. "Hey, how come you think these guys play *batuque* so good? They all been to Boa Vista! They know Jenise's uncle there!"

I went over to the trio's table. "Thanks for your sublime performance. Whatever Nellie agreed to pay you, I'm sure you deserve twice as much."

Lothar grinned. "You want us back here, I'm gonna hold you to that, man."

We shook hands all around, and then the group got all their gear packed away in the ramshackle van and drove off.

Jenise stood up and said, "We're supposed to be serving breakfast starting at eight. Glen, do you think we could open an hour later? I need at least a few minutes' sleep. And the cleanup is going to be immense."

"Of course. Don't kill yourself. I don't think you're going to get many early risers today. And if they show up, they can have some coffee and wait."

Jenise gave a cavernous yawn and ambled off to the dormitory trailer.

Nellie said, "I gotta crash, too."

"Just go lie down," I said. "I got this."

She kissed me again and went off to Sandy's cabin, where we had just been screwing our brains out.

Somehow, my earlier epiphany upon hearing Sandralene's words had given me an inexplicable reservoir of energy. I felt wired, but without any accompanying turbulence of thought.

I collapsed all the folding chairs and stacked them for return to storage. I pushed all the indoor tables and chairs into some approximation of their usual places, then got a push broom and swept all the detritus on the floor out onto the grass for pickup. I secured several big rubber bus tubs and loaded all the dirty dishes and glasses and flatware into them. But before I could carry them into the kitchen, where our expensive dishwashing machine lay waiting, all my strength suddenly dissipated. Good enough. When the staff arrived, they would find a lot less to do.

I returned to my room. Ray Zerkin was sleeping like a baby. Without the eyeglasses, his face looked even younger. I had a shower, and the hot water invigorated me again. I still couldn't sleep, so I got my clothes back on and headed out the door.

On the edge of the manicured lawn (the industrial riding mower that handyman Bethinho Fonseca drove had chewed up three thousand dollars of Uncle Ralph's line of credit), I found the start of one of the trails favored by hikers. My all-consuming focus on our scam had never left me any time to venture far off the property in all the weeks we had been here. But now, somehow, I felt I could.

The well-marked path led through meadows fragrant with late-season wildflowers, shadowy alleys of birches, a small rocky brook. Eventually, the trail began to ascend, and I found myself climbing a low hill.

The crest was bare granite. I had a view mostly of treetops, a slice of Nutbush Lake, and a few of the lodge buildings. Here and there, the stone bulk of the hill broke through the skin of dirt and grass, like cobbler peeking out between sections of crust. I dropped down onto a smooth stretch of rock already warmed by the sun. Still hypersensitive, I felt a deep connection, through the boulder, to this whole eternal globe spinning ceaselessly through space.

When I awoke, the sun was a bit past the zenith. If I had dreamed of anything, nothing remained with me.

42

I had to hand it to Nancarrow. For the rest of Saturday, after I returned from my walk, he convincingly played the part of a lazy, happy tourist swept up in a "shipboard romance." His patience was exemplary and galling. He gave no sign that he was visiting this place with any ulterior motive. And all I wanted was for him to make the next move so we could proceed toward the endgame.

Any lofty certainty I had felt after my magical sense of oneness with my own destiny had evaporated. No handy animal spirit guide shored me up. I was just my own shaky self once more, with no resources beyond what I had cultivated inside me. Not even Stan was around to reassure me. My ass was hanging out in the breeze all alone.

Arriving back at the lodge in the early afternoon, I found all evidence of last night's festivities cleaned up and the whole place humming along on an even keel, as it had ever since we opened. I could not fault the zeal and ability of the Caboverdeans whom Nellie had directed me to hire. Her boasting about their work ethic had been totally justified. Every one of them seemed almost as dedicated as she was to making this place successful. The lodge's legacy must still reverberate throughout their community, and their appreciation for a paycheck in tough times remained undimmed.

I tried not to think about how we were going to pull the rug out from under all this.

Families frolicked on the beach. A volleyball net had been erected on one stretch of lawn, and a friendly game with three players on a side was under way. Diners came and went from the hall. Some cars bearing day-trippers arrived, each a potential word-of-mouth advertiser to encourage future overnighters.

I encountered Nancarrow and Vee returning from a swim. Rushlow and Digweed were nowhere to be seen, and I surmised that they and their boss now deemed this place safe, allowing the strong-arm boys a little R&R.

Nancarrow's gym-honed muscles and studio tan made me feel like a sack of oatmeal. Vee's white-and-black bathing suit featured an abstract pattern resembling sedimentary strata in a cliff face. An ostensibly demure one-piece, the almost backless suit was cut away totally on both sides above her hips, while the small swatches designed to cover her breasts were joined in back and yoked in front by a slender shoelace whose knot looked ridiculously easy to undo. Her water-slicked hair, pasted to her head, revealed the elegant lines of her jaw and neck.

Nancarrow seemed none the worse for last night's extensive imbibing. "Glen, let me congratulate you again!" he said. "That was a splendid affair last night. You and your assistant have a natural flair for entertaining. It seems to me that if you had some capital to expand, you could really turn this place into something big."

I tried to sound both flattered at his interest and mildly offended. "Well, sure, but money's always the obstacle, right? I probably shouldn't tell you this, but we're in pretty deep to a local bank already. Keeps me up nights, worrying if we can make a go of the place."

Midway between lake and lodge, Nancarrow turned slowly and ostentatiously in a circle, making a show of appraising his surroundings. "You know what, Glen? I think I might be able to offer you some advice. As I said, I've tried my hand at a fair number of ventures, with some small successes. Let's make some time to talk."

Nancarrow encircled Vee's waist with one arm, and she nestled enthusiastically into his slimy embrace. Her face showed nothing but the adoration of money and status and good times that motivated any shortsighted striver who had come up the hard way. I marveled again at her acting talent. The mask was perfect. Wearing a shield against all humanity for so many years had obviously rendered her capable of the most convincing charade. I wondered whether I had even seen her true self that night of the party, when we screwed under the dark canopy of the big beech tree.

"But we won't talk business now," Nancarrow continued. "I promised the lovely Miss Pomestu a hearty meal after our swim. Plus, there's still champagne on ice. And afterward, imagine, she threatened to—and I quote—'whip my ass at badminton.' But first, to counteract those brisk lake waters of yours, a nice, long hot shower."

Nancarrow was not so smarmy as to wink, but he didn't need to. The implication that he would be slithering all over Vee in the same shower stall did not fly over my head.

I wondered whether there was some way to sabotage the pipes to his unit alone. Where was Elbert Tighe when I needed him?

As the pair moved away, Vee looked back over her shoulder and said, "Oh, Mr. McClinton? Could you please have housekeeping change the sheets in my room? They've seen a lot of use."

I had to turn away before giving a combined chuckle and pained grunt. But the women in my life were not done with me. I encountered Sandralene in a totally unnatural position.

Rather than reclining like a big lazy animal, half naked and soaking up the sun, she was dressed in jeans and a plain white T-shirt, sitting upright in her lawn chair and reading a book.

I looked at the cover, expecting some piece of fluff, but was surprised to see that she was well into one of Vee's Italian novels.

She seemed genuinely absorbed, and I had to stand by the chair for half a minute till she registered my presence.

"Oh, Glen, hello. It's nice to see you. How are you after your busy night?"

My knees went semiliquid. "I'm fine. Wonderful, in fact. And you?"

"I always try to feel good, Glen."

I cast an eye at the book. "Are you enjoying that?"

Her face, as guileless as Vee's was calculated, showed mixed puzzlement and dedication to soldier on. "I don't totally get it, but I'm thinking I should try. And it's good to have things to talk about when you're with people. I notice you like to talk about all sorts of things."

"Yes, sure, when I'm not otherwise busy."

Sandralene's laugh belled out big and hearty. "Actions speak louder than words, my friend."

I left her with lines of concentration furrowing her brow.

* * *

Nellie sat behind her office divider. I hadn't seen her since she went back to her cabin for a morning nap, and I was a little worried that maybe something in the room would have alerted her to my overnight presence there with Sandy. But her happy embrace told me she had discerned nothing of the sort.

"Glen, you should see the take from last night! We made such a profit! We have to do this every weekend!"

"You don't think we'll saturate the market and run out of customers?"

"Who doesn't like to have a good time every single weekend? But when the cold weather comes, we can't use outdoor seating no more. And the hall will only fit so many. Glen, do you think we can build on to that room? I know we just finished one renovation, but I don't see any other way to handle everyone who might want to come."

If I had been running this place for real, of course I would have hesitated and said I needed to study the matter. But out of guilt at my infidelity, and because I would soon be seeing Bigelow Junction Motor Lodge for the last time in my rearview mirror, I said, "Nellie, I don't see how we can *not* do it!"

My reward came in the usual smoking-hot currency.

I puttered around for the rest of the afternoon, until about five. I couldn't rush Nancarrow. I just had to be patient. Luckily, the lodge presented no end of chores to keep me busy.

Around five, an unexpected visitor arrived, in the person of Sheriff Broadstairs.

He crossed the lawn toward me with his usual gait: not exactly a swagger, but a kind of take-charge stride that brooked no interference.

"McClinton, I heard you had a hell of a shindig out here last night. Did you get all the proper licenses?"

My heart sank into my shoes. Was this how we would get tripped up?

Seeing my dismay, Broadstairs laughed uproariously. "Son of a bitch! Did I scare you, or what? Did you forget, my friend, that you are sitting on unincorporated land? Centerdale's got no jurisdiction here. You can run a strip joint for all I can say about it. Not that it would be the smartest idea. There's ways your neighbors can express an opinion that don't rightly follow the law books. Am I making sense?"

I was so relieved that we had not tripped up, I didn't even mind Broadstairs' blunt intimidation. "Absolutely."

"Now, to the real reason for my visit. I understand those two hunter guys are back. They after bear or moose? Because they only had licenses for turkey, deer, and geese, as I recall."

"Oh, you don't have to worry about them. They're not hunting anything other than quail this time."

Broadstairs' puzzlement lasted only a second before he grinned. "I see. Nice work if you can get it. Still, maybe I oughta just check in with them anyways."

I didn't want to draw attention to Nancarrow's presence, but felt I should mention it, given that the sheriff would inevitably find out. "They're here with their boss. Some guy named Nancarrow."

"He a hunter, too?"

"More or less the same as his underlings."

"Y'know," Broadstairs observed, "lots a times those kinda guys end up the hunted."

From the sheriff's lips to God's ear, I hoped.

43

Toting me along as his passport, Sheriff Broadstairs found Digweed and Rushlow in the kitchen. They had been fishing and
caught a good stringer of yellow perch. Now they had sweet-
talked Jenise and her staff into cleaning and even preparing the
fish for their exclusive supper. The way a couple of our female
kitchen employees hung close by the two thugs informed me
plainly enough how they had spent their night.

"Nice catch, gentlemen," Broadstairs said with apparent jollity.
"Good thing those babies are in season for licensed fishermen."

Digweed frowned, highlighting the pale scars more clearly
against his dark skin. Rushlow began to stammer. "Well, now,
you see—"

Broadstairs interrupted. "I only wish I could've gone fishing
today and had similar luck, for I surely do favor me some perch. I
find it best rolled in cornmeal and fried in a hot skillet—cast iron,
of course. Mighty good eating."

It seemed to take all Digweed's self-control to project polite
and spontaneous generosity.

"Sheriff, we'd be happy if you'd take a few for yourself."

"Why, that's awfully kind of you fellas."

Digweed appropriated a big sheet of aluminum foil and began piling scaled and gutted perch on it. With every fish, he would look to Broadstairs for the nod that this was enough. By the time he finally got it, there was just one perch apiece left for him and Rushlow.

Carrying the package under one arm, Sheriff Broadstairs tipped his anomalous bush hat and strolled off with me.

The muted swearing emanating from the kitchen was almost musical.

* * *

Once Broadstairs drove off, I went back to my cabin to check in on Ray and freshen up for dinner. In the gloom of the drawn window shades, his face glowed eerily in the radiance of his iPad. The illumination showed no color, just shades of gray, making me curious. He was sitting upright on the edge of his bed while tinny play-by-play emerged from the speakers.

Ray paused the video. "Are you familiar with this YouTube channel, Mr. Glen? It's called Major League Baseball Classics. I am a subscriber. They feature nothing but old games. Right now, I'm watching game six of the 1952 World Series. Yankees versus the Brooklyn Dodgers. This was before they became the Los Angeles Dodgers, you know."

I sat down on the bed beside Ray, and he resumed the program. The video was hypnotic. The frequent panoramas of the crowd, which appeared to be 90 percent suited white males. The breezy homespun chatter of the announcers, and their genuine excitement at the high points of the game. The leisurely daytime holiday ambience and the deliberate slowness and skills of the nonshowboating players.

Maybe I was still extra sensitive from my earlier epiphany. Maybe it was just fatigue and the darkened room. But whatever the cause, I felt cast back almost bodily to a time long before I was born, into a world that, whatever complicated realities it might have manifested to the citizens of that era, seemed simpler and more clear-cut, less harsh and mean, closer to some essential rhythm of life and civilization. I found myself yearning to escape this day and age—not just my present circumstances, but the whole matrix out of which my messed-up duties and schemes had arisen.

I must have watched about forty minutes of that game before I found the resolve to pull myself out of the nostalgic fantasy. I ran the shower on cold and eventually came around to my normal self.

Ray was still watching that old game or another.

"Ray, what can I bring you for supper?"

"Will there be pizza tonight?"

Ray had asked for pizza every night for the past week, without success. I suddenly felt extra sad for the boy, although he surely would have questioned what he could possibly find to be sad about in his own life. "Ray, pizza is not on the menu, but I will have a special order made and sent to you."

"Could you please have any pepperoni sliced extra thin, Mr. Glen? I don't like it too thick."

I did not think I had ever seen pepperoni on the provision invoices, but I knew we had several kinds of Portuguese sausage. "I'll see what I can do."

* * *

The dining hall that night was a considerably quieter place, never more than half full at any given hour. I was present throughout, including when Vee and Nancarrow dined. They leaned into each other, touching and laughing and necking, while the Dom Pérignon flowed.

Rushlow and Digweed scarfed down their meager perch apiece, accompanied by a goodly heap of coleslaw, then sated the rest of their hunger with three mushroom-and-cheese burgers each and a bucket of onion rings.

Nellie and I dined together with the kitchen staff after the dining-hall doors were closed. I listened with half an ear as she described her day, and then we parted for our separate, celibate quarters.

Ray had demolished his special-order pizza with gusto, although several slices of chorizo, apparently just a millimeter too thick, had been neatly discarded in the nearest receptacle: the basket for his dirty laundry.

I undressed and got into bed and went under as fast as if I had never napped on that warm hilltop earlier in the day, during what seemed another lifetime.

* * *

Sunday dawned colder than any previous day of the month, and I knew that our little arcadian extension of summer was at an end. I doubted that anyone but the hardiest would be swimming today, and when I stopped in at the front office, two couples were turning in their keys before an early departure, even though our generous checkout time was not until 2:00 p.m.

For a moment, a few entrepreneurial schemes raced through my brain as I speculated on what we might offer by way of new amusements to encourage autumn visitors. But then I kicked myself. This whole charade would soon be over, one way or another.

Out in the yard, seeing Nancarrow without Vee was almost jarring. She had glued herself to his side so effectively, and he had seemed so taken with her, that her absence seemed to hint at some kind of falling-out, which would do our scheme no good.

But Nancarrow showed no sign of a lovers' spat. Quite the opposite.

"Good morning, Glen. Brilliant weather, isn't it?"

I looked at the shimmering birches. "Yep, time to dig out the long underwear soon."

"Or fly south for the winter."

My guilty conscience made the commonplace joke sound too close to our plan to flee for the tropics after skinning this suave jerk. But Nancarrow seemed to intend nothing oblique with his pleasantry.

"You must be wondering why I'm uncommonly single this morning, without the vibrant company of Miss Pomestu. And by the way, I really should thank you for being the agent, however accidental, of our meeting—you and that imagined snake. She has been a very, ah, stimulating companion. Not the sharpest tool in the shed, of course, but with a certain rough intelligence and verve and no end of enthusiasm. To reward what is, in all likelihood, the start of the end of our little assignation, I've sent her out with my other companions. They're on a shopping trip to various boutiques some miles away—the best this backwater can offer."

"I don't generally comment on the doings of our guests, Barnaby, but I will say that it seems a classy move. I'm glad the lodge proved congenial for your, um, impromptu liaison."

"Ah, yes, your rough-edged jewel of an establishment. Now that I have my hands free, so to speak, let's talk about this place."

Nancarrow leaned in closer, as if to share a confidence.

"I know everything about you, McClinton, so you might as well just lay all your cards on the table."

44

Before my brain could unfreeze and offer even a lame-ass reply, Nancarrow continued. But, astonishingly, instead of the threats or accusations I half expected, he offered confidences and reassurances. I began to relax a mite, my pulse hammering less fiercely in my temples with every word. Maybe our plan was still on track.

We continued to walk across the yard in a kind of automatic reflex of motion, heading randomly toward the lakeshore.

"To encourage absolute candor between us, Glen—and I hope you'll pardon my wielding your last name a minute ago in that jarring manner, but I couldn't resist, strictly for dramatic effect!—I am going to disclose a few facts about myself before we turn to an analysis of your current condition.

"First, I did not come here on a pleasure trip. That is, not entirely for pleasure, although I anticipated some and actually got more than I hoped for, as you know. But there was always a business side to my trip. I sent my men up here last week with the express purpose of checking out your place and reporting back on it."

"But why?"

"Simply because I had heard rumors that the lodge was reopening and that it was showing some potential for success."

"But exactly how does that concern you?"

Nancarrow eyed me piercingly as we strolled. "You really don't recognize my name? It has some prominence back in the city we once shared. And in fact, I think I might even have had occasional dealings with your old employers. Ghent, Goolsbee, and Saikiri, that is, not the federal institution that deployed you on its highway work crew during your stint as its guest."

I winced—convincingly, because those memories of hot, sweaty days whacking weeds, with the armed guards never far removed and the driver and riders of every passing car eyeing us as if we were animals in a wildlife safari, still hurt. But I said nothing.

"Well, no matter. Perhaps you once knew my name but had its relevance purged from your mind by your troubles. I can appreciate how that might happen. But be that as it may, all you need to know now, Glen, is that I am a real estate developer—one of the biggest in the region. And I am always on the alert for any properties that hold the potential for a good return on investment. Here, let me show you some of my bona fides."

Nancarrow took out his phone—the latest, sleekest model, of course, as opposed to my flip-top hunk of junk—and mounted a slideshow of many of his properties, each with the hallmark bronze plaque proclaiming the building to be under his reign.

"Rather impressive, if I may allow myself to say so. Perhaps you agree?"

We had paused in our stroll around the edges of the property to look at Nancarrow's CV. I manifested a sudden interest in a sagging fence post before responding to his boast. "Well, sure, absolutely! That's a pretty awesome portfolio and track record, Barnaby."

"I'm glad you concur. So I think you'll admit that I have a good instinct for valuable properties, Glen. Especially if a property is underperforming. That's when I'm able to turn it around and maximize profits even more. I like to zero in on such deals. And my gut is telling me that the Bigelow Junction Motor Lodge is just such an opportunity."

"You really think so? I mean, I've gotten kinda fond of the place, but I never really had the sense that anyone else thought much of it."

"Well, I do. But at the rate you're going with your very limited resources, both financial and managerial, you're doomed to failure. Bankruptcy or worse. And then that disaster will taint the lodge, and even someone of my reputation and skills will not be able to relaunch it successfully. I think that would be a shame. Don't you?"

"Sure. A lot's riding on this place. My future, the jobs of the employees …"

"Totally. And to be frank, Glen, you're just not the fellow to bring it off. I know you're doing it to help your uncle, who was the actual purchaser of the lodge. I've done my research, you see. But you're just not fitted for the assignment."

I tried to look hurt. "I think I'm doing a pretty decent job up here. What makes you feel I'm wrong for the place?"

"Let's have a little tour of your past, shall we, Glen? All the facts I alluded to possessing a few minutes ago."

He then proceeded to document my entire sordid career in painful detail. Not even the prosecuting district attorney had laid out the case against me so thoroughly. Nancarrow named all my victims, all my maneuvers, all my profits and restitutions. He even guessed fairly accurately at the amount I had socked away on the sly. It took a crook to know one. Then he chronicled my miserable prison years and the lackluster, hangdog existence I had led since getting out, right down to my arrival at the lodge in a new role that I was singularly ill suited for.

During all this spilling of my past, I had been holding my breath against any mention of Stan Hasso. That was the key secret that had to remain undiscovered. If Nancarrow had ever connected me to Stan, the game was surely lost. But we had done all we could to keep him in the dark about our affiliation.

Back in the city, my December Good Samaritan turn, dosing Stan with the Narcan, had gone unrecorded in any media report, occurring only in the police log for that night. Three people back home knew of our joint business venture: Uncle Ralph, Suzy Lam, and Anton Paget. I could not imagine Nancarrow had access to any of them, or that they would aid him if he reached out.

In Centerdale, of course, Sheriff Broadstairs and Wilson Schreiber could connect Stan and me. I deemed them equally closemouthed, even should Nancarrow seek them out. And that was all the people up here who could link us. We had wisely kept Stan in the background with all the contractors and suppliers. I had conducted all the dealings and negotiations with the locals. If they had ever seen or noticed Stan, it was probably just as some nameless guest or hanger-on at the lodge, a wastrel cousin, or a drinking buddy. Probably, they all had been too busy ogling Sandralene even to note her boyfriend's existence. We had even kept Nellie unclear on his true status. She thought he was something like a silent investor. And now, despite politely sharing Nancarrow's champagne on Friday night, Nellie was still under the belief—ultimately correct—that he wanted to do Stan some harm. There was no way she would spill the beans.

Nancarrow was warming to his peroration, and without once mentioning Stan. I smelled success! As an ex-attorney, I admired the clarity of his closing arguments. As the subject—or, rather, miserable object—of his wrap-up, I was less pleased.

"I said I'd be frank, Glen, and so I intend to be. You are a washed-up ex-lawyer and ex-junkie with very few useful life skills in your quiver. You're still constrained by the terms of your parole and can't even leave this place for a break. Somehow, you've fallen into this job, and you're giving it your all. But your all is not enough. And you know what else? I don't think your heart is really in this venture. I think you're doing it to please your uncle, who probably just wants to see you become a useful member of society again. But be honest with me, Glen. Is your heart really in this gig? You once knew a pretty lush life—more like what I experience, if not quite so glamorous. Moving with the people who really matter, who are smart and hip and who can show you a good time. Even if, by some miracle, you were to succeed with this, is that the limit of your vision? Are you really going to be content owning a lousy little motel in East Nowhere, hanging out with these losers?"

We had arrived at the beach. As I had predicted, no one was about in the autumn chill. A few early colored leaves floated on the wavelets. I stayed mute, as if contemplating the sharp, painful wisdom of Nancarrow's speech.

"Maybe you're right," I said at last. "But what are you offering me instead of this place, which is at least some honest work?"

"Let's say almost three times what you paid for it. Half a million dollars. And something else: a chance to be a lawyer again."

45

I certainly wasn't Jesus. And Nancarrow, despite his egomania, avarice, dangerous outlaw behavior, and disdain for those weaker than he, was no Satan. And yet, I couldn't avoid likening this to the temptation of Christ. The lodge was my wilderness. I hadn't been fasting forty days and forty nights like the Son of God, but my stomach was a little growly from skipping breakfast.

Nancarrow and I seemed to be enclosed in an invisible bubble, some private universe or force field activated by his words. I couldn't even really hear the lapping waters of Nutbush Lake or the breeze in the trees, so focused was I on this new, unconsidered possibility.

"How ... how the hell could I be a lawyer again?"

"The relevant laws offer reinstatement after disbarment, after sufficient rehabilitation. Didn't you know that? Not every state has that option, but we do. You have to jump through a lot of hoops, of course, and there's only a 10 percent approval rate. But I do believe that if you had a sponsor such as myself, and if I were to call in certain favors, those odds would increase significantly in your favor. In fact, they would approach certainty."

Wisely, Nancarrow stopped talking then. Having made his pitch, he was not going to oversell it. He could see I was intrigued, and he was just going to let the seed of the notion flower within the dark, poisoned soil of my heart. So he just stood there, complacent in his head-to-toe Burberry gear—the devil in a thousand-dollar cotton field jacket.

And I *was* intrigued. A scenario leaped entire into my head.

Cut Stan, Sandralene, Ray, and Vee right out of the picture. They had no legal holds on me or the lodge. They could hardly sue me for violating the terms of our illegal conspiracy. Sure, they'd be enraged, hurt, pissed. But I doubted whether any of them, even Stan, would bother to come after me in the end. Nothing to gain. Maybe I could even use a hundred K of Nancarrow's money to soothe them. Twenty-five thousand apiece. That would be a decent payoff for a few weeks' work, right? Not five million each, true. But some modicum of revenge would still be had. Nancarrow would be out half a million. The hurt would not be as great as losing twenty million. But still, when the imaginary Prynne offer for the lodge failed to materialize, he would look and feel like a fool, which is what everyone really wanted.

Uncle Ralph would let me do anything I wanted. After all, the lodge had been purchased with my money, not his. I could sell it to Nancarrow and just walk away with almost triple my investment—a bigger stake to relaunch my life. My new life as a lawyer. This time, though, I would skip the dope and the chicanery. Concentrate on the legit pleasures: the cars, the suits, the bespoke shoes, the fine restaurants and finer women.

The women. What about Nellie? Maybe I could take her away into my restored paradise. Surely she would appreciate being with a successful lawyer. I could already see my new office, taste the rich cigars and fine liquor …

Nancarrow shattered my fantasy by speaking. "I can throw a lot of business your way, too, Glen, once you're practicing again. I can always use a guy who has proved that he's not averse to taking a few shortcuts to get things done more efficiently. Someone who knows that rules were made to be broken."

Nancarrow's words were the tipping point. Our little pocket universe fell apart, and the world I knew reasserted itself. He had pushed the sale too hard. I liked to believe that I would have discarded all my traitorous thoughts in the next second or two on my own after running through the scenario. After all, you had to consider all the angles before making a decision, didn't you? I really hadn't been about to betray my friends, had I?

But if I *had* been about to do something so vile, Nancarrow himself had swung me back to the other pole. The image of me sucking up to this creepy bastard for the rest of my life, having lunch with him and his bully boys, hanging out with him in clubs and at parties, giving forced laughter at his jokes, and false congratulation for his cheap victories—it turned my stomach and allowed me to reaffirm where my loyalties lay. I hadn't entered this scheme with any notions of revenge—just money. After all, I had no grudge against Barnaby Nancarrow. But his cavalier sleazy treatment of Vee had started me down the same road of getting even that Stan and Vee had embarked on long ago.

No way would I accept this offer.

Which, of course, was why I had to sound positively giddy about it.

"Barnaby, I—I don't know what to say. I didn't really think it was possible for me to practice law again. To have my career back, plus a profit on this dump—it's almost like a dream come true."

Nancarrow dropped an avuncular hand on my shoulder. "Dreams *can* come true, Glen. If your vision and willpower are strong enough. And if you have good allies. My own life is proof of that, I think. So I take it that you find my offer at least mildly tantalizing."

"Why, sure, yeah, of course!" I thought to interject some note of caution or suspicion that it all was too good to be true. After all, anyone in my position would at least consider the possibility that he might be getting taken for a ride.

"But maybe there's something you're not telling me. Are you really doing this out of the goodness of your heart? Is the challenge really so fascinating? I can't really believe you can make this place so huge it will earn you back half a million over a reasonable time. Are there mineral rights here, or something crazy like that?"

We started away from the lake, back toward the buildings. Nancarrow radiated a palpable air of deliberating and weighing all his options, to impress me with his weighty solemnity, before he spoke.

"All right, Glen, I can see that to close this deal I am going to have to lay all my cards on the table, just as I asked you to do. Yes, I do have some insider information that you were not privy to. But I don't think that knowing it will change your options. Here's what's going on. I've learned this from my contacts in the legislature. The land adjacent to your property is going to become a national park, about ten thousand acres in size. It's been donated by the current owner. And new exit and entrance ramps will be built off the interstate to facilitate access. Can you imagine how popular the lodge will be then? But here's the rub for you. These developments are over a five-year time frame, contingent on federal funding and such. Undercapitalized as you are, you can't possibly hang in there that long. I can. That's why I'm willing to invest half a million now."

I pretended to ponder this revelation for a few dozen more steps. "Makes sense, I guess."

"Then we have a deal?"

We came to a stop, and I stuck out my hand. "We have a deal."

Surprisingly, Nancarrow's grip was neither slimy nor scaled, neither fevered nor icy, but rather bold and pleasant. The shake of a fellow who was used to people liking him—or at least kowtowing to him. I tried to picture him fondling Vee with that hand, running it up and down her haunch, cupping her strong jaw. Maybe such elegance and style was actually more representative of the devil than horns or hooves or scales.

"Fabulous! Then nothing's left but the paperwork. I'll get back to the city today and start the process."

I had to exert all my self-control to conceal the jolt that Nancarrow's words sent through me. He couldn't leave now! Our whole subterfuge of getting the Prynne letter delivered under his nose, then confronting him with it, would be out the window. We had been relying on catching him off-balance, out of his native environment. Employing a kind of shock-and-awe outrage on our part that would motivate him to immediate consent for fear of losing the deal. But for all that to happen, he had to be on the premises. We couldn't let him leave.

I realized then that only Vee could keep him here.

46

The Escalade, driven by Rushlow, with Digweed riding shotgun and Vee ensconced like royalty in the back seat, arrived back around 2:00 p.m. After nearly four hours of nervous waiting, I hurried over. Everyone else I had to worry about was accounted for, leaving just Vee to talk to.

We had the usual Sunday influx of day-trippers, and Nellie was being run ragged with various errands that only she could handle. Not that she figured in the conspiracy exactly, but I just needed to know she wouldn't intrude on anything. After briefing Sandralene, I had sent her off into the woods—on foot, since both rowboats had customers—to apprise Stan of what was happening. Maybe he would have some insights into setting the hook deeper in Nancarrow's jaw. And although Ray was growing a tad antsy, he continued to cooperate by remaining room-bound. Arranging that homemade pizza for him had gone a long way toward satisfying his creature comforts—three times a day. His laundry basket continued to accumulate sausage slices that failed quality assurance.

Evidently missing his gym time, Nancarrow himself had

embarked on a hike. "I might as well get a wider look at what I'm buying," he told me before setting off. The kitchen had put up some sandwiches and bottled water for him. I was bemused by his backpack—a small, supple leather creation that featured two cartoonish yet somehow malign monster eyes on the closure flaps—until I saw the Fendi label. Fifteen hundred or thereabouts, I guessed, at Neiman Marcus and other exclusive outlets.

I went over to the SUV. Rushlow and Digweed were fumbling various packages bearing designer names out of the back, while Vee stood beside them, supervising.

"Need a hand?" I asked.

The wide boys glared at me as if I were questioning their manhood, bringing them down to my lowly servant level.

"We got this, cuz," said Digweed. "You just mind your room keys."

"Well, I'm actually glad you mentioned my job, Mr. Digweed. That's exactly why I'm here. Miss Pomestu, I'm afraid I need to talk to you about your bill."

Vee peered over the top of her sunglasses at me. "My bill? What about it?"

"I think you'd prefer we discuss it in private. You see, your last check—well there was some difficulty ..."

Rushlow and Digweed made barely muffled snickers. It was obvious they were getting a little tired of their boss' infatuation, and of their role as handmaidens in this boring rustic setting. As active city boys, they plainly longed for a return to breaking legs and feeling up strippers while their boss schmoozed politicians at "gentlemen's clubs." And they surely knew that Vee's reign as queen of Nancarrow's libido was nearing its predetermined end, giving them license to be slyly dismissive of her.

"This is ridiculous and insulting," said Vee. "Where's Barnaby? He'll straighten matters out."

I interpreted Vee's question as *Is it safe to talk?* "He's not available right now."

She huffed. "Then I suppose I'll have to go with you and listen to your mean-spirited accusations. But just wait until he hears of this!" She turned to address her reluctant assistants. "Please bring those things to my room." She tossed them her key. "You can just leave the door unlocked and the key on my dresser."

In the lodge's office, Anildo Pereira emerged from the screen of his phone only hazily, as if half his attention were still ensorcelled in some Narnia or Middle Earth. I sent him off to make sure the dirty laundry had been picked up from the men's and women's dormitory trailers. Then I made certain the windows were closed and the door to the office locked.

Vee had perched on a corner of Nellie's desk behind the privacy screen, holding her sunglasses wearily by one stem. Her limbs seemed limp as noodles, and her face looked so different from its hardened gold-digger guise of a moment ago that it was as if she had peeled off one of those full prosthetic masks featured in Hollywood spy films.

"How are you holding up?"

"I feel like I've spent a lifetime under a filthy rock with all the creepy, crawling things. I don't think I can ever wash this stink off. Has it been only three days?"

"Yes, only that. But you've got to know that you're doing a magnificent job. Nancarrow is much less alert, less sharp-edged, than I suspect he would be back in his neighborhood. He's not cutting this deal with killer instinct. You've lulled him into a kind of complacency about the whole affair. He thinks we're a bunch of rubes and you're the farmer's daughter."

"Huh! I don't feel like anyone's daughter anymore."

I held her free hand. "Just hang in there. It's almost over. But there's one last hurdle. You've got to keep him here tonight and into tomorrow."

I explained what I hadn't been able to tell Vee before: that the FedEx envelope would arrive only before noon on Monday— tomorrow. When Nancarrow had shown up on Friday, we alerted Ray's Vegas confederate to send the envelope by overnight rate on Saturday.

"As soon as it comes, we'll shove the harpoon in, and with any luck, the whole schmear will come to closure. He'll sign the contract, wire us the money, and that's the last we'll see of him."

"I sure hope it plays out that way," she said. "But what am I going to do to make him stay? Believe me, I've shown him a real good time—every position I know, and then all over again. But I'm just one woman."

Vee's words triggered an immediate picture in my head, but I hesitated to say aloud what I was envisioning. Yet, as it proved, I needn't have been so shy or fussy. Vee herself immediately recognized the same implication and could not deny that route as our best scheme. Still, even acknowledging the reality of the situation, she couldn't stop herself from slumping more despondently.

She fleshed out what so far was only hypothetical. "Those two simpletons of his have hooked up with a couple of the girls here, I suppose?"

"Yes."

"And I likewise suppose, what with the limited quarters and the lack of privacy in the trailers, that all four of them have been busy in their one room?"

"It would appear so."

"Then what's two more? I'm sure Nancarrow has been eyeing their young bods, even if he had the good manners not to make it obvious. I'm pretty good, but I'm not eighteen anymore. So if

I bring up the possibility of an orgy, he's bound to jump. I just hope your furniture girlfriend—whatshername, Bethune—chose sturdy beds. But they do all look top of the line. I'm sure she wanted to sell you the best and maximize her profits. Just like all of us, I guess."

Vee arose from the desk, and her transformation back to her hardboiled self was as remarkable and unnerving as her deflation had been. Her voice reeked of self-assurance and contempt for any who would interfere with her desires.

"Well, Mr. McClinton, I'm glad we got that all straightened out. Now I know just what I have to do to satisfy everyone."

I saw her out of the office just as Anildo Pereira was returning. Entranced by the jiggle of her hips, the boy gave a low whistle.

"*Ai*, she is something else!"

"You don't know the half of it, *minha amigu.*"

Sandralene got back from her sortie around the lake, and we met by the water's edge. Flashing on my moment of temptation earlier in the day, I winced at the memory of how close I had come to succumbing.

Sandralene plopped down in a lawn chair, weary from bush-whacking through a mile and a half of woods and back. I stood beside her, anxious for her report. "Stan says you're doing great, Glen. Just don't let down your guard. He doesn't think there's much he can offer, except this. When it gets dark, he's going to come right to the edge of the property and keep watch from behind those bushes next to the garage. If anything goes screwy, he says, just send for him. He doesn't want to blow the deal, but he doesn't want anyone getting hurt, either."

"That's generous," I said. "But it's a little late to stop anyone from getting hurt."

47

I had expected Nancarrow, with his lord-of-the-manor sensibilities, to swagger boldly and proudly out of Rushlow and Digweed's unit the morning after, strutting his status, allure, and sexual prowess. But he had been surprisingly tactful and low-key about the whole matter. It made sense, for a man used to keeping up his public image. Whatever his less-savory private indulgences, he still had to maintain his pillar-of-the-community persona as developer, contributor to charities, socialite, and friend to the rich and powerful.

Rather than assemble en masse, the six orgiasts had come in separately, starting around ten o'clock, after the kids and most of the adults were tucked into their tasteful, well-made Brenda Bethune beds. The wanton revelry had not blown any shutters off, thanks in part to the cinder-block construction of the rooms, paired with the sound-damping hangings from Aphrodite Fabric Creations on the shared walls. About the only outward sign of the proceedings had been the delivery to the unit of the remaining champagne, on ice. And when the carousing finally wound down, around 5:00 a.m., Nancarrow had escorted Vee back to her room, away from prying eyes, before returning for whatever last decadent spasms were to be had.

I tried to feel sorry for the only two innocent participants: our kitchen staff members Irina and Litzy. But in the end, I couldn't summon up too much pity for them. Though oblivious to the evil nature of the three men they were consorting with, they were no babes in the woods and had entered into the affair willingly, looking for thrills unavailable to them back in Centerdale, under the censorious eyes of family and community.

I had such detailed knowledge because I had spent the night in the bushes with Stan, monitoring all the comings and goings.

* * *

I joined him there around nine thirty. I carried a couple of brisket sandwiches and some bottled drinks—but nothing alcoholic, not even a beer. Approaching the shrubbery from behind—rhododendrons, I think, with woody stems and big, flat leaves and, mercifully, no thorns—I squirmed into the center of the growth. There, the space opened up a little to provide a decent line of sight to the two main residential wings extending from either side of the office.

Of course, Stan had heard me coming, though he said nothing while I worked my way in. Though it was hard to make out the big guy's features in the thin starlight and spillage from the distant exterior light fixtures, I thought I detected a wry smile. He seemed genuinely pleased to see me, and I realized again how much I had come to rely on his presence. I felt reassured that maybe we could bring this crazy plot off.

He greeted me silently with a mock punch to the jaw, then snatched up a sandwich.

"Fresh grub!" he whispered. "You rock, Glen boy! You don't

know how sick I am of cold canned beans. And it's starting to get cold nights."

"You can have mine, too," I said. "Not much appetite."

Speaking around mouthfuls, Stan said, "This action with Vee getting you down, huh? Pretty skeevy, I admit. But if she's willing and it's working, then we can't afford to suddenly let our scruples queer the deal. Just gotta take it in stride."

"I suppose so. I just wish there had been another way."

"Listen, kid. With a guy like Nancarrow, there are three ways to get past his defenses: profit, pride, and pussy. You're stroking his pride, and he's convinced himself that the profit angle is solid. And Vee is providing the sex. We mighta relied on just the first two avenues. But it's like a stool with three legs versus two. This way's much more solid and secure."

"I guess."

"Shhh! Here comes Needles and Buck."

The two toughs entered their room, and the other participants trickled in over the next half hour.

"Okay," said Stan, "you can go now. Get some sleep so you can be fresh for the big play tomorrow."

"I'll stick around. I want to make sure nothing goes wrong and no one gets hurt."

"Leave that to me."

"No. I feel responsible for all this."

"You're not gonna change your mind?"

"Nope."

"Well, then, you're gonna need these if you wanna stay sharp."

Stan held out a grimy palm, and I could make out two gelcaps.

"What's that?"

"Adderall. Keeps you flying high and wide-eyed, but smooth. Take one now and one in the morning."

"I thought we were finished with drugs."

"*Pfft!* I said I was done with *smack*. This stuff is candy. Every other college kid scarfs 'em by the handful."

I sighed. "Well, all right." I swallowed the first pill, and we settled into our guard duty.

Sometime after midnight, feeling wide awake and guilty, I said, "Stan, I'm sure Sandralene told y—"

"Sandy don't have to tell me nothing. The great and powerful Hasso knows all. So I will surely be aware in the future if you come sniffing around my woman uninvited. Besides, there is no way a skinny, weak bastard like you's gonna be able to keep Nellie and Sandy both happy. Just focus on the bush of your own bird, if you get me."

"Okay, clear enough. But I just wanted to say—"

"Will you shut up about your sex life for once so I can concentrate! Kee-*rist*, you'd think nobody ever done you a favor before."

I found myself grinning. "Whatever you say, boss."

The rest of the night passed in a strange fugue—a blend of alertness and a kind of dissociative state, where I seemed to be both watching the scene from behind my eyes, and watching myself from outside my body.

At last, the horizon beyond the lake began to show the faintest hint of dawn.

"Okay," Stan said, "I gotta get out of here before anyone spots me. But if you manage to pull this off today, I'll be back before much longer. And then we're outta here permanent-like. Good luck."

Stan decamped with uncommon stealth for a man his size.

I watched Nancarrow deliver Vee back to her room at 5:00 a.m. and then rejoin his pals. I eased out of the bushes and returned to my own quarters. Ray Zerkin slept the sleep of an innocent lamb. I used the shower and got dressed nicely, popped the second amphetamine capsule, and went out.

Much to my surprise, I felt confident and at ease. Maybe being with Stan had charged me up, or maybe it was just the drug. Whatever the cause, I seemed to have tapped into some cosmic Tao, to ride the surging forces of fate, that famously unstoppable power over the affairs of men. The last time I had felt like this was at the apex of my thieving career, on the day I convinced a supposedly savvy businessman to invest two million dollars in my absurd Ponzi scheme. Now I only had to rake in ten times that amount, and all would be perfect. Incredibly, I felt as if it would be no trouble at all. As we slid closer to cool October, our occupancy rate had gone down. And this being Monday, people had departed already to get back to jobs and schools. So the dining hall, with its big windows shut against the chill, had only a handful of diners. We quit serving breakfast at eleven, so I was counting on Nancarrow and company to show by then. I ate and then puttered about while waiting for them to make an appearance.

Irina and Litzy, having worked all weekend, had today off from their kitchen duties, and I'm sure they were appreciating the holiday at the moment.

At ten past eleven, confident that his charm would secure him an exemption from all rules, Nancarrow and his cronies showed. They looked like a team of mountaineers who have descended from a Himalayan peak after an arduous battle with the elements—proud but exhausted.

I greeted them like the pleasant host they expected, but with even more fawning, given the big favor Nancarrow was conferring on me.

"Barnaby, I just want to thank you again for this opportunity," I said. "It's immense."

"No need for that, Glen." Affable smile. "All of us stand to profit."

I had expected Digweed and Rushlow to eat like half-starved

animals, but they just poked sleepily at their food as if still mired in some narcotic sexual la-la land.

Outside the windows, a FedEx truck pulled up. I had never wanted to kiss a deliveryman before.

"Let me see what this is, Barnaby."

"Certainly."

I got the FedEx envelope from the uniformed driver and, after signing his tablet, headed toward the office. I entered the office through the front door, on the side facing the dining hall, then went out the door facing the lake. Out of sight now, I went to the rear door of my room and knocked. Ray opened the door, holding the fake Steve Prynne letter in his hand as I had instructed. I nodded my thanks, took it wordlessly, then went back inside the office, unseen. There I waited alone, having given Anildo the day off, and made sure Nellie was occupied elsewhere.

Nancarrow came to me, as I knew he must if only to say goodbye.

"Glen, I'm leaving now for the city, to begin the transfer of the lodge. I don't anticipate any problems, of course, but if I might have your cell number, just in case—"

I glared at him. Here was where we pulled the carpet out from under him so fast, he would have no real time to react.

"No problems, huh? Of course not, you son of a bitch! The deal is off!"

Clearly unused to such treatment, Nancarrow bristled. But still with his eye on the prize, and still a little hazy from lack of sleep and his night's exertions, he summoned enough control to speak calmly.

"Glen, I don't understand. Why this sudden change in attitude?"

"Maybe you'll find this to be reason enough. Pretty shitty move you tried—and it almost worked."

I slid the envelope across the desk. He picked it up, and his eyes went wide when he saw Steve Prynne's return address. Then he fished the letter out and began to read.

48

The letter was short and to the point, and Nancarrow, now fully alert, assimilated it quickly. I had to give him props for chutzpah. He didn't look guilty or chagrined or indecisive or repentant. Annealed by a thousand hurdles and setbacks overcome, his rough-hewn Gulch-born-and-bred character veneered with a canny cosmopolitan sophistication, he instantly regrouped and opened his attack on another front, like a general who has never once entertained the prospect of defeat.

He calmly tucked the letter back into its envelope, then slid it back across my desk.

"This is a most unwelcome development."

"No shit, Shylock! From your perspective, of course it's not welcome! To me, it's a lifesaver. National Park, my ass! You're not gonna insult my intelligence by pretending you didn't know anything about this, are you? I don't think I could stand such a big laugh this early in the day."

"Please, Glen, give me some credit for not trying to deny what is now obvious. And do not demean my professional gamesmanship. If you'd had the wit, you would have done the same thing in my shoes. It's true, I had pieced together information from various sources showing that Steve Prynne had an interest in your land. But I had no clue to the actual amount he might offer. If I had, I might have been a bit more generous in my own price."

"Yeah, like what? A cool *million*? Leaving you with the other nineteen? Well, you're out of the picture now, Barnaby. I can conduct business with Steve Prynne just as easily as I can with you."

Nancarrow pulled up a chair and sat down, all calm deliberation. He crossed one elegantly trousered leg over the other, adjusting the crease of the fabric, and took a monogrammed platinum case bearing his trademark piano imagery from his jacket pocket. The case proved to contain nothing more exotic than Altoids. He took one out with grave precision and slipped it between his lips. Bastard didn't even offer me a mint. All this, I knew, was just stalling for time while he formulated his new strategy.

"Glen, perhaps you recall how I gave an appraisal of your abilities and nature yesterday, leading up to our handshake deal for this land. You might have found my estimation of your business acumen unduly harsh. But even if my candor now causes me to lose all participation in this sale of the lodge, I have to reaffirm my earlier assessment. You are not fit to conduct the important sale of this property. Why, just look at how easily I tricked you. If it weren't for this chance intervention, you would have practically given away this immensely valuable property. As a lawyer, you surely recognize the term 'due diligence.' Yet you did nothing along those lines. In light of this naive behavior, how can you possibly imagine you could negotiate with a genius megashark like Steve Prynne?"

I did my best to sound stubbornly obtuse. "I don't have to negotiate anything! I've got his offer of twenty million, right here in writing!" I slapped the envelope for emphasis.

Nancarrow sighed tragically, as if witnessing a toddler about to shoot its head off with a loaded pistol while he debated whether to interfere, or allow hard-edged Darwinism to play out.

"That's just it, Glen. You have Steve Prynne's opening gambit. If you had any negotiating skills or business savvy, you'd realize that you could get him to go much higher. But you're not fit to conduct such a deal. You'd blow it entirely. You might even cause him to lose interest in your property altogether. There's other land in this region, you know. Maybe not as ideal as the lodge, but still tenable."

I appeared to ponder Nancarrow's argument. "Okay, so I can't milk him for more. What do I care? Twenty million is a fortune! That's plenty for me *and* Uncle Ralph."

"Glen, you are an utter fool and a perfect idiot. Letting Prynne get this land for his opening offer is an insult to every deal maker who ever lived. I can't sit by and let you do this. I'll be up front with you: I want every penny from Vegas that we can squeeze out of Prynne. He can't be allowed to think we're just hayseeds that he can bamboozle. But beyond that, I want to impress the man with my own abilities. This is a chance for me to make important connections, to enter a whole new level of dealings, to break out of this petty statewide arena. I need this deal, Glen. There, I've admitted it. You are sitting on something I want, and I intend to get it."

"Well, what if we went partners? You do the negotiating, and we split the dough."

"No, Glen, that's not how I work. This has to be a Nancarrow Logistics project, not a Nancarrow-McClinton deal."

I moved around the stapler and tape dispenser on my desk, as if I and not Nancarrow were the general disposing his surrogate forces. "Suppose you're right about everything. How are you going to sweeten the pot for me?"

"Glen, I am prepared to offer you twenty-one million for this land. And just to continue our new policy of complete honesty and openness, I will reveal that I am convinced I can get Prynne to cough up at least thirty million."

"Then make it twenty-two."

"No, Glen, this is where we draw the line. It pains me to give a lucky buffoon like you even twenty-one million. It can't be a penny more."

"Okay, I guess that's fair. Let me just call Uncle Ralph—"

"Do we really need to involve him? He's just a front, isn't he?"

"Yeah, that's true. And I did make sure to hold all the papers on this place. But I just wanted his advice."

"The advice of a senile track rat? Come now, Glen. Family loyalty is one thing, but this is ridiculous. You're not trying to put me off, hoping to find another buyer who'll offer more, are you? Because it's just not possible. No individual in this state has more liquidity than I. We can bring this whole deal to closure very quickly if only you acknowledge that I am your best and only bet." Nancarrow paused in his sales pitch for a second as he caught up to the meaning of my words. "Exactly what do you mean, you 'hold the papers' for the lodge?"

"Just that I got a signed blank sales agreement from Uncle Ralph as part of the conditions of me coming up here. I wanted to dump the place quick if it got to be a burden, and I figured I could find some local sucker to take it on. I never counted on a deal like this, though."

"Might I see these papers?"

"Yeah, sure, they're back in my room. I'll go get them."

"Very good. That will give me a minute to tell my associates about our change in plans. We'll meet back here in ten minutes."

We parted, and I hurried to my room.

Ray exhibited as much excitement as he ever did, which was

equivalent to anyone else's genial indifference. "Mr. Glen, I hope all the documents are proving successful."

"Working like a charm, Ray. You'd better start thinking about how you're going to spend all your dough."

"I do already have a spreadsheet, Mr. Glen, which I would be happy to show you."

"Soon, my man, soon."

Heading back to the office, I ran into Nellie. She held a sheaf of invoices in her hand and was arrowing toward her desk.

"Nellie, honey, can I use the office privately for just a few minutes? There's something going down with that Nancarrow guy. I think I can negotiate a solution to Stan's troubles with him. But it's a little touchy."

"Oh, *seguro*! Good luck. I'll camp out in the dining room. You just let me know what happens, okay?"

"Of course."

I hadn't exactly told her yet another lie, so I didn't feel bad about deceiving her. And as close as I was to pulling this off, my blood was racing too fast for regrets.

Nancarrow rejoined me and I handed over the sales agreement. He gave it the precise scrutiny of a gemologist studying a rare diamond.

"This is acceptable. Allow me to fill out the specifics."

He used his own Montblanc pen to execute both copies of the agreement. I looked at the figure of twenty-one million and giddily imagined spending my share.

"Satisfactory?"

"Sure."

Nancarrow signed twice. Then he took one copy and began to fold it to put in his pocket.

I snatched it back. "Nuh-uh. I want to see the money first."

He looked wounded. "This is practically an insult, Glen. You possess a legal document with my signature on it. I have never reneged on a signed contract."

"There's always a first time. And like you said, I'm pretty naive. There might be some way for you to get this land without me getting paid. But if I'm holding the money, then everything's kosher."

"Well, what do you want me to do? Write a check?"

"Is there a branch of your bank in Centerdale?" Of course, I knew the answer to that question already.

"Right."

"Go into town, make an electronic funds transfer into Uncle Ralph's line of credit at Midland Trust Bank, and we are golden."

Nancarrow contemplated this demand. "I could have my associates simply take that contract from you, Glen."

"I don't think so. They wouldn't pull any rough stuff with so many witnesses."

Seconds ticked by as I fretted about whether Nancarrow would comply with this crucial demand. We had to have money in hand before he left.

"Glen, I am about to show you the difference between a peasant and a nobleman, between low-grade cunning like yours and genius instincts such as I possess. Fortune favors the bold, you see. And despite any amount of money I give you, you will never be anything other than a simpering, cowardly, unambitious lout."

"You can insult me all you want, just so long as I see that money in my account."

Nancarrow sighed dramatically and stood up.

"Give me the details of your account. Then wait right here, my little friend."

49

I watched the Escalade bearing Nancarrow and his bully boys depart. If they proceeded with maximum efficiency—no traffic, no trouble at the banks—I figured we had about three hours before they got back. That was more time than I really needed to cover all the bases, and spending the excess minutes biting my nails would be hard. But the thought of screwing over Nancarrow and having all his money to spend bolstered my resolve to endure the tedium and anxiety.

The first thing I did was to search out Nellie. She was in the kitchen, having a sandwich and a glass of milk at the butcher-block counter while she shuffled papers and worked a calculator.

I kissed her forehead and received a bright smile. "Your desk is free now, if you want it."

"Great! How did everything work out with Nancarrow? Is Stan in the clear? Can he come out of hiding?"

"*Tudu bem,*" I said. "But it's still wise not to get too chummy with Nancarrow if you see him when he returns. You could say something by accident that sets him off."

I really did not need Nellie to hear from Nancarrow that he was the lodge's new owner.

"That is awesome! I'm so glad for Stan. And don't worry, I'll keep my lips zipped!"

"Not permanently, I hope!"

"*Sempre aberto para o seu pixota!*"

I relished the pleasant spinal tingles that her sexy words provided. We kissed again, and I set off.

Sandralene opened the door to her cabin before I could even knock. She must have been watching for me. Her generally placid and contented face registered the first traces of anticipation and anxiousness I had ever seen there.

"We did it. Our pigeon's going into Centerdale to transfer the funds right now. Go tell Stan. He might want to hang out closer to the lodge in about three hours, but still hidden, so he can join us as soon as he sees Nancarrow take off again."

Sandralene wrapped me in her bountiful flesh and squeezed like a starving anaconda before planting a fat kiss on my lips. The night we had spent together rushed back upon me like a perfumed tsunami. Somehow, knowing that the incredible experience could never be repeated didn't even bother me.

Even isolated in our shared room, Ray had picked up the almost palpable excitement of the payoff. Handing over the documents he had worked so hard to concoct must have made him feel useful and important and brought our scam out of the abstract and into physical, tangible reality. As the big get-even raced toward its culmination, all our hard work, arduous and demanding and uncertain though it had been at the time, seemed to recede into the mythic realm, like some fabulous odyssey now ended.

Ray had his tablet at the ready, doing regular refreshes on the status of the account at Midland.

"Nothing yet, Mr. Glen."

"Relax, Ray; they just drove off. It'll be a while yet. But you know what to do when you see the money arrive, right?"

"Correct, I do know. First, I transfer almost all of it into our offshore account. I leave behind enough to zero out Uncle Ralph's line of credit, plus a bonus of two hundred thousand dollars."

That money would come out of my share. I would hardly feel it, since we had that extra million now to split four ways. I figured it was the least I could do for Ralph Sickert and his lady love, Suzy Lam. I pictured them happy at the track, the Bermuda mai tais flowing like Niagara Falls, Uncle Ralph no longer having to stoop for discarded slips.

"Then," Ray continued, "I buy four tickets on the next flight to any Cape Verde destination, so long as the departure time is at least eight hours in the future."

"You've got all the personal information the airlines need? For Stan, Sandy, Nellie, and me."

"Yes, of course."

I had gotten Nellie's data on the sly. I still had to tell her she was returning to her ancestral islands on such short notice, and explain the circumstances of our bidding farewell to the lodge. But I wasn't worried.

A bigger fool had never lived.

I regarded Ray's blankly earnest face. "Ray, are you sure you wouldn't like to come with us? If you came along, I bet Vee would, too. Life would be pretty easy for you in Cape Verde."

"Mr. Glen, that is a fine offer. But I could not desert my friends in the group home. I have big plans for us all. And there is another matter. There is no Major League Baseball in the islands. Although both Davey Lopes and Wayne Gomes are of Cape Verdean descent and had excellent records when they played in America."

"Okay, Ray. But you can always change your mind."

* * *

Consciously or unconsciously, I had been saving Vee for last. I couldn't bear the thought of finding her emotionally and physically wiped out, some crumpled, trembling wreck, a shadow of her old indomitable self.

My imagination should have known better.

Vee looked crisp and functional and pulled together when she came to the door of her unit. She might have just awoken from a solid eight hours' sleep following a church social where lemonade and cookies provided the main thrills. She still manifested the gold-digger vibe, from outfit to posture to makeup. I realized that Nancarrow's dealings with me had left him no time to break it off with Vee and say, "Gotta run, girl, that was fine, see you again maybe someday," and that she was anticipating at least a brief tête-à-tête.

I stepped inside her room, and she shut the door. I took out the contract for the lodge's sale.

"Signed, thanks to you."

Vee took out a cigarette, lit it, and took a drag. "Amazing what half a dozen decent blow jobs can accomplish."

I did not endorse or dispute her harsh calculus.

"Ray tells me you're going to make over your identity. Will you promise to stay in touch with us?"

"Why?"

"Well, I can't say right now. But that's the whole point. You never know what the future will bring. We might need to talk someday."

"Not too likely."

"Still, what could it hurt?"

"That's another thing you can't predict."

"Just consider it, okay?"

"Consider it considered."

I wanted to hug her at least. But with one arm barricading her chest (fingertips clamped under her opposite armpit) and the other holding the lit cigarette in front of her face like a red-tipped spear, there was no possibility.

I went back to the room. I figured Ray could use my expert help hitting the refresh button.

When the money showed up on the screen, the victory seemed both real and unreal. Ray quickly followed through as we had discussed earlier, and the money was hidden in a place where Nancarrow could never find it.

I went back to the front office to tell Nellie some more lies.

"Nell, I just got a phone call from Nancarrow. He's coming back from Centerdale, where he went to straighten out this mess with Stan. Everything's all settled. But he wants to see me for one last talk. Would you mind giving up the office again?"

"No problem, Glen! I got to help Bethinho with one of the rowboats that sprung a leak. He figures we might as well give both of them some love. They been used hard."

The Escalade did not even park in the assigned area but pulled even with the door of the office. Nancarrow got out alone from the back seat while Rushlow and Digweed remained in the idling vehicle.

"You have your money," he said inside. "I took it out of petty cash."

Right. Although Nancarrow surely had plenty of illicit funds hidden away, his net worth was well known, and twenty million represented a significant hit.

"Hand me that contract now."

I passed it over.

"As the lodge's new owner, I am giving you twenty-four

hours to leave. And please do not attempt to convince any of my employees, such as your very competent manager, Miss Firmino, to leave with you. That would be actionable under the relevant noncompete clauses of this very agreement. I am relying on the staffing to continue just as it is while I return to the city and prepare to negotiate with Prynne. No sense in shutting down a functioning enterprise prematurely. In fact, the sustainability of this operation will be one of my bargaining chips with Vegas."

"Well, Barnaby, I can't say we're parting as friends. But I hope there's no real hard feelings."

"Since when does a winner experience hard feelings?"

We did not shake hands. I watched him go to Vee's unit and spend about ninety seconds inside.

Then the Escalade drove off, taking Barnaby Nancarrow out of our lives forever.

50

We were celebrating Nancarrow's monumental gullibility, and his stinging loss of twenty-one million dollars, with his own champagne. He had left two unopened bottles behind in the room after last night's orgy. We chilled them down quickly in a big ice bucket and were now relishing the sweet taste of victory.

He had driven off only twenty minutes ago, and already he was receding in importance. In a year from now, lolling on a Caboverdean beach, I would have a hard time even remembering what our benefactor looked like.

Inside the stand-alone cabin that Stan and Sandralene had occupied from the first (lately shared with Nellie during Stan's exile), five of us together made for cozy company, as we had when we assembled at the start of this caper. Was it only a few days ago that Stan had been lecturing us on how to bring this off? And now it was over. The time involved seemed both compressed and infinite.

It felt good to be rich again. I hoped Stan and Vee were enjoying their revenge as well as their wealth.

Stan clearly was. In rumpled clothes and with bits of leaf and twig in his dense beard, he could nonetheless have been attending the Oscars as the odds-on winner for best actor. He was sitting on the bed with a grinning Sandralene, one arm around her waist, and letting out a series of war whoops.

"*Shhh!*" I cautioned. "You'll have the whole staff over here."

"Can't help it, Glen boy! This is the first time in my life I had a win this big."

Vee had not given in to any such displays—at least, not so it showed. She sat meticulously sipping her champagne, one leg crossed over the other knee, the airborne foot oscillating nervously. She had reverted to her natural style and appearance.

"Well, everything's relative," she said. "And fucking over Nancarrow and sitting on his money feels better than if we had failed."

Ray had made his way through half a glass of bubbly and seemed bemused. Bobbing in place in his chair, he started to hum some disco tune I vaguely recognized.

Stan was drinking his champagne from an eight-ounce tumbler. After polishing off his third, he wiped his mouth and stood. "Okay, people, this has been big fun. But we can't hang on here. We've got to get going. I don't really imagine Nancarrow is going to find out he's been shafted for days yet. But the quicker we're abroad, the happier I'll be."

He turned to me. "You know what this means, Glen. Time to get your honey bunny up to speed."

Maybe it was only the champagne, but I felt confident of success.

"I'll go get her."

When Nellie entered the cabin, she went first to embrace Stan.

"Ay, *grande homem*! It's so good to have you back. The place was not the same without you. Now we will have some real fun and make the lodge spin."

"I hear ya, Nell. There's plenty of fun ahead, you got that

right. But maybe not the exact way you think. Tell her, Glen boy."

If I had had to be a con artist with Nancarrow, that applied doubly now. Using all my guile and affability and powers of persuasion, I laid down the cover story more or less as Stan had concocted it for me.

The only way we had seen to resolve Stan's troubles, I explained, had been to sell the lodge to Nancarrow. It was too complicated to give all the details right this minute. But we had made a good profit, and the new owner promised to retain all the Caboverde help and run the place just as if it were his own baby from the beginning. Now it was time for Nellie and me to retire to her beautiful islands, yada yada yada.

I laid down the patter as smooth as locally sourced butter. At first, she looked confused and hurt. But as the prospect of living a life of leisure began to open wide in her mind, she started to come around.

"Oh, *minha nossa*, this is all happening so fast! Glen, I want to show you Cape Verde, I do! But I was building this place up into something fine. Not just for me, but for everyone and the whole area. You think it will really be okay without me?"

I put an arm around her. "Nellie, there is no one as good as you for this job. But there are plenty of people who are *almost* as good. Look at it this way: you're opening up a new employment slot for another Caboverdean. The lodge will keep right on improving. And we can always visit whenever we want, just to make sure."

"All right, then! I am so in!"

Ray Zerkin spoke. "But, Mr. Glen, none of that is true."

The silence that instantly suffused the room was as thick as cold oatmeal.

Nellie looked worried and uncertain. "What's he mean? What do you mean, Ray? Glen, tell me he doesn't know what he's saying!"

Stan stepped forward. "Listen to me, Nell. The kid is right. We've been stringing you along for your own good and your own comfort. But you may as well hear the real deal."

Stan spilled it all.

Nellie's face looked like a china plate that someone had taken a hammer to. "You mean Nancarrow don't really care nothing about this place? He just thinks the land is worth money, and so he's going to throw everything down the toilet when he learns about the scam?"

"Well, now, no one can rightly say for sure …"

The next second, I recalled the original pretext for bringing Nellie here: to give us language lessons. Evidently, she was now trying to make up for lost time. Because the flood of high-speed Portuguese invective that poured forth from those sweet lips was a semester's worth of instruction. I could not catch more than a fraction. I heard *"monte de merda," "vai para o caralho," "cabrão,"* and *"olho do cu."* And then she was out the door.

I started to go after her. Stan stopped me with a hand on my shoulder.

"No use, bro. You got to let her calm down. It'll be fine, you'll see."

And then we heard a car engine roar to life, followed by the sound of gravel spinning up against metal.

I was out the door just in time to watch the Impala fishtail down the drive.

I looked weakly at the others, clustered in the doorway. "She had the keys to run some errands."

Stan took charge. "Okay, this is no problem. So she's going home to Mommy and Daddy for a shoulder to cry on. Big deal. Once we're set up in the islands and she sees what her choices are—go down with a sinking ship, or hang out in the lap of luxury—then you'll have her sitting on your knee again. I promise you, Glen boy. Have I ever been wrong about anything before?"

My heart was broken. But I wasn't about to throw away every-thing we had worked so hard for.

"I guess you're right …"

"Damn straight I'm right! Okay, now that we got the soap opera stuff out of the way, let's think about how we're going to work this. There's no way the five of us are going to cram into Vee's bug. So this is what we'll do. Vee will drive me into Centerdale and I'll rent a car for us. It's only three o'clock now. We got plenty of time. With luck, we'll all be on the road by seven."

It seemed like a decent plan. But I was so distraught over losing Nellie, even temporarily, I couldn't really focus on it.

"All of you wait out here for me. No splitting up. I just gotta shave and shower. No one would rent a car to me looking like this."

Stan went into the cabin's tiny bathroom. The champagne had lost its appeal for the rest of us. We sat listening to the shower run. Eventually, Ray said, "Did I do wrong, Mr. Glen? I know we had to lie to Mr. Nancarrow, but I thought the rest of us were all friends. Vee taught me never to lie to my friends."

"No, Ray, you did the right thing."

The shower stopped, and I could hear Stan humming. I had to admire his unflagging enthusiasm, although I could not match it.

About forty minutes had passed since Nellie's stormy depar-ture when we all heard a car pull up outside, skidding on the gravel.

"It must be her!" I said, and hurried to open the door.

I was knocked flat by Buck Rushlow, bowling through like a human tornado, with Needles Digweed right behind him. Some steps behind them, moving at a more leisurely pace, was Barnaby Nancarrow, dragging Nellie by the wrist.

As I got shakily to my feet, I focused on the compact but lethal-looking pistol in Rushlow's fist. I had always figured him for a .45, but being on vacation, he must have felt safe traveling light.

Stan came out of the bathroom then with just a towel around his waist. "Hey, what the—"

Without a second's hesitation, Rushlow conked Stan on the side of the head with his gun, which proved heavy enough for the job. Stan went down like a poleaxed steer.

Nancarrow came into the cabin with Nellie and shut the door. The little room was packed tighter than a sardine mosh pit.

He addressed me first. "Mr. McClinton, your girlfriend was most naively informative, in hopes of persuading me to do the right thing. For that, I am most appreciative."

Nancarrow took a moment to size up the rest of us.

"Haul Mr. Hasso up onto the bed. Put the boy and the other two women inside the bathroom. But leave Miss Pomestu and Mr. McClinton where they are."

Sandralene, Nellie, and Ray wisely put up no resistance to being stuffed into the tiny windowless bathroom, and Digweed locked them inside.

Stan looked woozy, rubbing his head where Rushlow had bashed him. I grabbed some ice from the champagne tub, wrapped it in a cup towel, and had him hold it to his seeping wound.

"Mr. McClinton, allow me to congratulate you. And kudos to my old employee and schoolyard pal Mr. Hasso as well. Who would ever have believed that either of you had the imagination or the skills to bring this off? Your ruse appealed cunningly to all my ambitions. All my buttons were duly pressed. Well played. Not many people can say they bested Barnaby Nancarrow, even temporarily. But now this mildly amusing game is over. I will take back my money, and that will put an end to our intercourse."

Nancarrow smiled as he said the final word, and leered at Vee. "I don't mean to minimize your part, either, Miss Pomestu. You played your role quite well. In fact, you showed definite talent as a whore."

Throughout the invasion, Vee had exhibited a superhuman unflappability. I don't think she even jumped when Rushlow barged in, although I had been in no position to observe. Now she stood slowly up, drawing the attention of Rushlow's gun barrel.

Her voice seemed like a steel rod. "That is not my name. My name is Varvara Aptekar. And you caused the deaths of my mother and father."

Nancarrow actually blanched then before recovering his aplomb. But he didn't show quite the same seamless sangfroid as before.

"Little Vee. How you've grown! If only your worthless parents could still be around to witness their daughter's accomplishments. I'm sure they would be immensely proud." Vee sat stiffly back down, saying nothing.

"Okay, Glen, you are going to go online and transfer my money right back, this instant. After that, I will allow you all to depart, although, naturally, I will insist that all of you bid my state goodbye forever. If I ever learn that you are anywhere within a hundred miles of these borders, it will not go well for you."

Somehow, I found the courage to say, "I won't do it—that is, I can't. The money's locked up tight behind a lot of crypto."

"Don't be ridiculous. You have access to it for yourselves, I'm sure. That means you can send it back to me."

"And—and what if I refuse?"

"Mr. McClinton, I have never found it necessary to have any of my rivals killed. But I will admit that I have caused several of them intense pain. Oh, not by my own hands. I leave that to Mr. Digweed."

I looked to Needles. His scarred face split into a wicked grin as he reached into a coat pocket and took out a long, narrow metal case. He opened it to reveal a glittering array of slender chrome lances, like the kit of some satanic acupuncturist.

"Mr. Digweed is capable of causing intense pain and even crippling outcomes while leaving barely a mark. I have known eminent physicians who were unable even to determine the original points of entry when their patients dragged their shattered bodies in. Now, do I get my money back, or does Mr. Digweed start his, um, probing?"

Stan leaped up then, aiming to tackle Rushlow. But his injury slowed him just enough for Rushlow to get off a shot. In the tight space, it sounded like a lightning strike. Nellie screamed from behind the bathroom door as once again Stan went down like a sack of potatoes.

"That was most entertaining," Nancarrow said. "But now back to business. Needles, please proceed."

Digweed made a show of selecting just the right lance and examining it for any imperfections, then brought its tip up to my eye. This close, it looked like a twenty-penny nail.

Then, from the corner of that same imperiled eyeball, I caught a blur of motion—Vee, hurling herself onto Nancarrow.

I jumped back from Digweed, who was now intent on helping his boss but was stymied by the flailing whirl of bodies in close quarters.

Vee was on Nancarrow's back, with her legs wrapped around his waist. She had her left arm around his throat, and the stiletto in her right hand.

As the blade arced down toward Nancarrow's chest, Rushlow's gun boomed again. The bullet hit her upraised arm somewhere between elbow and shoulder, and she fell to the floor to join a white-faced Stan Hasso. Blood was everywhere.

Incredibly, Nancarrow seemed more concerned about his

appearance than anything else. He brushed himself off, straightened his clothing, then turned to Digweed. But before he could order the torturing to commence, a voice outside boomed from a bullhorn.

"This is Sheriff Broadstairs! I want everyone in that cabin to come out with your hands up!"

"Someone must have called the cops," Digweed theorized. "Just our luck, this douche musta been close by."

Rushlow peeked around the drawn curtain. "It's just Andy of Mayberry, all alone. No backup. Guess he figures that toy-soldier SWAT helmet he's got on is s'posed to scare us. What a fucking idiot! Let me take him out, Mr. Nancarrow. There won't be any witnesses. The rest of these people are holed up tight, and it's pretty dark out there. Even if they claim they saw our car here, we can bullshit our way out of it."

Nancarrow's composure seemed to be cracking a bit. Vee's assault was probably the first time in years he had found himself in personal danger.

"Do it. Then we will depart with Mr. McClinton, to continue this discussion elsewhere."

Rushlow eased the window open just enough to poke the gun muzzle through. He took his time aiming, then squeezed off a shot.

"He's down! Right in the chest! I'll finish him before we leave if I hafta."

Digweed had put away his kit and now had my arms pinned behind me by the wrists, both of which fit into one big hand, leaving the other free to bash me if needed. He marched me ahead of him. Rushlow followed, with Nancarrow bringing up the rear.

I cast a backward glance at Vee and Stan on the reddened floor. She had passed out, and Stan would soon join her.

Digweed pushed me out of the cabin, and the others followed.

There was movement at both corners of the cabin as, from either side, a man with a weapon stepped out.

Elbert Tighe, the well digger, carried a double-barreled shotgun, while his skinny young assistant, Kirwan Allen, had a handgun of some sort.

"Gentlemen," Tighe said, "please don't try anything loco. For starters, you can release that young feller, and drop your gun. Then head toward the squad car."

Freed from Digweed's grasp, I dashed back inside. Both Stan and Vee were unconscious but breathing. I fumbled out my phone to call 911, but a siren was already approaching.

Sandralene banged on the bathroom door, shouting, "Let us out!" Ignoring her for the moment, I raced back outside.

Sheriff Broadstairs, miraculously unharmed, was busy bundling the handcuffed trio into the back of the squad car.

Elbert Tighe walked up with the sheriff's precious bush hat. Broadstairs doffed his Kevlar helmet and took the hat.

"Thanks kindly, Deputy Tighe. You, too, Kirwan."

Broadstairs turned to me and rapped his knuckles against his chest, producing a resonant thump.

"Ain't quite as fat as I appear—vest adds a few pounds. Course, they could've aimed for my face, but professionals usually don't. And I didn't think either of them hunter boys was much of a shot, if all they could bag was one sorry turkey between 'em."

The ambulance pulled up, and the EMTs hurried toward the cabin as employees and some guests began cautiously to appear, goggling at the scene.

The EMTs brought out the wounded on stretchers. Sandralene, Nellie, and Ray followed under their own power.

Sheriff Broadstairs regarded me pleasantly enough, but his words were ominous.

"Now, you and me, son, we got a lot to discuss."

EPILOGUE

The main hospital in Centerdale proved to be a well-run institution: light, clean, and cheery despite the downtrodden economy
of the region. Stan's knee had been repaired nicely, although the
surgeon told him he would "not be running any marathons ever
again."

Stan sounded unusually sober. "That's okay, Doc. This last
one near did me in."

Stan's history with heroin caused the doctors to prescribe fewer
opioids, and the pain got to him more some days than others.

They tended to Vee's lesser but nonetheless serious injury even
more efficiently, and she had been released a week ago, after just a
couple of days in the hospital. She and Ray Zerkin had driven off
in her blue Volkswagen without any goodbyes.

For a day or so, I was hurt by her cold departure. But then
I realized there was really nothing between us left to say at this
moment and place. Which did not necessarily mean we would
never talk again. I had a sense that Nancarrow's satisfying arrest
had removed some vital component from her obsessive psyche, and
she was struggling to realize who she had to be, who she *could* be.

Now it was Stan's mustering-out day, and I was here to drive him back to the lodge. Once there, we would have to figure out what to do next.

I just found it strangely wonderful that we were alive and free.

I walked into the room. Sandralene was sitting on the edge of his bed, fussing with his meal, making sure he was eating properly. She looked like a zaftig Valkyrie from some Eastern Valhalla.

I said, "Did that bullet in the knee affect your hand-eye coordination somehow? Or did brain damage during the operation regress you back to childhood?"

Stan's glower might have intimidated someone who had not crouched shoulder-to-shoulder with him staked out in a rhododendron thicket. But I found myself cheerfully immune.

"Listen, Glen boy, I know this pampering ain't gonna go on forever, so I aim to make the most of it while I can. You'd do the same thing in my shoes."

"Fair enough. Now, chow down so we can leave. I want to see Nellie."

Everything was still unsettled between Nellie and me. I had been here in Centerdale since the night of the home invasion, and she had been back at the lodge. We had talked a couple of times, keeping it formal and businesslike. She had told me that since the headline-making incident, the lodge had been booked solid, and visits from day-trippers had doubled. But I was sure our popularity would die down as the notoriety waned, and that even with the extra business, we were probably still running in the red.

Stan finished his meal, and the nurse officially discharged him. Her assistant got him into a wheelchair and delivered him to the sidewalk, where he switched to crutches. Sandralene and I helped him into the Impala, and we motored off.

"You know I want to help you all I can, Glen. But I'm gonna be busy back in the city for a while once ol' Algy's trial gets under way."

"Yeah, I do realize that."

The law had been playing Stan and me for suckers all along. We had not been masters of our fates for one minute. Paget, Broadstairs, Schreiber, and a host of others behind the scenes, all the way to the state attorney general, had taken us for a ride.

The government had been gunning for Nancarrow for years, it turned out. A few too many lucrative fires had at last piqued their interest. But they had no solid case against him. They knew that Stan had been his firebug, but also that Stan wouldn't cooperate in any prosecution. Still, they had begun keeping tabs on Stan after his release from prison, in the hope that he would lead them somewhere. So once Stan and I began conspiring against Nancarrow, the authorities tumbled to our scheme. Their cybersquad, for one, had followed Ray Zerkin's moves with ease. So much for secrecy and stealth. The locals and even the feds used us as bait, hoping to trip Nancarrow up on some lesser charge that would open up a wider case against him. And now they had him in jail on the home invasion and could count on Stan's testimony in the larger set of charges. Stan's loyalty to the Gulch ethos of "snitches get stitches" had been utterly undone by his shattered knee.

All these things Broadstairs related to me during several recorded sessions at the local courthouse, with many interested law and court officers present.

When Broadstairs had finally finished, and I had recovered somewhat from feeling very stupid, I said, "And what about any charges against all of us, for our scam? All the false pretenses, like our line of credit?"

"Scam? What scam? All's I can see is a couple of entrepreneurs who bought a business, then tried to sell it. The DA's got no interest in such innocent affairs. And as far as false pretenses go—why, if you stick to what you claimed you set out to do, then there's no false pretenses at all, is there?"

"No, I guess not."

"But that twenty-one million dollars, Glen—that is all gone."

"So I suspected. How did you get hold of it? Ray swore that account was impenetrable."

"Probably woulda been, if it was the genuine Swiss thing. But the Feds spoofed your boy right along. He never was dealing with any foreign bank. You see, they need all of Nancarrow's money they can claw back."

None of us in the car said much as we got closer to the lodge. Then Stan spoke. He sounded uncommonly downbeat.

"This trip reminds me of that day we drove around the city with me showing you all the buildings I torched. Only back then we had prospects. We were gonna get rich *and* get even. Now where are we? A couple of stumblebums stuck with Camp Who-Gives-a-Fuck. And what's worse, we had a taste of the good stuff. Only for a few minutes, but you can't forget."

"Aw, Stan, don't look at it that way. Count your blessings. We could be dead or in jail. Instead, it's the status quo ante. Back to square one. We can make it work somehow."

Stan heaved a mournful sigh. "Yeah, the sunny side of the street." He visibly hoisted himself together. "Oh, well, I got a woman and a buddy and a roof over my head, and I ain't taking orders from some jumped-up mortgage monkey. We'll take it from there."

I was touched to be included in Stan's inventory of benedictions.

We pulled into the lodge, which seemed to be just as hopping as promised. Music issued from the dining hall, and I thought I recognized the cool strains of the Lucky Graves trio.

Stan and Sandralene headed toward their cabin. I hoped all the blood had been washed away, but knowing Nellie's efficiency, I wasn't too worried.

Stan's loping gait with the crutches somehow conveyed his

renewed zeal for life. "See you at dinner, Glen boy. If we're a little late, don't come looking for us. Me and this lady ain't knocked boots in way too long."

I grinned, shook my head, and went to the office.

Nellie was sitting at her desk. She didn't jump up to greet me, but she didn't run away in disgust, either.

"So. We had a serious misunderstanding."

"You lied to me big-time, Glen."

"Not about loving you."

"I don't know if that makes up for the rest."

"I guess we'll just have to see, then."

"Day by day, one step at a time. That's the way I feel."

It wasn't a honeymoon, but it would have to do.

There was a pile of mail on the desk, all addressed to me. For something to do to cover the awkward moment, I started sorting through it. Bills, bills, bills …

The office phone rang. Nellie looked at the caller ID.

"*Merda!* This guy been calling for you for days, Glen. Won't say nothing to me."

"I'll take it."

"Hello, Mr. McClinton? This is Rafe Lonergan, from Ghent, Goolsbee, and Saikiri."

It took me a few seconds to wrap my mind around the caller's affiliation. Was I being offered my job back? Getting sued? Luckily, Rafe Lonergan continued his spiel. I switched to speakerphone so Nellie could hear.

"Mr. McClinton, we've been retained as the local representative of MGM Resorts International. Our client has some potential business to discuss with you. Could you name a convenient place and time?"

I stammered out something about getting back to him, then hung up.

Nellie came at me like a rugby player. She shoved me in the chest with both hands, and I staggered backward.

"*Filho da puta!* You even *think* of selling this place, I will finish up what that Needles started—only I'll use a rotisserie spit!"

I gave her a wary smile. "Oh, baby, we got so much to talk about. We've got to figure out what's best for everyone now!"